DEATH OF A SALESMAN

Arthur Miller was born in N̲ ̲ ̲ ̲
1915 and studied at the ̲ ̲ ̲ ̲ ̲ ̲ ̲ ̲
His plays include *All M* ̲ ̲ ̲ ̲ ̲ ̲ ̲ ̲ a
Salesman (1949), *The Cru* ̲ ̲ ̲ ̲ ̲ ̲ , *A Memory of
Two Mondays* (1955), *A View from the Bridge*
(1955), *After the Fall* (1963), *Incident at Vichy*
(1964), *The Price* (1968), *The Archbishop's Ceiling*
(1977), *The American Clock* (1980), *Playing for
Time* (1981), which won the Peabody Award,
and *Two-Way Mirror* (1985). He has twice won
the New York Drama Critics' Award and in 1949
he was awarded the Pulitzer Prize. His play *The
Creation of the World and Other Business* (1972) was
made into a musical, *Up from Paradise*, in 1974.
Arthur Miller is the author of *Focus*, a novel; *The
Misfits*, a film screenplay; *I Don't Need You Anymore*, a collection of short stories; and, in collab-
oration with his wife, the photographer Inge
Morath, *In Russia* (1969), *In the Country* (1977),
Chinese Encounters (1979) and *Salesman in Beijing*
(1984). His autobiography, *Timebends*, was published in 1987.

ARTHUR MILLER

Death of a Salesman

CERTAIN PRIVATE
CONVERSATIONS IN TWO ACTS
AND A REQUIEM

PENGUIN BOOKS

PENGUIN BOOKS

Published by the Penguin Group
Penguin Books Ltd, 27 Wrights Lane, London W8 5TZ, England
Penguin Books USA Inc., 375 Hudson Street, New York, New York 10014, USA
Penguin Books Australia Ltd, Ringwood, Victoria, Australia
Penguin Books Canada Ltd, 10 Alcorn Avenue, Toronto, Ontario, Canada M4V 3B2
Penguin Books (NZ) Ltd, 182–190 Wairau Road, Auckland 10, New Zealand

Penguin Books Ltd, Registered Offices: Harmondsworth, Middlesex, England

First published 1949
Published in Great Britain by the Cresset Press 1949
Published in Penguin Books 1961
43 45 47 49 50 48 46 44 42

All applications for a licence to perform this play must be made either to the
International Creative Management Ltd, 22 Grafton Street, London W1 (for professional
performance), or to Chappel Plays Ltd, 129 Park Street, London W1Y 3FA (for amateur
performance). No performance may take place unless a licence has been obtained.

Printed in England by Clays Ltd, St Ives plc
Set in Monotype Bembo

DEATH OF A SALESMAN

First presented in England at the Phoenix Theatre,
London, on 28 July 1949, with the following cast:

WILLY LOMAN	*Paul Muni*
LINDA	*Katherine Alexander*
BIFF	*Kevin McCarthy*
HAPPY	*Frank Maxwell*
BERNARD	*Sam Main*
THE WOMAN	*Bessie Love*
CHARLEY	*Ralph Theadore*
UNCLE BEN	*Henry Oscar*
HOWARD WAGNER	*J. Anthony La Penna*
JENNY	*Joan MacArthur*
STANLEY	*George Margo*
MISS FORSYTHE	*Mary Laura Wood*
LETTA	*Barbara Cummings*
WAITER	*Ronald Frazer*

Produced by ELIA KAZAN

CHARACTERS

WILLY LOMAN   CHARLEY
LINDA   UNCLE BEN
BIFF   HOWARD WAGNER
HAPPY   JENNY
BERNARD   STANLEY
THE WOMAN   MISS FORSYTHE
LETTA   WAITER

SCENE: The action takes place in Willy Loman's house and yard and in various places he visits in the New York and Boston of today.

ACT ONE

A melody is heard, played upon a flute. It is small and fine, telling of grass and trees and the horizon. The curtain rises.

Before us is the SALESMAN'S *house. We are aware of towering, angular shapes behind it, surrounding it on all sides. Only the blue light of the sky falls upon the house and forestage; the surrounding area shows an angry glow of orange. As more light appears, we see a solid vault of apartment houses around the small, fragile-seeming home. An air of the dream clings to the place, a dream rising out of reality. The kitchen at centre seems actual enough, for there is a kitchen table with three chairs, and a refrigerator. But no other fixtures are seen. At the back of the kitchen there is a draped entrance, which leads to the living-room. To the right of the kitchen, on a level raised two feet, is a bedroom furnished only with a brass bedstead and a straight chair. On a shelf over the bed a silver athletic trophy stands. A window opens on to the apartment house at the side.*

Behind the kitchen, on a level raised six and a half feet, is the boys' bedroom, at present barely visible. Two beds are dimly seen, and at the back of the room a dormer window. (This bedroom is above the unseen living-room.) At the left a stairway curves up to it from the kitchen.

The entire setting is wholly or, in some places, partially transparent. The roof-line of the house is one-dimensional; under and over it we see the apartment buildings. Before the house lies an apron, curving beyond the forestage into the orchestra. This forward area serves as the back yard as well as the locale of all Willy's imaginings and of his city scenes. Whenever the action is in the present the actors observe the imaginary wall-lines, entering the house only through its door at the left. But in the scenes of the past these boundaries are broken, and characters enter or leave a room by stepping 'through' a wall on to the forestage.

[*From the right,* WILLY LOMAN, *the Salesman, enters, carry-ing two large sample cases. The flute plays on. He hears but is not aware of it. He is past sixty years of age, dressed quietly. Even as he crosses the stage to the doorway of the house, his exhaustion is apparent. He unlocks the door, comes into the kitchen, and thankfully lets his burden down, feeling the sore-ness of his palms. A word-sigh escapes his lips – it might be* 'Oh, boy, oh, boy.' *He closes the door, then carries his cases out into the living-room, through the draped kitchen doorway.*

LINDA, *his wife, has stirred in her bed at the right. She gets out and puts on a robe, listening. Most often jovial, she has developed an iron repression of her exceptions to* WILLY'S *behaviour – she more than loves him, she admires him, as though his mercurial nature, his temper, his massive dreams and little cruelties, served her only as sharp reminders of the turbulent longings within him, longings which she shares but lacks the temperament to utter and follow to their end.*]

LINDA [*hearing* WILLY *outside the bedroom, calls with some trepidation*]: Willy!

WILLY: It's all right. I came back.

LINDA: Why? What happened? [*Slight pause.*] Did something happen, Willy?

WILLY: No, nothing happened.

LINDA: You didn't smash the car, did you?

WILLY [*with casual irritation*]: I said nothing happened. Didn't you hear me?

LINDA: Don't you feel well?

WILLY: I'm tired to the death. [*The flute has faded away. He sits on the bed beside her, a little numb.*] I couldn't make it. I just couldn't make it, Linda.

LINDA [*very carefully, delicately*]: Where were you all day? You look terrible.

WILLY: I got as far as a little above Yonkers. I stopped for a cup of coffee. Maybe it was the coffee.

LINDA: What?

WILLY [*after a pause*]: I suddenly couldn't drive any more. The car kept going off on to the shoulder, y'know?

LINDA [*helpfully*]: Oh. Maybe it was the steering again. I don't think Angelo knows the Studebaker.

WILLY: No, it's me, it's me. Suddenly I realize I'm goin' sixty miles an hour and I don't remember the last five minutes. I'm – I can't seem to – keep my mind to it.

LINDA: Maybe it's your glasses. You never went for your new glasses.

WILLY: No, I see everything. I came back ten miles an hour. It took me nearly four hours from Yonkers.

LINDA [*resigned*]: Well, you'll just have to take a rest, Willy, you can't continue this way.

WILLY: I just got back from Florida.

LINDA: But you didn't rest your mind. Your mind is over-active, and the mind is what counts, dear.

WILLY: I'll start out in the morning. Maybe I'll feel better in the morning. [*She is taking off his shoes.*] These goddam arch supports are killing me.

LINDA: Take an aspirin. Should I get you an aspirin? It'll soothe you.

WILLY [*with wonder*]: I was driving along, you understand? And I was fine. I was even observing the scenery. You can imagine, me looking at scenery, on the road every week of my life. But it's so beautiful up there, Linda, the trees are so thick, and the sun is warm. I opened the windshield and just let the warm air bathe over me. And then all of a sudden I'm going' off the road! I'm tellin' ya, I absolutely forgot I was driving. If I'd've gone the other way over the white line I might've killed somebody. So I went on again – and five minutes later I'm dreamin' again, and I nearly – [*He presses two fingers against his eyes.*] I have such thoughts, I have such strange thoughts.

LINDA: Willy, dear. Talk to them again. There's no reason why you can't work in New York.

WILLY: They don't need me in New York. I'm the New England man. I'm vital in New England.

LINDA: But you're sixty years old. They can't expect you to keep travelling every week.

WILLY: I'll have to send a wire to Portland. I'm supposed to see Brown and Morrison tomorrow morning at ten o'clock to show the line. Goddammit, I could sell them! [*He starts putting on his jacket.*]

LINDA [*taking the jacket from him*]: Why don't you go down to the place tomorrow and tell Howard you've simply got to work in New York? You're too accommodating, dear.

WILLY: If old man Wagner was alive I'd a been in charge of New York now! That man was a prince, he was a masterful man. But that boy of his, that Howard, he don't appreciate. When I went north the first time, the Wagner Company didn't know where New England was!

LINDA: Why don't you tell those things to Howard, dear?

WILLY [*encouraged*]: I will, I definitely will. Is there any cheese?

LINDA: I'll make you a sandwich.

WILLY: No, go to sleep. I'll take some milk. I'll be up right away. The boys in?

LINDA: They're sleeping. Happy took Biff on a date tonight.

WILLY [*interested*]: That so?

LINDA: It was so nice to see them shaving together, one behind the other, in the bathroom. And going out together. You notice? The whole house smells of shaving lotion.

WILLY: Figure it out. Work a lifetime to pay off a house. You finally own it, and there's nobody to live in it.

LINDA: Well, dear, life is a casting off. It's always that way.

WILLY: No, no, some people – some people accomplish something. Did Biff say anything after I went this morning?

LINDA: You shouldn't have criticized him, Willy, especially after he just got off the train. You mustn't lose your temper with him.

WILLY: When the hell did I lose my temper? I simply asked him if he was making any money. Is that a criticism?

LINDA: But, dear, how could he make any money?

WILLY [*worried and angered*]: There's such an undercurrent in him. He became a moody man. Did he apologize when I left this morning?

LINDA: He was crestfallen, Willy. You know how he admires you. I think if he finds himself, then you'll both be happier and not fight any more.

WILLY: How can he find himself on a farm? Is that a life? A farmhand? In the beginning, when he was young, I thought, well, a young man, it's good for him to tramp around, take a lot of different jobs. But it's more than ten years now and he has yet to make thirty-five dollars a week!

LINDA: He's finding himself, Willy.

WILLY: Not finding yourself at the age of thirty-four is a disgrace!

LINDA: Shh!

WILLY: The trouble is he's lazy, goddammit!

LINDA: Willy, please!

WILLY: Biff is a lazy bum!

LINDA: They're sleeping. Get something to eat. Go on down.

WILLY: Why did he come home? I would like to know what brought him home.

LINDA: I don't know. I think he's still lost, Willy. I think he's very lost.

WILLY: Biff Loman is lost. In the greatest country in the world a young man with such – personal attractiveness, gets lost. And such a hard worker. There's one thing about Biff – he's not lazy.

LINDA: Never.

WILLY [*with pity and resolve*]: I'll see him in the morning; I'll have a nice talk with him. I'll get him a job selling. He could be big in no time. My God! Remember how they used to follow him around in high school? When he smiled at one of them their faces lit up. When he walked down the street . . . [*He loses himself in reminiscences.*]

LINDA [*trying to bring him out of it*]: Willy, dear, I got a new kind of American-type cheese today. It's whipped.

WILLY: Why do you get American when I like Swiss?

LINDA: I just thought you'd like a change –

WILLY: I don't want a change! I want Swiss cheese. Why am I always being contradicted?

LINDA [*with a covering laugh*]: I thought it would be a surprise.

WILLY: Why don't you open a window in here, for God's sake?

LINDA [*with infinite patience*]: They're all open, dear.

WILLY: The way they boxed us in here. Bricks and windows, windows and bricks.

LINDA: We should've bought the land next door.

WILLY: The street is lined with cars. There's not a breath of fresh air in the neighbourhood. The grass don't grow any more, you can't raise a carrot in the backyard. They should've had a law against apartment houses. Remember those two beautiful elm trees out there? When I and Biff hung the swing between them?

LINDA: Yeah, like being a million miles from the city.

WILLY: They should've arrested the builder for cutting those down. They massacred the neighbourhood. [*Lost*] More and more I think of those days, Linda. This time of year it was lilac and wistaria. And then the peonies would come out, and the daffodils. What a fragrance in this room!

LINDA: Well, after all, people had to move somewhere.

WILLY: No, there's more people now.

LINDA: I don't think there's more people, I think –

WILLY: There's more people! That's what's ruining this country! Population is getting out of control. The competition is maddening! Smell the stink from that apartment house! And another one on the other side ... How can they whip cheese?

[*On* WILLY'S *last line*, BIFF *and* HAPPY *raise themselves up in their beds, listening.*]

LINDA: Go down, try it. And be quiet.

WILLY [*turning to* LINDA, *guiltily*]: You're not worried about me, are you, sweetheart?

BIFF: What's the matter?

HAPPY: Listen!

LINDA: You've got too much on the ball to worry about.

WILLY: You're my foundation and my support, Linda.

LINDA: Just try to relax, dear. You make mountains out of molehills.

WILLY: I won't fight with him any more. If he wants to go back to Texas, let him go.

LINDA: He'll find his way.

WILLY: Sure. Certain men just don't get started till later in life. Like Thomas Edison, I think. Or B. F. Goodrich. One of them was deaf. [*He starts for the bedroom doorway.*] I'll put my money on Biff.

LINDA: And Willy – if it's warm Sunday we'll drive in the country. And we'll open the windshield, and take lunch.

WILLY: No, the windshields don't open on the new cars.

LINDA: But you opened it today.

WILLY: Me? I didn't. [*He stops.*] Now isn't that peculiar! Isn't that a remarkable – [*He breaks off in amazement and fright as the flute is heard distantly.*]

LINDA: What, darling?

WILLY: That is the most remarkable thing.

LINDA: What, dear?

WILLY: I was thinking of the Chevvy. [*Slight pause.*] Nineteen twenty-eight ... when I had that red Chevvy – [*Breaks off.*] That funny? I coulda sworn I was driving that Chevvy today.

LINDA: Well, that's nothing. Something must've reminded you.

WILLY: Remarkable. Ts. Remember those days? The way Biff used to simonize that car? The dealer refused to believe there was eighty thousand miles on it. [*He shakes his head.*] Heh! [*To* LINDA] Close your eyes, I'll be right up. [*He walks out of the bedroom.*]

HAPPY [*to* BIFF]: Jesus, maybe he smashed up the car again!

LINDA [*calling after* WILLY]: Be careful on the stairs, dear! The cheese is on the middle shelf! [*She turns, goes over to the bed, takes his jacket, and goes out of the bedroom.*]

[*Light has risen on the boys' room. Unseen,* WILLY *is heard talking to himself, 'Eighty thousand miles,' and a little laugh.* BIFF *gets out of bed, comes downstage a bit, and stands attentively.* BIFF *is two years older than his brother* HAPPY, *well built, but in these days bears a worn air and seems less self-assured. He has succeeded less, and his dreams are stronger and less acceptable than* HAPPY'S. HAPPY *is tall, powerfully made. Sexuality is like a visible colour on him, or a scent that many women have discovered. He, like his brother, is lost, but in a different way, for he has never allowed himself to turn his face toward defeat and is thus more confused and hard-skinned, although seemingly more content.*]

HAPPY [*getting out of bed*]: He's going to get his licence taken away if he keeps that up. I'm getting nervous about him, y'know, Biff?

BIFF: His eyes are going.

HAPPY: No, I've driven with him. He sees all right. He just doesn't keep his mind on it. I drove into the city with him last week. He stops at a green light and then it turns red and he goes. [*He laughs.*]

BIFF: Maybe he's colour-blind.

HAPPY: Pop? Why, he's got the finest eye for colour in the business. You know that.

BIFF [*sitting down on his bed*]: I'm going to sleep.

HAPPY: You're not still sour on Dad, are you, Biff?

BIFF: He's all right, I guess.

WILLY [*underneath them, in the living-room*]: Yes, sir, eighty thousand miles – eighty-two thousand!

BIFF: You smoking?

HAPPY [*holding out a pack of cigarettes*]: Want one?

BIFF [*taking a cigarette*]: I can never sleep when I smell it.

WILLY: What a simonizing job, heh!

HAPPY [*with deep sentiment*]: Funny, Biff, y'know? Us sleeping in here again? The old beds. [*He pats his bed affectionately.*] All the talk that went across those two beds, huh? Our whole lives.

BIFF: Yeah. Lotta dreams and plans.

HAPPY [*with a deep and masculine laugh*]: About five hundred women would like to know what was said in this room.

[*They share a soft laugh.*]

BIFF: Remember that big Betsy something – what the hell was her name – over on Bushwick Avenue?

HAPPY [*combing his hair*]: With the collie dog!

BIFF: That's the one. I got you in there, remember?

HAPPY: Yeah, that was my first time – I think. Boy, there was a pig! [*They laugh, almost crudely.*] You taught me everything I know about women. Don't forget that.

BIFF: I bet you forgot how bashful you used to be. Especially with girls.

HAPPY: Oh, I still am, Biff.

BIFF: Oh, go on.

HAPPY: I just control it, that's all. I think I got less bashful and you got more so. What happened, Biff? Where's the old humour, the old confidence? [*He shakes* BIFF'S *knee.* BIFF *gets up and moves restlessly about the room.*] What's the matter?

BIFF: Why does Dad mock me all the time?

HAPPY: He's not mocking you, he –

BIFF: Everything I say there's a twist of mockery on his face. I can't get near him.

HAPPY: He just wants you to make good, that's all. I wanted to talk to you about Dad for a long time, Biff. Something's – happening to him. He – talks to himself.

BIFF: I noticed that this morning. But he always mumbled.

HAPPY: But not so noticeable. It got so embarrassing I sent him to Florida. And you know something? Most of the time he's talking to you.

BIFF: What's he say about me?

HAPPY: I can't make it out.

BIFF: What's he say about me?

HAPPY: I think the fact that you're not settled, that you're still kind of up in the air . . .

BIFF: There's one or two other things depressing him, Happy.

HAPPY: What do you mean?

BIFF: Never mind. Just don't lay it all to me.

HAPPY: But I think if you got started – I mean – is there any future for you out there?

BIFF: I tell ya, Hap, I don't know what the future is. I don't know – what I'm supposed to want.

HAPPY: What do you mean?

BIFF: Well, I spent six or seven years after high school trying to work myself up. Shipping clerk, salesman, business of one kind or another. And it's a measly manner of existence. To get on that subway on the hot mornings in summer. To devote your whole life to keeping stock, or making phone calls, or selling or buying. To suffer fifty weeks of the year for the sake of a two-week vacation, when all you really desire is to be outdoors, with your shirt off. And always to have to get ahead of the next fella. And still – that's how you build a future.

HAPPY: Well, you really enjoy it on a farm? Are you content out there?

BIFF [*with rising agitation*]: Hap, I've had twenty or thirty different kinds of job since I left home before the war, and it always turns out the same. I just realized it lately. In Nebraska when I herded cattle, and the Dakotas, and Arizona, and now in Texas. It's why I came home now, I guess, because I realized it. This farm I work on, it's spring there now, see? And they've got about fifteen new colts. There's nothing more inspiring or – beautiful than the sight of a mare and a new colt. And it's cool there now, see? Texas is cool now, and it's spring. And whenever spring comes to where I am, I suddenly get the feeling, my God, I'm not gettin' anywhere. What the hell am I doing, playing around with horses, twenty-eight dollars a week! I'm thirty-four years old, I oughta be makin' my future. That's when I come running home. And now, I get here, and I don't know what to do with myself. [*After a pause*] I've always made a point of not wasting my life, and everytime I come back here I know that all I've done is to waste my life.

HAPPY: You're a poet, you know that, Biff? You're a – you're an idealist!

BIFF: No, I'm mixed up very bad. Maybe I oughta get married. Maybe I oughta get stuck into something. Maybe that's my trouble. I'm like a boy. I'm not married, I'm not in business, I just – I'm like a boy. Are you content, Hap? You're a success, aren't you? Are you content?

HAPPY: Hell, no!

BIFF: Why? You're making money, aren't you?

HAPPY [*moving about with energy, expressiveness*]: All I can do now is wait for the merchandise manager to die. And suppose I get to be merchandise manager? He's a good friend of mine, and he just built a terrific estate on Long Island. And he lived there about two months and sold it, and now he's building another one. He can't enjoy it once it's finished. And I know that's just what I would do. I don't know what the hell I'm workin' for. Sometimes I sit in my apartment – all alone. And I think of the rent I'm paying. And it's crazy. But then, it's what I always wanted. My own apartment, a car, and plenty of women. And still, goddammit, I'm lonely.

BIFF [*with enthusiasm*]: Listen, why don't you come out West with me?

HAPPY: You and I, heh?

BIFF: Sure, maybe we could buy a ranch. Raise cattle, use our muscles. Men built like we are should be working out in the open.

HAPPY [*avidly*]: The Loman Brothers, heh?

BIFF [*with vast affection*]: Sure, we'd be known all over the counties!

HAPPY [*enthralled*]: That's what I dream about, Biff. Sometimes I want to just rip my clothes off in the middle of the store and outbox that goddam merchandise manager. I mean I can outbox, outrun, and outlift anybody in that store, and I have to take orders from those common, petty sons-of-bitches till I can't stand it any more.

BIFF: I'm tellin' you, kid, if you were with me I'd be happy out there.

HAPPY [*enthused*]: See, Biff, everybody around me is so false that I'm constantly lowering my ideals . . .

BIFF: Baby, together we'd stand up for one another, we'd have someone to trust.

HAPPY: If I were around you –

BIFF: Hap, the trouble is we weren't brought up to grub for money. I don't know how to do it

HAPPY: Neither can I!

BIFF: Then let's go!

HAPPY: The only thing is – what can you make out there?

BIFF: But look at your friend. Builds an estate and then hasn't the peace of mind to live in it.

HAPPY: Yeah, but when he walks into the store the waves part in front of him. That's fifty-two thousand dollars a year coming through the revolving door, and I got more in my pinky finger than he's got in his head.

BIFF: Yeah, but you just said –

HAPPY: I gotta show some of those pompous, self-important executives over there that Hap Loman can make the grade. I want to walk into the store the way he walks in. Then I'll go with you, Biff. We'll be together yet, I swear. But take those two we had tonight. Now weren't they gorgeous creatures?

BIFF: Yeah, yeah, most gorgeous I've had in years.

HAPPY: I get that any time I want, Biff. Whenever I feel disgusted. The only trouble is, it gets like bowling or something. I just keep knockin' them over and it doesn't mean anything. You still run around a lot?

BIFF: Naa. I'd like to find a girl – steady, somebody with substance.

HAPPY: That's what I long for.

BIFF: Go on! You'd never come home.

HAPPY: I would! Somebody with character, with resistance! Like Mom, y'know? You're gonna call me a bastard when I tell you this. That girl Charlotte I was with tonight is engaged to be married in five weeks. [*He tries on his new hat.*]

BIFF: No kiddin'!

HAPPY: Sure, the guy's in line for the vice-presidency of the store. I don't know what gets into me, maybe I just have an over-developed sense of competition or something, but I went and ruined her, and furthermore I can't get rid of her. And he's the third executive I've done that to. Isn't that a crummy characteristic? And to top it all, I go to their weddings! [*Indignantly, but laughing*] Like I'm not supposed to take bribes. Manufacturers offer me a hundred-dollar bill now and then to throw an order their way. You know how honest I am, but it's like this girl, see. I hate myself for it. Because I don't want the girl, and, still, I take it and – I love it!

BIFF: Let's go to sleep.

HAPPY: I guess we didn't settle anything, heh?

BIFF: I just got one idea that I think I'm going to try.

HAPPY: What's that?

BIFF: Remember Bill Oliver?

HAPPY: Sure, Oliver is very big now. You want to work for him again?

BIFF: No, but when I quit he said something to me. He put his arm on my shoulder, and he said, 'Biff, if you ever need anything, come to me.'

HAPPY: I remember that. That sounds good.

BIFF: I think I'll go to see him. If I could get ten thousand or even seven or eight thousand dollars I could buy a beautiful ranch.

HAPPY: I bet he'd back you. 'Cause he thought highly of you, Biff. I mean, they all do. You're well liked, Biff. That's why I say to come back here, and we both have the apartment. And I'm tellin' you, Biff, any babe you want . . .

BIFF: No, with a ranch I could do the work I like and still be something. I just wonder though. I wonder if Oliver still thinks I stole that carton of basketballs.

HAPPY: Oh, he probably forgot that long ago. It's almost ten years. You're too sensitive. Anyway, he didn't really fire you.

BIFF: Well, I think he was going to. I think that's why I quit. I was never sure whether he knew or not. I know he thought the world of me, though. I was the only one he'd let lock up the place.

WILLY [*below*]: You gonna wash the engine, Biff?

HAPPY: Shh!

[BIFF *looks at* HAPPY, *who is gazing down, listening.* WILLY *is mumbling in the parlour.*]

HAPPY: You hear that?

[*They listen.* WILLY *laughs warmly.*]

BIFF [*growing angry*]: Doesn't he know Mom can hear that?

WILLY: Don't get your sweater dirty, Biff!

[*A look of pain crosses* BIFF'S *face.*]

HAPPY: Isn't that terrible? Don't leave again, will you? You'll find a job here. You gotta stick around. I don't know what to do about him, it's getting embarrassing.

WILLY: What a simonizing job!

BIFF: Mom's hearing that!

WILLY: No kiddin', Biff, you got a date? Wonderful!

HAPPY: Go on to sleep. But talk to him in the morning, will you?

BIFF [*reluctantly getting into bed*]: With her in the house. Brother!

HAPPY [*getting into bed*]: I wish you'd have a good talk with him.

[*The light on their room begins to fade.*]

BIFF [*to himself in bed*]: That selfish, stupid . . .

HAPPY: Sh . . . Sleep, Biff.

[*Their light is out. Well before they have finished speaking,* WILLY'S *form is dimly seen below in the darkened kitchen. He opens the refrigerator, searches in there, and takes out a bottle of milk. The apartment houses are fading out, and the entire house and surroundings become covered with leaves. Music insinuates itself as the leaves appear.*]

WILLY: Just wanna be careful with those girls, Biff, that's all. Don't make any promises. No promises of any kind. Because a girl, y'know, they always believe what you tell 'em, and you're very young, Biff, you're too young to be talking seriously to girls.

[*Light rises on the kitchen.* WILLY, *talking, shuts the refrigerator door and comes downstage to the kitchen table. He pours milk into a glass. He is totally immersed in himself, smiling faintly.*]

WILLY: Too young entirely, Biff. You want to watch your schooling first. Then when you're all set, there'll be plenty of girls for a boy like you. [*He smiles broadly at a kitchen chair.*] That so? The girls pay for you? [*He laughs.*] Boy, you must really be makin' a hit.

[WILLY *is gradually addressing – physically – a point offstage, speaking through the wall of the kitchen, and his voice has been rising in volume to that of a normal conversation.*]

WILLY: I been wondering why you polish the car so careful. Ha! Don't leave the hubcaps, boys. Get the chamois to the hubcaps. Happy, use newspaper on the windows, it's the easiest thing. Show him how to do it, Biff! You see, Happy? Pad it up, use it like a pad. That's it, that's it, good work. You're doin' all right, Hap. [*He pauses, then nods in approbation for a few seconds, then looks upward.*] Biff, first thing we gotta do when we get time is clip that big branch over the house. Afraid it's gonna fall in a storm and hit the roof. Tell you what. We get a rope and sling her around, and then we climb up there with a couple of saws and take her down. Soon as you finish the car, boys, I wanna see ya. I got a surprise for you, boys.

BIFF [*offstage*]: Whatta ya got, Dad?

WILLY: No, you finish first. Never leave a job till you're finished – remember that. [*Looking toward the 'big trees'*] Biff, up in Albany I saw a beautiful hammock. I think I'll buy it next trip, and we'll hang it right between those two elms. Wouldn't that be something? Just swingin' there under those branches. Boy, that would be . . .

[YOUNG BIFF *and* YOUNG HAPPY *appear from the direction* WILLY *was addressing.* HAPPY *carries rags and a pail of water.* BIFF, *wearing a sweater with a block 'S', carries a football.*]

BIFF [*pointing in the direction of the car offstage*]: How's that, Pop, professional?

WILLY: Terrific. Terrific job, boys. Good work, Biff.

HAPPY: Where's the surprise, Pop?

WILLY: In the back seat of the car.

HAPPY: Boy! [*He runs off.*]

BIFF: What is it, Dad? Tell me, what'd you buy?

WILLY [*laughing, cuffs him*]: Never mind, something I want you to have.

BIFF [*turns and starts off*]: What is it, Hap?

HAPPY [*offstage*]: It's a punching bag!

BIFF: Oh, Pop!

WILLY: It's got Gene Tunney's signature on it!

[HAPPY *runs onstage with a punching bag.*]

BIFF: Gee, how'd you know we wanted a punching bag?

WILLY: Well, it's the finest thing for the timing.

HAPPY [*lies down on his back and pedals with his feet*]: I'm losing weight, you notice, Pop?

WILLY [*to* HAPPY]: Jumping rope is good too.

BIFF: Did you see the new football I got?

WILLY [*examining the ball*]: Where'd you get a new ball?

BIFF: The coach told me to practise my passing.

WILLY: That so? And he gave you the ball, heh?

BIFF: Well, I borrowed it from the locker room. [*He laughs confidentially.*]

WILLY [*laughing with him at the theft*]: I want you to return that.

HAPPY: I told you he wouldn't like it!

BIFF [*angrily*]: Well, I'm bringing it back!

WILLY [*stopping the incipient argument, to* HAPPY]: Sure, he's gotta practise with a regulation ball, doesn't he? [*To* BIFF] Coach'll probably congratulate you on your initiative!

BIFF: Oh, he keeps congratulating my initiative all the time, Pop.

WILLY: That's because he likes you. If somebody else took that ball there'd be an uproar. So what's the report, boys, what's the report?

BIFF: Where'd you go this time, Dad? Gee, we were lonesome for you.

WILLY [*pleased, puts an arm around each boy and they come down to the apron*]: Lonesome, heh?

BIFF: Missed you every minute.

WILLY: Don't say? Tell you a secret, boys. Don't breathe it to a soul. Someday I'll have my own business, and I'll never have to leave home any more.

HAPPY: Like Uncle Charley, heh?

WILLY: Bigger than Uncle Charley! Because Charley is not – liked. He's liked, but he's not – well liked.

BIFF: Where'd you go this time, Dad?

WILLY: Well, I got on the road, and I went north to Providence. Met the Mayor.

BIFF: The Mayor of Providence!

WILLY: He was sitting in the hotel lobby.

BIFF: What'd he say?

WILLY: He said, 'Morning!' And I said, 'You got a fine city here, Mayor.' And then he had coffee with me. And then I went to Waterbury. Waterbury is a fine city. Big clock city, the famous Waterbury clock. Sold a nice bill there. And then Boston – Boston is the cradle of the Revolution.

A fine city. And a couple of other towns in Mass., and on to Portland and Bangor and straight home!

BIFF: Gee, I'd love to go with you sometime, Dad.

WILLY: Soon as summer comes.

HAPPY: Promise?

WILLY: You and Hap and I, and I'll show you all the towns. America is full of beautiful towns and fine, upstanding people. And they know me, boys, they know me up and down New England. The finest people. And when I bring you fellas up, there'll be open sesame for all of us, 'cause one thing, boys: I have friends. I can park my car in any street in New England, and the cops protect it like their own. This summer, heh?

BIFF and HAPPY [*together*]: Yeah! You bet!

WILLY: We'll take our bathing-suits.

HAPPY: We'll carry your bags, Pop!

WILLY: Oh, won't that be something! Me comin' into the Boston stores with you boys carryin' my bags. What a sensation!

[BIFF *is prancing around, practising passing the ball.*]

WILLY: You nervous, Biff, about the game?

BIFF: Not if you're gonna be there.

WILLY: What do they say about you in school, now that they made you captain?

HAPPY: There's a crowd of girls behind him every time the classes change.

BIFF [*taking* WILLY'S *hand*]: This Saturday, Pop, this Saturday – just for you, I'm going to break through for a touchdown.

HAPPY: You're supposed to pass.

BIFF: I'm takin' one play for Pop. You watch me, Pop, and when I take off my helmet, that means I'm breakin' out. Then watch me crash through that line!

WILLY [*kisses* BIFF]: Oh, wait'll I tell this in Boston!

[BERNARD *enters in knickers. He is younger than* BIFF, *earnest and loyal, a worried boy.*]

BERNARD: Biff, where are you? You're supposed to study with me today.

WILLY: Hey, looka Bernard. What're you lookin' so anaemic about, Bernard?

BERNARD: He's gotta study, Uncle Willy. He's got Regents next week.

HAPPY [*tauntingly, spinning* BERNARD *around*]: Let's box, Bernard!

BERNARD: Biff! [*He gets away from* HAPPY.] Listen, Biff, I heard Mr Birnbaum say that if you don't start studyin' math he's gonna flunk you, and you won't graduate. I heard him!

WILLY: You better study with him, Biff. Go ahead now.

BERNARD: I heard him!

BIFF: Oh, Pop, you didn't see my sneakers! [*He holds up a foot for* WILLY *to look at.*]

WILLY: Hey, that's a beautiful job of printing!

BERNARD [*wiping his glasses*]: Just because he printed University of Virginia on his sneakers doesn't mean they've got to graduate him, Uncle Willy!

WILLY [*angrily*]: What're you talking about? With scholarships to three universities they're gonna flunk him?

BERNARD: But I heard Mr Birnbaum say –

WILLY: Don't be a pest, Bernard! [*To his boys*] What an anaemic!

BERNARD: Okay, I'm waiting for you in my house, Biff.

[BERNARD *goes off. The* LOMANS *laugh.*]

WILLY: Bernard is not well liked, is he?

BIFF: He's liked, but he's not well liked.

HAPPY: That's right, Pop.

WILLY: That's just what I mean, Bernard can get the best marks in school, y'understand, but when he gets out in the business world, y'understand, you are going to be five times ahead of him. That's why I thank Almighty God you're both built like Adonises. Because the man who makes an appearance in the business world, the man who creates personal interest, is the man who gets ahead. Be liked and you will never want. You take me, for instance. I never have to wait in line to see a buyer. 'Willy Loman is here!' That's all they have to know, and I go right through.

BIFF: Did you knock them dead, Pop?

WILLY: Knocked 'em cold in Providence, slaughtered 'em in Boston.

HAPPY [*on his back, pedalling again*]: I'm losing weight, you notice, Pop?

[LINDA *enters, as of old, a ribbon in her hair, carrying a basket of washing.*]

LINDA [*with youthful energy*]: Hello, dear!

WILLY: Sweetheart!

LINDA: How'd the Chevvy run?

WILLY: Chevrolet, Linda, is the greatest car ever built. [*To the boys*] Since when do you let your mother carry wash up the stairs?

BIFF: Grab hold there, boy!

HAPPY: Where to, Mom?

LINDA: Hang them up on the line. And you better go down to your friends, Biff. The cellar is full of boys. They don't know what to do with themselves.

BIFF: Ah, when Pop comes home they can wait!

WILLY [*laughs appreciatively*]: You better go down and tell them what to do, Biff.

BIFF: I think I'll have them sweep out the furnace room.

WILLY: Good work, Biff.

BIFF [*goes through wall-line of kitchen to doorway at back and calls down*]: Fellas! Everybody sweep out the furnace room! I'll be right down!

VOICES: All right! Okay, Biff.

BIFF: George and Sam and Frank, come out back! We're hangin' up the wash! Come on, Hap, on the double! [*He and* HAPPY *carry out the basket.*]

LINDA: The way they obey him!

WILLY: Well, that's training, the training. I'm tellin' you, I was sellin' thousands and thousands, but I had to come home.

LINDA: Oh, the whole block'll be at that game. Did you sell anything?

WILLY: I did five hundred gross in Providence and seven hundred gross in Boston.

LINDA: No! Wait a minute, I've got a pencil. [*She pulls pencil and paper out of her apron pocket.*] That makes your commission ... Two hundred – my God! Two hundred and twelve dollars!

WILLY: Well, I didn't figure it yet, but ...

LINDA: How much did you do?

WILLY: Well, I – I did – about a hundred and eighty gross in Providence. Well, no – it came to – roughly two hundred gross on the whole trip.

LINDA [*without hesitation*]: Two hundred gross. That's ... [*She figures.*]

WILLY: The trouble was that three of the stores were half-closed for inventory in Boston. Otherwise I woulda broke records.

LINDA: Well, it makes seventy dollars and some pennies. That's very good.

WILLY: What do we owe?

LINDA: Well, on the first there's sixteen dollars on the refrigerator –

WILLY: Why sixteen?

LINDA: Well, the fan belt broke, so it was a dollar eighty.

WILLY: But it's brand new.

LINDA: Well, the man said that's the way it is. Till they work themselves in, y'know.

[*They move through the wall-line into the kitchen.*]

WILLY: I hope we didn't get stuck on that machine.

LINDA: They got the biggest ads of any of them!

WILLY: I know, it's a fine machine. What else?

LINDA: Well, there's nine-sixty for the washing-machine. And for the vacuum cleaner there's three and a half due on the fifteenth. Then the roof, you got twenty-one dollars remaining.

WILLY: It don't leak, does it?

LINDA: No, they did a wonderful job. Then you owe Frank for the carburettor.

WILLY: I'm not going to pay that man! That goddam Chevrolet, they ought to prohibit the manufacture of that car!

LINDA: Well, you owe him three and a half. And odds and ends, comes to around a hundred and twenty dollars by the fifteenth.

WILLY: A hundred and twenty dollars! My God, if business don't pick up I don't know what I'm gonna do!

LINDA: Well, next week you'll do better.

WILLY: Oh, I'll knock 'em dead next week. I'll go to Hartford. I'm very well liked in Hartford. You know, the trouble is, Linda, people don't seem to take to me.

[*They move on to the forestage.*]

LINDA: Oh, don't be foolish.

WILLY: I know it when I walk in. They seem to laugh at me.

LINDA: Why? Why would they laugh at you? Don't talk that way, Willy.

[WILLY *moves to the edge of the stage.* LINDA *goes into the kitchen and starts to darn stockings.*]

WILLY: I don't know the reason for it, but they just pass me by. I'm not noticed.

LINDA: But you're doing wonderful, dear. You're making seventy to a hundred dollars a week.

WILLY: But I gotta be at it ten, twelve hours a day. Other men – I don't know – they do it easier. I don't know why – I can't stop myself – I talk too much. A man oughta come in with a few words. One thing about Charley. He's a man of few words, and they respect him.

LINDA: You don't talk too much, you're just lively.

WILLY [*smiling*]: Well, I figure, what the hell, life is short, a couple of jokes. [*To himself*] I joke too much! [*The smile goes.*]

LINDA: Why? You're –

WILLY: I'm fat. I'm very – foolish to look at, Linda. I didn't tell you, but Christmas-time I happened to be calling on F. H. Stewarts, and a salesman I know, as I was going in to see the buyer I heard him say something about – walrus. And I – I cracked him right across the face. I won't take that. I simply will not take that. But they do laugh at me. I know that.

LINDA: Darling . . .

WILLY: I gotta overcome it. I know I gotta overcome it. I'm not dressing to advantage, maybe.

LINDA: Willy, darling, you're the handsomest man in the* world –

WILLY: Oh, no, Linda.

LINDA: To me you are. [*Slight pause.*] The handsomest.

[*From the darkness is heard the laughter of a woman.* WILLY *doesn't turn to it, but it continues through* LINDA'S *lines.*]

LINDA: And the boys, Willy. Few men are idolized by their children the way you are.

[*Music is heard as behind a scrim, to the left of the house, the* WOMAN, *dimly seen, is dressing.*]

WILLY [*with great feeling*]: You're the best there is, Linda, you're a pal, you know that? On the road – on the road I want to grab you sometimes and just kiss the life outa you.

[*The laughter is loud now, and he moves into a brightening area at the left, where the* WOMAN *has come from behind the scrim and is standing, putting on her hat, looking into a 'mirror', and laughing.*]

WILLY: 'Cause I get so lonely – especially when business is bad and there's nobody to talk to. I get the feeling that I'll never sell anything again, that I won't make a living for you, or a business, a business for the boys. [*He talks through the* WOMAN'S *subsiding laughter; the* WOMAN *primps at the 'mirror'.*] There's so much I want to make for –

THE WOMAN: Me? You didn't make me, Willy. I picked you.

WILLY [*pleased*]: You picked me?

THE WOMAN [*who is quite proper-looking, Willy's age*]: I did.

I've been sitting at that desk watching all the salesmen go by, day in, day out. But you've got such a sense of humour, and we do have such a good time together, don't we?

WILLY: Sure, sure. [*He takes her in his arms.*] Why do you have to go now?

THE WOMAN: It's two o'clock . . .

WILLY: No, come on in! [*He pulls her.*]

THE WOMAN: . . . my sisters'll be scandalized. When'll you be back?

WILLY: Oh, two weeks about. Will you come up again?

THE WOMAN: Sure thing. You do make me laugh. It's good for me. [*She squeezes his arm, kisses him.*] And I think you're a wonderful man.

WILLY: You picked me, heh?

THE WOMAN: Sure. Because you're so sweet. And such a kidder.

WILLY: Well, I'll see you next time I'm in Boston.

THE WOMAN: I'll put you right through to the buyers.

WILLY [*slapping her bottom*]: Right. Well, bottoms up!

THE WOMAN [*slaps him gently and laughs*]: You just kill me, Willy. [*He suddenly grabs her and kisses her roughly.*] You kill me. And thanks for the stockings. I love a lot of stockings. Well, good night.

WILLY: Good night. And keep your pores open!

THE WOMAN: Oh, Willy!

[*The* WOMAN *bursts out laughing, and* LINDA's *laughter blends in. The* WOMAN *disappears into the dark. Now the area at the kitchen table brightens.* LINDA *is sitting where she was at the kitchen table, but now is mending a pair of her silk stockings.*]

LINDA: You are, Willy. The handsomest man. You've got no reason to feel that –

WILLY [*coming out of the* WOMAN's *dimming area and going over to* LINDA]: I'll make it all up to you, Linda, I'll –

LINDA: There's nothing to make up, dear. You're doing fine, better than –

WILLY [*noticing her mending*]: What's that?

LINDA: Just mending my stockings. They're so expensive –

WILLY [*angrily, taking them from her*]: I won't have you mending stockings in this house! Now throw them out!

[LINDA *puts the stockings in her pocket.*]

BERNARD [*entering on the run*]: Where is he? If he doesn't study!

WILLY [*moving to the forestage, with great agitation*]: You'll give him the answers!

BERNARD: I do, but I can't on a Regents! That's a state exam! They're liable to arrest me!

WILLY: Where is he? I'll whip him, I'll whip him!

LINDA: And he'd better give back that football, Willy, it's not nice.

WILLY: Biff! Where is he? Why is he taking everything?

LINDA: He's too rough with the girls, Willy. All the mothers are afraid of him!

WILLY: I'll whip him!

BERNARD: He's driving the car without a licence!

[*The* WOMAN'S *laugh is heard.*]

WILLY: Shut up!

LINDA: All the mothers –

WILLY: Shut up!

BERNARD [*backing quietly away and out*]: Mr Birnbaum says he's stuck up.

WILLY: Get outa here!

BERNARD: If he doesn't buckle down he'll flunk math! [*He goes off.*]

LINDA: He's right, Willy, you've gotta –

WILLY [*exploding at her*]: There's nothing the matter with him! You want him to be a worm like Bernard? He's got spirit, personality . . .

[*As he speaks,* LINDA, *almost in tears, exits into the living-room.* WILLY *is alone in the kitchen, wilting and staring. The leaves are gone. It is night again, and the apartment houses look down from behind.*]

WILLY: Loaded with it. Loaded! What is he stealing? He's giving it back, isn't he? Why is he stealing? What did I tell him? I never in my life told him anything but decent things.

[HAPPY *in pyjamas has come down the stairs;* WILLY *suddenly becomes aware of* HAPPY'S *presence.*]

HAPPY: Let's go now, come on.

WILLY [*sitting down at the kitchen table*]: Huh! Why did she have to wax the floors herself? Everytime she waxes the floors she keels over. She knows that!

HAPPY: Shh! Take it easy. What brought you back tonight?

WILLY: I got an awful scare. Nearly hit a kid in Yonkers. God! Why didn't I go to Alaska with my brother Ben that time! Ben! That man was a genius, that man was success incarnate! What a mistake! He begged me to go.

HAPPY: Well, there's no use in –

WILLY: You guys! There was a man started with the clothes on his back and ended up with diamond mines?

HAPPY: Boy, someday I'd like to know how he did it.

WILLY: What's the mystery? The man knew what he wanted and went out and got it! Walked into a jungle, and comes out, the age of twenty-one, and he's rich! The world is an oyster, but you don't crack it open on a mattress!

HAPPY: Pop, I told you I'm gonna retire you for life.

WILLY: You'll retire me for life on seventy goddam dollars a week? And your women and your car and your apartment, and you'll retire me for life! Christ's sake, I couldn't get past Yonkers today! Where are you guys, where are you? The woods are burning! I can't drive a car!

[CHARLEY *has appeared in the doorway. He is a large man, slow of speech, laconic, immovable. In all he says, despite what he says, there is pity, and now, trepidation. He has a robe over pyjamas, slippers on his feet. He enters the kitchen.*]

CHARLEY: Everything all right?

HAPPY: Yeah, Charley, everything's . . .

WILLY: What's the matter?

CHARLEY: I heard some noise. I thought something happened. Can't we do something about the walls? You sneeze in here, and in my house hats blow off.

HAPPY: Let's go to bed, Dad. Come on.

[CHARLEY *signals to* HAPPY *to go.*]

WILLY: You go ahead, I'm not tired at the moment.

HAPPY [*to* WILLY]: Take it easy, huh? [*He exits.*]

WILLY: What're you doin' up?

CHARLEY [*sitting down at the kitchen table opposite* WILLY]: Couldn't sleep good. I had a heartburn.

WILLY: Well, you don't know how to eat.

CHARLEY: I eat with my mouth.

WILLY: No, you're ignorant. You gotta know about vitamins and things like that.

CHARLEY: Come on, let's shoot. Tire you out a little.

WILLY [*hesitantly*]: All right. You got cards?

CHARLEY [*taking a deck from his pocket*]: Yeah, I got them. Someplace. What is it with those vitamins?

WILLY [*dealing*]: They build up your bones. Chemistry.

CHARLEY: Yeah, but there's no bones in a heartburn.

WILLY: What are you talkin' about? Do you know the first thing about it?

CHARLEY: Don't get insulted.

WILLY: Don't talk about something you don't know anything about.

[*They are playing. Pause.*]

CHARLEY: What're you doin' home?

WILLY: A little trouble with the car.

CHARLEY: Oh. [*Pause.*] I'd like to take a trip to California.

WILLY: Don't say.

CHARLEY: You want a job?

WILLY: I got a job, I told you that. [*After a slight pause*] What the hell are you offering me a job for?

CHARLEY: Don't get insulted.

WILLY: Don't insult me.

CHARLEY: I don't see no sense in it. You don't have to go on this way.

WILLY: I got a good job. [*Slight pause.*] What do you keep comin' in here for?

CHARLEY: You want me to go?

WILLY [*after a pause, withering*]: I can't understand it. He's going back to Texas again. What the hell is that?

CHARLEY: Let him go.

WILLY: I got nothin' to give him, Charley, I'm clean, I'm clean.

CHARLEY: He won't starve. None of them starve. Forget about him.

WILLY: Then what have I got to remember?

CHARLEY: You take it too hard. To hell with it. When a deposit bottle is broken you don't get your nickel back.

WILLY: That's easy enough for you to say.

CHARLEY: That ain't easy for me to say.

WILLY: Did you see the ceiling I put up in the living-room?

CHARLEY: Yeah, that's a piece of work. To put up a ceiling is a mystery to me. How do you do it?

WILLY: What's the difference?

CHARLEY: Well, talk about it.

WILLY: You gonna put up a ceiling?

CHARLEY: How could I put up a ceiling?

WILLY: Then what the hell are you bothering me for?

CHARLEY: You're insulted again.

WILLY: A man who can't handle tools is not a man. You're disgusting.

CHARLEY: Don't call me disgusting, Willy.

[UNCLE BEN, *carrying a valise and an umbrella, enters the forestage from around the right corner of the house. He is a stolid man, in his sixties, with a moustache and an authoritative air. He is utterly certain of his destiny, and there is an aura of far places about him. He enters exactly as* WILLY *speaks.*]

WILLY: I'm getting awfully tired, Ben.

[BEN'S *music is heard.* BEN *looks around at everything.*]

CHARLEY: Good, keep playing; you'll sleep better. Did you call me Ben?

[BEN *looks at his watch.*]

WILLY: That's funny. For a second there you reminded me of my brother Ben.

BEN: I only have a few minutes. [*He strolls, inspecting the place.* WILEY *and* CHARLEY *continue playing.*]

CHARLEY: You never heard from him again, heh? Since that time?

WILLY: Didn't Linda tell you? Couple of weeks ago we got a letter from his wife in Africa. He died.

CHARLEY: That so.

BEN [*chuckling*]: So this is Brooklyn, eh?

CHARLEY: Maybe you're in for some of his money.

WILLY: Naa, he had seven sons. There's just one opportunity I had with that man . . .

BEN: I must make a train, William. There are several properties I'm looking at in Alaska.

WILLY: Sure, sure! If I'd gone with him to Alaska that time, everything would've been totally different.

CHARLEY: Go on, you'd froze to death up there.

WILLY: What're you talking about?

BEN: Opportunity is tremendous in Alaska, William. Surprised you're not up there.

WILLY: Sure, tremendous.

CHARLEY: Heh?

WILLY: There was the only man I ever met who knew the answers.

CHARLEY: Who?

BEN: How are you all?

WILLY [*taking a pot, smiling*]: Fine, fine.

CHARLEY: Pretty sharp tonight.

BEN: Is Mother living with you?

WILLY: No, she died a long time ago.

CHARLEY: Who?

BEN: That's too bad. Fine specimen of a lady, Mother.

WILLY [*to* CHARLEY]: Heh?

BEN: I'd hoped to see the old girl.

CHARLEY: Who died?

BEN: Heard anything from Father, have you?

WILLY [*unnerved*]: What do you mean, who died?

CHARLEY [*taking a pot*]: What're you talkin' about?

BEN [*looking at his watch*]: William, it's half past eight!

WILLY [*as though to dispel his confusion he angrily stops* CHAR-
LEY'S *hand*]: That's my build!

CHARLEY: I put the ace —

WILLY: If you don't know how to play the game I'm not
gonna throw my money away on you!

CHARLEY [*rising*]: It was my ace, for God's sake!

WILLY: I'm through, I'm through!

BEN: When did Mother die?

WILLY: Long ago. Since the beginning you never knew how
to play cards.

CHARLEY [*picks up the cards and goes to the door*]: All right!
Next time I'll bring a deck with five aces.

WILLY: I don't play that kind of game!

CHARLEY [*turning to him*]: You ought to be ashamed of yourself!

WILLY: Yeah?

CHARLEY: Yeah! [*He goes out.*]

WILLY [*slamming the door after him*]: Ignoramus!

BEN [*as* WILLY *comes toward him through the wall-line of the
kitchen*]: So you're William.

WILLY [*shaking* BEN'S *hand*]: Ben! I've been waiting for you
so long! What's the answer? How did you do it?

BEN: Oh, there's a story in that.

   [LINDA *enters the forestage, as of old, carrying the wash
   basket.*]

LINDA: Is this Ben?

BEN [*gallantly*]: How do you do, my dear?

LINDA: Where've you been all these years? Willy's always
wondered why you —

WILLY [*pulling* BEN *away from her impatiently*]: Where is Dad? Didn't you follow him? How did you get started?

BEN: Well, I don't know how much you remember.

WILLY: Well, I was just a baby, of course, only three or four years old –

BEN: Three years and eleven months.

WILLY: What a memory, Ben!

BEN: I have many enterprises, William, and I have never kept books.

WILLY: I remember I was sitting under the wagon in – was it Nebraska?

BEN: It was South Dakota, and I gave you a bunch of wild flowers.

WILLY: I remember you walking away down some open road.

BEN [*laughing*]: I was going to find Father in Alaska.

WILLY: Where is he?

BEN: At that age I had a very faulty view of geography, William. I discovered after a few days that I was heading due south, so instead of Alaska, I ended up in Africa.

LINDA: Africa!

WILLY: The Gold Coast!

BEN: Principally diamond mines.

LINDA: Diamond mines!

BEN: Yes, my dear. But I've only a few minutes –

WILLY: No! Boys! Boys! [YOUNG BIFF *and* HAPPY *appear*.] Listen to this. This is your Uncle Ben, a great man! Tell my boys, Ben!

BEN: Why boys, when I was seventeen I walked into the jungle, and when I was twenty-one I walked out. [*He laughs*.] And by God I was rich.

WILLY [*to the boys*]: You see what I been talking about? The greatest things can happen!

BEN [*glancing at his watch*]: I have an appointment in Ketchikan Tuesday week.

WILLY: No, Ben! Please tell about Dad. I want my boys to

hear. I want them to know the kind of stock they spring from. All I remember is a man with a big beard, and I was in Mamma's lap, sitting around a fire, and some kind of high music.

BEN: His flute. He played the flute.

WILLY: Sure, the flute, that's right!

[*New music is heard, a high, rollicking tune.*]

BEN: Father was a very great and a very wild-hearted man. We would start in Boston, and he'd toss the whole family into the wagon, and then he'd drive the team right across the country; through Ohio, and Indiana, Michigan, Illinois, and all the Western states. And we'd stop in the towns and sell the flutes that he'd made on the way. Great inventor, Father. With one gadget he made more in a week than a man like you could make in a lifetime.

WILLY: That's just the way I'm bringing them up, Ben – rugged, well liked, all-around.

BEN: Yeah? [*To* BIFF] Hit that, boy – hard as you can. [*He pounds his stomach.*]

BIFF: Oh, no, sir!

BEN [*taking boxing stance*]: Come on, get to me! [*He laughs.*]

WILLY: Go to it, Biff! Go ahead, show him!

BIFF: Okay! [*He cocks his fists and starts in.*]

LINDA [*to* WILLY]: Why must he fight, dear?

BEN [*sparring with* BIFF]: Good boy! Good boy!

WILLY: How's that, Ben, heh?

HAPPY: Give him the left, Biff!

LINDA: Why are you fighting?

BEN: Good boy! [*Suddenly comes in, trips* BIFF, *and stands over him, the point of his umbrella poised over* BIFF'S *eye.*]

LINDA: Look out, Biff!

BIFF: Gee!

BEN [*patting* BIFF'S *knee*]: Never fight fair with a stranger, boy. You'll never get out of the jungle that way. [*Taking* LINDA'S *hand and bowing*] It was an honour and a pleasure to meet you, Linda.

LINDA [*withdrawing her hand coldly, frightened*]: Have a nice
– trip.

BEN [*to* WILLY]: And good luck with your – what do you
do?

WILLY: Selling.

BEN: Yes. Well . . . [*He raises his hand in farewell to all.*]

WILLY: No, Ben, I don't want you to think . . . [*He takes*
BEN'S *arm to show him.*] It's Brooklyn, I know, but we
hunt too.

BEN: Really, now.

WILLY: Oh, sure, there's snakes and rabbits and – that's why I
moved out here. Why, Biff can fell any one of these trees
in no time! Boys! Go right over to where they're building
the apartment house and get some sand. We're gonna
rebuild the entire front stoop right now! Watch this,
Ben!

BIFF: Yes, sir! On the double, Hap!

HAPPY [*as he and* BIFF *run off*]: I lost weight, Pop, you
notice?

[CHARLEY *enters in knickers, even before the boys are gone.*]

CHARLEY: Listen, if they steal any more from that building
the watchman'll put the cops on them!

LINDA [*to* WILLY]: Don't let Biff . . .

[BEN *laughs lustily.*]

WILLY: You shoulda seen the lumber they brought home
last week. At least a dozen six-by-tens worth all kinds a
money.

CHARLEY: Listen, if that watchman –

WILLY: I gave them hell, understand. But I got a couple of
fearless characters there.

CHARLEY: Willy, the jails are full of fearless characters.

BEN [*clapping* WILLY *on the back, with a laugh at* CHARLEY]:
And the stock exchange, friend!

WILLY [*joining in* BEN'S *laughter*]: Where are the rest of your
pants?

CHARLEY: My wife bought them.

WILLY: Now all you need is a golf club and you can go upstairs and go to sleep. [*To* BEN] Great athlete! Between him and his son Bernard they can't hammer a nail!

BERNARD [*rushing in*]: The watchman's chasing Biff!

WILLY [*angrily*]: Shut up! He's not stealing anything!

LINDA [*alarmed, hurrying off left*]: Where is he? Biff, dear! [*She exits.*]

WILLY [*moving toward the left, away from* BEN]: There's nothing wrong. What's the matter with you?

BEN: Nervy boy. Good!

WILLY [*laughing*]: Oh, nerves of iron, that Biff!

CHARLEY: Don't know what it is. My New England man comes back and he's bleedin', they murdered him up there.

WILLY: It's contacts, Charley, I got important contacts!

CHARLEY [*sarcastically*]: Glad to hear it, Willy. Come in later, we'll shoot a little casino. I'll take some of your Portland money. [*He laughs at* WILLY *and exits.*]

WILLY [*turning to* BEN]: Business is bad, it's murderous. But not for me, of course.

BEN: I'll stop by on my way back to Africa.

WILLY [*longingly*]: Can't you stay a few days? You're just what I need, Ben, because I – I have a fine position here, but I – well, Dad left when I was such a baby and I never had a chance to talk to him and I still feel – kind of temporary about myself.

BEN: I'll be late for my train.

[*They are at opposite ends of the stage.*]

WILLY: Ben, my boys – can't we talk? They'd go into the jaws of hell for me, see, but I –

BEN: William, you're being first-rate with your boys. Outstanding, manly chaps!

WILLY [*hanging on to his words*]: Oh, Ben, that's good to hear! Because sometimes I'm afraid that I'm not teaching them the right kind of – Ben, how should I teach them?

BEN [*giving great weight to each word, and with a certain vicious audacity*]: William, when I walked into the jungle, I was seventeen. When I walked out I was twenty-one. And, by God, I was rich! [*He goes off into darkness around the right corner of the house.*]

WILLY: ... was rich! That's just the spirit I want to imbue them with! To walk into a jungle! I was right! I was right! I was right!

[BEN *is gone, but* WILLY *is still speaking to him as* LINDA, *in nightgown and robe, enters the kitchen, glances around for* WILLY, *then goes to the door of the house, looks out and sees him. Comes down to his left. He looks at her.*]

LINDA: Willy, dear? Willy?

WILLY: I was right!

LINDA: Did you have some cheese? [*He can't answer.*] It's very late, darling. Come to bed, heh?

WILLY [*looking straight up*]: Gotta break your neck to see a star in this yard.

LINDA: You coming in?

WILLY: Whatever happened to that diamond watch fob? Remember? When Ben came from Africa that time? Didn't he give me a watch fob with a diamond in it?

LINDA: You pawned it, dear. Twelve, thirteen years ago. For Biff's radio correspondence course.

WILLY: Gee, that was a beautiful thing. I'll take a walk.

LINDA: But you're in your slippers.

WILLY [*starting to go around the house at the left*]: I was right! I was! [*Half to* LINDA, *as he goes, shaking his head*] What a man! There was a man worth talking to. I was right!

LINDA [*calling after* WILLY]: But in your slippers, Willy!

[WILLY *is almost gone when* BIFF, *in his pyjamas, comes down the stairs and enters the kitchen.*]

BIFF: What is he doing out there?

LINDA: Sh!

BIFF: God Almighty, Mom, how long has he been doing this?

LINDA: Don't, he'll hear you.

BIFF: What the hell is the matter with him?

LINDA: It'll pass by morning.

BIFF: Shouldn't we do anything?

LINDA: Oh, my dear, you should do a lot of things, but there's nothing to do, so go to sleep.

[HAPPY *comes down the stairs and sits on the steps.*]

HAPPY: I never heard him so loud, Mom.

LINDA: Well, come around more often; you'll hear him.

[*She sits down at the table and mends the lining of* WILLY'S *jacket.*]

BIFF: Why didn't you ever write me about this, Mom?

LINDA: How would I write to you? For over three months you had no address.

BIFF: I was on the move. But you know I thought of you all the time. You know that, don't you, pal?

LINDA: I know, dear, I know. But he likes to have a letter. Just to know that there's still a possibility for better things.

BIFF: He's not like this all the time, is he?

LINDA: It's when you come home he's always the worst.

BIFF: When I come home?

LINDA: When you write you're coming, he's all smiles, and talks about the future, and – he's just wonderful. And then the closer you seem to come, the more shaky he gets, and then, by the time you get here, he's arguing, and he seems angry at you. I think it's just that maybe he can't bring himself to – to open up to you. Why are you so hateful to each other? Why is that?

BIFF [*evasively*]: I'm not hateful, Mom.

LINDA: But you no sooner come in the door than you're fighting!

BIFF: I don't know why, I mean to change. I'm tryin', Mom; you understand?

LINDA: Are you home to stay now?

BIFF: I don't know. I want to look around, see what's doin'.

LINDA: Biff, you can't look around all your life, can you?

BIFF: I just can't take hold, Mom. I can't take hold of some kind of a life.

LINDA: Biff, a man is not a bird, to come and go with the springtime.

BIFF: Your hair ... [*He touches her hair.*] Your hair got so grey.

LINDA: Oh, it's been grey since you were in high school. I just stopped dyeing it, that's all.

BIFF: Dye it again, will ya? I don't want my pal looking old. [*He smiles.*]

LINDA: You're such a boy! You think you can go away for a year and ... You've got to get it into your head now that one day you'll knock on this door and there'll be strange people here –

BIFF: What are you talking about? You're not even sixty, Mom.

LINDA: But what about your father?

BIFF [*lamely*]: Well, I meant him too.

HAPPY: He admires Pop.

LINDA: Biff, dear, if you don't have any feeling for him, then you can't have any feeling for me.

BIFF: Sure I can, Mom.

LINDA: No. You can't just come to see me, because I love him. [*With a threat, but only a threat, of tears*] He's the dearest man in the world to me, and I won't have anyone making him feel unwanted and low and blue. You've got to make up your mind now, darling, there's no leeway any more. Either he's your father and you pay him that respect, or else you're not to come here. I know he's not easy to get along with – nobody knows that better than me – but ...

WILLY [*from the left, with a laugh*]: Hey, hey, Biffo!

BIFF [*starting to go out after* WILLY]: What the hell is the matter with him? [HAPPY *stops him.*]

LINDA: Don't – don't go near him!

BIFF: Stop making excuses for him! He always, always wiped the floor with you. Never had an ounce of respect for you.

HAPPY: He's always had respect for –

BIFF: What the hell do you know about it?

HAPPY [*surlily*]: Just don't call him crazy!

BIFF: He's got no character – Charley wouldn't do this. Not in his own house – spewing out that vomit from his mind.

HAPPY: Charley never had to cope with what he's got to.

BIFF: People are worse off than Willy Loman. Believe me, I've seen them!

LINDA: Then make Charley your father, Biff. You can't do that, can you? I don't say he's a great man. Willy Loman never made a lot of money. His name was never in the paper. He's not the finest character that ever lived. But he's a human being, and a terrible thing is happening to him. So attention must be paid. He's not to be allowed to fall into his grave like an old dog. Attention, attention must be finally paid to such a person. You called him crazy –

BIFF: I didn't mean –

LINDA: No, a lot of people think he's lost his – balance. But you don't have to be very smart to know what his trouble is. The man is exhausted.

HAPPY: Sure!

LINDA: A small man can be just as exhausted as a great man. He works for a company thirty-six years this March, opens up unheard-of territories to their trademark, and now in his old age they take his salary away.

HAPPY [*indignantly*]: I didn't know that, Mom.

LINDA: You never asked, my dear! Now that you get your spending money someplace else you don't trouble your mind with him.

HAPPY: But I gave you money last –

LINDA: Christmas-time, fifty dollars! To fix the hot water it cost ninety-seven fifty! For five weeks he's been on straight commission, like a beginner, an unknown!

BIFF: Those ungrateful bastards!

LINDA: Are they any worse than his sons? When he brought them business, when he was young, they were glad to see him. But now his old friends, the old buyers that loved him so and always found some order to hand him in a pinch –

they're all dead, retired. He used to be able to make six, seven calls a day in Boston. Now he takes his valises out of the car and puts them back and takes them out again and he's exhausted. Instead of walking he talks now. He drives seven hundred miles, and when he gets there no one knows him any more, no one welcomes him. And what goes through a man's mind, driving seven hundred miles home without having earned a cent? Why shouldn't he talk to himself? Why? When he has to go to Charley and borrow fifty dollars a week and pretend to me that it's his pay? How long can that go on? How long? You see what I'm sitting here and waiting for? And you tell me he has no character? The man who never worked a day but for your benefit? When does he get the medal for that? Is this his reward – to turn around at the age of sixty-three and find his sons, who he loved better than his life, one a philandering bum –

HAPPY: Mom!

LINDA: That's all you are, my baby! [*To* BIFF] And you! What happened to the love you had for him? You were such pals! How you used to talk to him on the phone every night! How lonely he was till he could come home to you!

BIFF: All right, Mom. I'll live here in my room, and I'll get a job. I'll keep away from him, that's all.

LINDA: No, Biff. You can't stay here and fight all the time.

BIFF: He threw me out of this house, remember that.

LINDA: Why did he do that? I never knew why.

BIFF: Because I know he's a fake and he doesn't like anybody around who knows!

LINDA: Why a fake? In what way? What do you mean?

BIFF: Just don't lay it all at my feet. It's between me and him – that's all I have to say. I'll chip in from now on. He'll settle for half my pay cheque. He'll be all right. I'm going to bed. [*He starts for the stairs.*]

LINDA: He won't be all right.

BIFF [*turning on the stairs, furiously*]: I hate this city and I'll stay here. Now what do you want?

LINDA: He's dying, Biff.

[HAPPY *turns quickly to her, shocked.*]

BIFF [*after a pause*]: Why is he dying?

LINDA: He's been trying to kill himself.

BIFF [*with great horror*]: How?

LINDA: I live from day to day.

BIFF: What're you talking about?

LINDA: Remember I wrote you that he smashed up the car again? In February?

BIFF: Well?

LINDA: The insurance inspector came. He said that they have evidence. That all these accidents in the last year – weren't – weren't – accidents.

HAPPY: How can they tell that? That's a lie.

LINDA: It seems there's a woman . . . [*She takes a breath as*]

BIFF [*sharply but contained*]: ⎫ What woman?

LINDA [*simultaneously*]:   ⎭ . . . and this woman . . .

LINDA: What?

BIFF: Nothing. Go ahead.

LINDA: What did you say?

BIFF: Nothing. I just said what woman?

HAPPY: What about her?

LINDA: Well, it seems she was walking down the road and saw his car. She says that he wasn't driving fast at all, and that he didn't skid. She says he came to that little bridge, and then deliberately smashed into the railing, and it was only the shallowness of the water that saved him.

BIFF: Ch, no, he probably just fell asleep again.

LINDA: I don't think he fell asleep.

BIFF: Why not?

LINDA: Last month . . . [*With great difficulty*] Oh, boys, it's so hard to say a thing like this! He's just a big stupid man to you, but I tell you there's more good in him than in many other people. [*She chokes, wipes her eyes.*] I was looking for a fuse. The lights blew out, and I went down the cellar.

And behind the fuse-box – it happened to fall out – was a length of rubber pipe – just short.

HAPPY: No kidding?

LINDA: There's a little attachment on the end of it. I knew right away. And sure enough, on the bottom of the water heater there's a new little nipple on the gas pipe.

HAPPY [angrily]: That – jerk.

BIFF: Did you have it taken off?

LINDA: I'm – I'm ashamed to. How can I mention it to him? Every day I go down and take away that little rubber pipe. But, when he comes home, I put it back where it was. How can I insult him that way? I don't know what to do. I live from day to day, boys. I tell you, I know every thought in his mind. It sounds so old-fashioned and silly, but I tell you he put his whole life into you and you've turned your backs on him. [She is bent over in the chair, weeping, her face in her hands.] Biff, I swear to God! Biff, his life is in your hands!

HAPPY [to BIFF]: How do you like that damned fool!

BIFF [kissing her]: All right, pal, all right. It's all settled now. I've been remiss. I know that, Mom. But now I'll stay, and I swear to you, I'll apply myself. [Kneeling in front of her, in a fever of self-reproach] It's just – you see, Mom, I don't fit in business. Not that I won't try. I'll try, and I'll make good.

HAPPY: Sure you will. The trouble with you in business was you never tried to please people.

BIFF: I know, I –

HAPPY: Like when you worked for Harrison's. Bob Harrison said you were tops, and then you go and do some damn fool thing like whistling whole songs in the elevator like a comedian.

BIFF [against HAPPY]: So what? I like to whistle sometimes.

HAPPY: You don't raise a guy to a responsible job who whistles in the elevator!

LINDA: Well, don't argue about it now.

HAPPY: Like when you'd go off and swim in the middle of the day instead of taking the line around.

BIFF [*his resentment rising*]: Well, don't you run off? You take off sometimes, don't you? On a nice summer day?

HAPPY: Yeah, but I cover myself!

LINDA: Boys!

HAPPY: If I'm going to take a fade the boss can call any number where I'm supposed to be and they'll swear to him that I just left. I'll tell you something that I hate to say, Biff, but in the business world some of them think you're crazy.

BIFF [*angered*]: Screw the business world!

HAPPY: All right, screw it! Great, but cover yourself!

LINDA: Hap, Hap!

BIFF: I don't care what they think! They've laughed at Dad for years, and you know why? Because we don't belong in this nuthouse of a city! We should be mixing cement on some open plain, or – or carpenters. A carpenter is allowed to whistle!

[WILLY *walks in from the entrance of the house, at left.*]

WILLY: Even your grandfather was better than a carpenter. [*Pause. They watch him.*] You never grew up. Bernard does not whistle in the elevator, I assure you.

BIFF [*as though to laugh* WILLY *out of it*]: Yeah, but you do, Pop.

WILLY: I never in my life whistled in an elevator! And who in the business world thinks I'm crazy?

BIFF: I didn't mean it like that, Pop. Now don't make a whole thing out of it, will ya?

WILLY: Go back to the West? Be a carpenter, a cowboy, enjoy yourself!

LINDA: Willy, he was just saying –

WILLY: I heard what he said!

HAPPY [*trying to quiet* WILLY]: Hey, Pop, come on now . . .

WILLY [*continuing over* HAPPY's *line*]: They laugh at me, heh? Go to Filene's, go to the Hub, go to Slattery's, Boston. Call out the name Willy Loman and see what happens! Big shot!

BIFF: All right, Pop.

WILLY: Big!

BIFF: All right!

WILLY: Why do you always insult me?

BIFF: I didn't say a word. [*To* LINDA] Did I say a word?

LINDA: He didn't say anything, Willy.

WILLY [*going to the doorway of the living-room*]: All right, good night, good night.

LINDA: Willy, dear, he just decided . . .

WILLY [*to* BIFF]: If you get tired hanging around tomorrow, paint the ceiling I put up in the living-room.

BIFF: I'm leaving early tomorrow.

HAPPY: He's going to see Bill Oliver, Pop.

WILLY [*interestedly*]: Oliver? For what?

BIFF [*with reserve, but trying, trying*]: He always said he'd stake me. I'd like to go into business, so maybe I can take him up on it.

LINDA: Isn't that wonderful?

WILLY: Don't interrupt. What's wonderful about it? There's fifty men in the City of New York who'd stake him. [*To* BIFF] Sporting goods?

BIFF: I guess so. I know something about it and –

WILLY: He knows something about it! You know sporting goods better than Spalding, for God's sake! How much is he giving you?

BIFF: I don't know, I didn't even see him yet, but –

WILLY: Then what're you talkin' about?

BIFF [*getting angry*]: Well, all I said was I'm gonna see him, that's all!

WILLY [*turning away*]: Ah, you're counting your chickens again.

BIFF [*starting left for the stairs*]: Oh, Jesus, I'm going to sleep!

WILLY [*calling after him*]: Don't curse in this house!

BIFF [*turning*]: Since when did you get so clean?

HAPPY [*trying to stop them*]: Wait a . . .

WILLY: Don't use that language to me! I won't have it!

HAPPY [*grabbing* BIFF, *shouts*]: Wait a minute! I got an idea.

I got a feasible idea. Come here, Biff, let's talk this over now, let's talk some sense here. When I was down in Florida last time, I thought of a great idea to sell sporting goods. It just came back to me. You and I, Biff – we have a line, the Loman Line. We train a couple of weeks, and put on a couple of exhibitions, see?

WILLY: That's an idea!

HAPPY: Wait! We form two basketball teams, see? Two water-polo teams. We play each other. It's a million dollars' worth of publicity. Two brothers, see? The Loman Brothers. Displays in the Royal Palms – all the hotels. And banners over the ring and the basketball court: 'Loman Brothers'. Baby, we could sell sporting goods!

WILLY: That is a one-million-dollar idea!

LINDA: Marvellous!

BIFF: I'm in great shape as far as that's concerned.

HAPPY: And the beauty of it is, Biff, it wouldn't be like a business. We'd be out playin' ball again . . .

BIFF [enthused]: Yeah, that's . . .

WILLY: Million-dollar . . .

HAPPY: And you wouldn't get fed up with it, Biff. It'd be the family again. There'd be the old honour, and comrade-ship, and if you wanted to go off for a swim or somethin' – well you'd do it! Without some smart cooky gettin' up ahead of you!

WILLY: Lick the world! You guys together could absolutely lick the civilized world.

BIFF: I'll see Oliver tomorrow. Hap, if we could work that out . . .

LINDA: Maybe things are beginning to –

WILLY [wildly enthused, to LINDA]: Stop interrupting! [To BIFF] But don't wear sport jacket and slacks when you see Oliver.

BIFF: No, I'll –

WILLY: A business suit, and talk as little as possible, and don't crack any jokes.

BIFF: He did like me. Always liked me.

LINDA: He loved you!

WILLY [to LINDA]: Will you stop! [To BIFF] Walk in very serious. You are not applying for a boy's job. Money is to pass. Be quiet, fine, and serious. Everybody likes a kidder, but nobody lends him money.

HAPPY: I'll try to get some myself, Biff. I'm sure I can.

WILLY: I see great things for you kids, I think your troubles are over. But remember, start big and you'll end big. Ask for fifteen. How much you gonna ask for?

BIFF: Gee, I don't know –

WILLY: And don't say 'Gee'. 'Gee' is a boy's word. A man walking in for fifteen thousand dollars does not say 'Gee'!

BIFF: Ten, I think, would be top though.

WILLY: Don't be so modest. You always started too low. Walk in with a big laugh. Don't look worried. Start off with a couple of your good stories to lighten things up. It's not what you say, it's how you say it – because personality always wins the day.

LINDA: Oliver always thought the highest of him –

WILLY: Will you let me talk?

BIFF: Don't yell at her, Pop, will ya?

WILLY [angrily]: I was talking, wasn't I?

BIFF: I don't like you yelling at her all the time, and I'm tellin' you, that's all.

WILLY: What're you, takin' over this house?

LINDA: Willy –

WILLY [turning on her]: Don't take his side all the time, goddammit!

BIFF [furiously]: Stop yelling at her!

WILLY [suddenly pulling on his cheek, beaten down, guilt ridden]: Give my best to Bill Oliver – he may remember me. [He exits through the living-room doorway.]

LINDA [her voice subdued]: What'd you have to start that for? [BIFF turns away.] You see how sweet he was as soon as you talked hopefully? [She goes over to BIFF.] Come up and say good night to him. Don't let him go to bed that way.

HAPPY: Come on, Biff, let's buck him up.

LINDA: Please, dear. Just say good night. It takes so little to make him happy. Come. [*She goes through the living-room doorway, calling upstairs from within the living-room.*] Your pyjamas are hanging in the bathroom, Willy!

HAPPY [*looking toward where* LINDA *went out*]: What a woman! They broke the mould when they made her. You know that, Biff?

BIFF: He's off salary. My God, working on commission!

HAPPY: Well, let's face it: he's no hot-shot selling man. Except that sometimes, you have to admit, he's a sweet personality.

BIFF [*deciding*]: Lend me ten bucks, will ya? I want to buy some new ties.

HAPPY: I'll take you to a place I know. Beautiful stuff. Wear one of my striped shirts tomorrow.

BIFF: She got grey. Mom got awful old. Gee. I'm gonna go in to Oliver tomorrow and knock him for a –

HAPPY: Come on up. Tell that to Dad. Let's give him a whirl. Come on.

BIFF [*steamed up*]: You know, with ten thousand bucks, boy!

HAPPY [*as they go into the living-room*]: That's the talk, Biff, that's the first time I've heard the old confidence out of you! [*From within the living-room, fading off*] You're gonna live with me, kid, and any babe you want just say the word . . . [*The last lines are hardly heard. They are mounting the stairs to their parents' bedroom.*]

LINDA [*entering her bedroom and addressing* WILLY, *who is in the bathroom. She is straightening the bed for him.*] Can you do anything about the shower? It drips.

WILLY [*from the bedroom*]: All of a sudden everything falls to pieces! Goddam plumbing, oughta be sued, those people. I hardly finished putting it in and the thing . . . [*His words rumble off.*]

LINDA: I'm just wondering if Oliver will remember him. You think he might?

WILLY [*coming out of the bathroom in his pyjamas*]: Remember him? What's the matter with you, you crazy? If he'd've stayed with Oliver he'd be on top by now! Wait'll Oliver gets a look at him. You don't know the average calibre any more. The average young man today – [*he is getting into bed*] – is got a calibre of zero. Greatest thing in the world for him was to bum around.

[BIFF *and* HAPPY *enter the bedroom. Slight pause.*]

WILLY [*stops short, looking at* BIFF]: Glad to hear it, boy.

HAPPY: He wanted to say good night to you, sport.

WILLY [*to* BIFF]: Yeah. Knock him dead, boy. What'd you want to tell me?

BIFF: Just take it easy, Pop. Good night. [*He turns to go.*]

WILLY [*unable to resist*]: And if anything falls off the desk while you're talking to him – like a package or something – don't you pick it up. They have office boys for that.

LINDA: I'll make a big breakfast –

WILLY: Will you let me finish? [*To* BIFF] Tell him you were in the business in the West. Not farm work.

BIFF: All right, Dad.

LINDA: I think everything –

WILLY [*going right through her speech*]: And don't undersell yourself. No less than fifteen thousand dollars.

BIFF [*unable to bear him*]: Okay. Good night, Mom. [*He starts moving.*]

WILLY: Because you got a greatness in you, Biff, remember that. You got all kinds a greatness . . . [*He lies back, exhausted.* BIFF *walks out.*]

LINDA [*calling after* BIFF]: Sleep well, darling!

HAPPY: I'm gonna get married, Mom. I wanted to tell you.

LINDA: Go to sleep, dear.

HAPPY [*going*]: I just wanted to tell you.

WILLY: Keep up the good work. [HAPPY *exits.*] God . . .

remember that Ebbets Field game? The championship of the city?

LINDA: Just rest. Should I sing to you?

WILLY: Yeah. Sing to me. [LINDA *hums a soft lullaby.*] When that team came out – he was the tallest, remember?

LINDA: Oh, yes. And in gold.

[BIFF *enters the darkened kitchen, takes a cigarette, and leaves the house. He comes downstage into a golden pool of light. He smokes, staring at the night.*]

WILLY: Like a young god. Hercules – something like that. And the sun, the sun all around him. Remember how he waved to me? Right up from the field, with the representatives of three colleges standing by? And the buyers I brought, and the cheers when he came out – Loman, Loman, Loman! God Almighty, he'll be great yet. A star like that, magnificent, can never really fade away!

[*The light on* WILLY *is fading. The gas heater begins to glow through the kitchen wall, near the stairs, a blue flame beneath red coils.*]

LINDA [*timidly*]: Willy dear, what has he got against you?

WILLY: I'm so tired. Don't talk any more.

[BIFF *slowly returns to the kitchen. He stops, stares toward the heater.*]

LINDA: Will you ask Howard to let you work in New York?

WILLY: First thing in the morning. Everything'll be all right.

[BIFF *reaches behind the heater and draws out a length of rubber tubing. He is horrified and turns his head toward* WILLY's *room, still dimly lit, from which the strains of* LINDA's *desperate but monotonous humming rise.*]

WILLY [*staring through the window into the moonlight*]: Gee, look at the moon moving between the buildings!

[BIFF *wraps the tubing around his hand and quickly goes up the stairs.*]

CURTAIN

ACT TWO

Music is heard, gay and bright. The curtain rises as the music fades away.

> [WILLY, *in shirt sleeves, is sitting at the kitchen table, sipping coffee, his hat in his lap.* LINDA *is filling his cup when she can.*]

WILLY: Wonderful coffee. Meal in itself.

LINDA: Can I make you some eggs?

WILLY: No. Take a breath.

LINDA: You look so rested, dear.

WILLY: I slept like a dead one. First time in months. Imagine, sleeping till ten on a Tuesday morning. Boys left nice and early, heh?

LINDA: They were out of here by eight o'clock.

WILLY: Good work!

LINDA: It was so thrilling to see them leaving together. I can't get over the shaving lotion in this house!

WILLY [*smiling*]: Mmm –

LINDA: Biff was very changed this morning. His whole attitude seemed to be hopeful. He couldn't wait to get downtown to see Oliver.

WILLY: He's heading for a change. There's no question, there simply are certain men that take longer to get – solidified. How did he dress?

LINDA: His blue suit. He's so handsome in that suit. He could be a – anything in that suit!

> [WILLY *gets up from the table.* LINDA *holds his jacket for him.*]

WILLY: There's no question, no question at all. Gee, on the way home tonight I'd like to buy some seeds.

LINDA [*laughing*]: That'd be wonderful. But not enough sun gets back there. Nothing'll grow any more.

WILLY: You wait, kid, before it's all over we're gonna get a little place out in the country, and I'll raise some vegetables, a couple of chickens . . .

LINDA: You'll do it yet, dear.

[WILLY *walks out of his jacket.* LINDA *follows him.*]

WILLY: And they'll get married, and come for a weekend. I'd build a little guest house. 'Cause I got so many fine tools, all I'd need would be a little lumber and some peace of mind.

LINDA [*joyfully*]: I sewed the lining . . .

WILLY: I could build two guest houses, so they'd both come. Did he decide how much he's going to ask Oliver for?

LINDA [*getting him into the jacket*]: He didn't mention it, but I imagine ten or fifteen thousand. You going to talk to Howard today?

WILLY: Yeah. I'll put it to him straight and simple. He'll just have to take me off the road.

LINDA: And Willy, don't forget to ask for a little advance, because we've got the insurance premium. It's the grace period now.

WILLY: That's a hundred . . .?

LINDA: A hundred and eight, sixty-eight. Because we're a little short again.

WILLY: Why are we short?

LINDA: Well, you had the motor job on the car . . .

WILLY: That goddam Studebaker!

LINDA: And you got one more payment on the refrigerator . . .

WILLY: But it just broke again!

LINDA: Well, it's old, dear.

WILLY: I told you we should've bought a well-advertised machine. Charley bought a General Electric and it's twenty years old and it's still good, that son-of-a-bitch.

LINDA: But, Willy –

WILLY: Whoever heard of a Hastings refrigerator? Once in my life I would like to own something outright before it's broken! I'm always in a race with the junkyard! I just finished paying for the car and it's on its last legs. The refrigerator consumes belts like a goddam maniac. They time those things. They time them so when you finally paid for them, they're used up.

LINDA [*buttoning up his jacket as he unbuttons it*]: All told, about two hundred dollars would carry us, dear. But that includes the last payment on the mortgage. After this payment, Willy, the house belongs to us.

WILLY: It's twenty-five years!

LINDA: Biff was nine years old when we bought it.

WILLY: Well, that's a great thing. To weather a twenty-five-year mortgage is –

LINDA: It's an accomplishment.

WILLY: All the cement, the lumber, the reconstruction I put in this house! There ain't a crack to be found in it any more.

LINDA: Well, it served its purpose.

WILLY: What purpose? Some stranger'll come along, move in, and that's that. If only Biff would take this house, and raise a family . . . [*He starts to go.*] Good-bye, I'm late.

LINDA [*suddenly remembering*]: Oh, I forgot! You're supposed to meet them for dinner.

WILLY: Me?

LINDA: At Frank's Chop House on Forty-eighth near Sixth Avenue.

WILLY: Is that so! How about you?

LINDA: No, just the three of you. They're gonna blow you to a big meal!

WILLY: Don't say! Who thought of that?

LINDA: Biff came to me this morning, Willy, and he said, 'Tell Dad, we want to blow him to a big meal.' Be there six o'clock. You and your two boys are going to have dinner.

WILLY: Gee whiz! That's really somethin'. I'm gonna knock Howard for a loop, kid. I'll get an advance, and I'll come home with a New York job. Goddammit, now I'm gonna do it!

LINDA: Oh, that's the spirit, Willy!

WILLY: I will never get behind a wheel the rest of my life!

LINDA: It's changing, Willy, I can feel it changing!

WILLY: Beyond a question. G'bye, I'm late. [*He starts to go again.*]

LINDA [*calling after him as she runs to the kitchen table for a handkerchief*]: You got your glasses?

WILLY [*feels for them, then comes back in*]: Yeah, yeah, got my glasses.

LINDA [*giving him the handkerchief*]: And a handkerchief.

WILLY: Yeah, handkerchief.

LINDA: And your saccharine?

WILLY: Yeah, my saccharine.

LINDA: Be careful on the subway stairs.

[*She kisses him, and a silk stocking is seen hanging from her hand.* WILLY *notices it.*]

WILLY: Will you stop mending stockings? At least while I'm in the house. It gets me nervous. I can't tell you. Please.

[LINDA *hides the stocking in her hand as she follows* WILLY *across the forestage in front of the house.*]

LINDA: Remember, Frank's Chop House.

WILLY [*passing the apron*]: Maybe beets would grow out there.

LINDA [*laughing*]: But you tried so many times.

WILLY: Yeah. Well, don't work hard today. [*He disappears around the right corner of the house.*]

LINDA: Be careful!

[*As* WILLY *vanishes,* LINDA *waves to him. Suddenly the phone rings. She runs across the stage and into the kitchen and lifts it.*]

LINDA: Hello? Oh, Biff! I'm so glad you called, I just . . . Yes, sure, I just told him. Yes, he'll be there for dinner at six o'clock, I didn't forget. Listen, I was just dying to tell you. You know that little rubber pipe I told you about? That he connected to the gas heater? I finally decided to go down the cellar this morning and take it away and destroy it. But it's gone! Imagine! He took it away himself, it isn't there! [*She listens.*] When? Oh, then you took it. Oh – nothing, it's just that I'd hoped he'd taken it away himself. Oh, I'm not worried, darling, because this morning he left in such high spirits, it was like the old days! I'm not afraid any more. Did Mr Oliver see you? ... Well, you wait there then. And make a nice impression on him, darling. Just don't perspire too much before you see him. And have a nice time with Dad. He may have big news too! ... That's right, a New York job. And be sweet to him tonight, dear. Be loving to him. Because he's only a little boat looking for a harbour. [*She is trembling with sorrow and joy.*] Oh, that's wonderful, Biff, you'll save his life. Thanks, darling. Just put your arms around him when he comes into the restaurant. Give him a smile. That's the boy ... Good-bye, dear ... You got your comb? ... That's fine. Good-bye, Biff dear.

[*In the middle of her speech,* HOWARD WAGNER, *thirty-six, wheels on a small typewriter table on which is a wire-recording machine and proceeds to plug it in. This is on the left forestage. Light slowly fades on* LINDA *as it rises on* HOWARD. HOWARD *is intent on threading the machine and only glances over his shoulder as* WILLY *appears.*]

WILLY: Pst! Pst!

HOWARD: Hello, Willy, come in.

WILLY: Like to have a little talk with you, Howard.

HOWARD: Sorry to keep you waiting. I'll be with you in a minute.

WILLY: What's that, Howard?

HOWARD: Didn't you ever see one of these? Wire recorder.

WILLY: Oh. Can we talk a minute?

HOWARD: Records things. Just got delivery yesterday. Been driving me crazy, the most terrific machine I ever saw in my life. I was up all night with it.

WILLY: What do you do with it?

HOWARD: I bought it for dictation, but you can do anything with it. Listen to this. I had it home last night. Listen to what I picked up. The first one is my daughter. Get this. [*He flicks the switch and 'Roll out the Barrel' is heard being whistled.*] Listen to that kid whistle.

WILLY: That is lifelike, isn't it?

HOWARD: Seven years old. Get that tone.

WILLY: Ts, ts. Like to ask a little favour if you . . .

[*The whistling breaks off, and the voice of* HOWARD'S *daughter is heard.*]

HIS DAUGHTER: 'Now you, Daddy.'

HOWARD: She's crazy for me! [*Again the same song is whistled.*] That's me! Ha! [*He winks.*]

WILLY: You're very good!

[*The whistling breaks off again. The machine runs silent for a moment.*]

HOWARD: Sh! Get this now, this is my son.

HIS SON: 'The capital of Alabama is Montgomery; the capital of Arizona is Phoenix; the capital of Arkansas is Little Rock; the capital of California is Sacramento . . .' [*and on, and on.*]

HOWARD [*holding up five fingers*]: Five years old, Willy!

WILLY: He'll make an announcer some day!

HIS SON [*continuing*]: 'The capital . . .'

HOWARD: Get that – alphabetical order! [*The machine breaks off suddenly.*] Wait a minute. The maid kicked the plug out.

WILLY: It certainly is a –

HOWARD: Sh, for God's sake!

HIS SON: 'It's nine o'clock, Bulova watch time. So I have to go to sleep.'

WILLY: That really is –

HOWARD: Wait a minute! The next is my wife.

[*They wait.*]

HOWARD'S VOICE: 'Go on, say something.' [*Pause.*] 'Well, you gonna talk?'

HIS WIFE: 'I can't think of anything.'

HOWARD'S VOICE: 'Well, talk – it's turning.'

HIS WIFE [*shyly, beaten*]: 'Hello.' [*Silence.*] 'Oh, Howard, I can't talk into this . . .'

HOWARD [*snapping the machine off*]: That was my wife.

WILLY: That is a wonderful machine. Can we –

HOWARD: I tell you, Willy, I'm gonna take my camera, and my bandsaw, and all my hobbies, and out they go. This is the most fascinating relaxation I ever found.

WILLY: I think I'll get one myself.

HOWARD: Sure, they're only a hundred and a half. You can't do without it. Supposing you wanna hear Jack Benny, see? But you can't be at home at that hour. So you tell the maid to turn the radio on when Jack Benny comes on, and this automatically goes on with the radio . . .

WILLY: And when you come home you . . .

HOWARD: You can come home twelve o'clock, one o'clock, any time you like, and you get yourself a Coke and sit yourself down, throw the switch, and there's Jack Benny's programme in the middle of the night!

WILLY: I'm definitely going to get one. Because lots of time I'm on the road, and I think to myself, what I must be missing on the radio!

HOWARD: Don't you have a radio in the car?

WILLY: Well, yeah, but who ever thinks of turning it on?

HOWARD: Say, aren't you supposed to be in Boston?

WILLY: That's what I want to talk to you about, Howard. You got a minute? [*He draws a chair in from the wing.*]

HOWARD: What happened? What're you doing here?

WILLY: Well . . .

HOWARD: You didn't crack up again, did you?

WILLY: Oh, no. No . . .

HOWARD: Geez, you had me worried there for a minute. What's the trouble?

WILLY: Well, tell you the truth, Howard. I've come to the decision that I'd rather not travel any more.

HOWARD: Not travel! Well, what'll you do?

WILLY: Remember, Christmas-time, when you had the party here? You said you'd try to think of some spot for me here in town.

HOWARD: With us?

WILLY: Well, sure.

HOWARD: Oh, yeah, yeah. I remember. Well, I couldn't think of anything for you, Willy.

WILLY: I tell ya, Howard. The kids are all grown up, y'know. I don't need much any more. If I could take home – well, sixty-five dollars a week, I could swing it.

HOWARD: Yeah, but Willy, see I –

WILLY: I tell ya why, Howard. Speaking frankly and between the two of us, y'know – I'm just a little tired.

HOWARD: Oh, I could understand that, Willy. But you're a road man, Willy, and we do a road business. We've only got a half-dozen salesmen on the floor here.

WILLY: God knows, Howard, I never asked a favour of any man. But I was with the firm when your father used to carry you in here in his arms.

HOWARD: I know that, Willy, but –

WILLY: Your father came to me the day you were born and asked me what I thought of the name of Howard, may he rest in peace.

HOWARD: I appreciate that, Willy, but there just is no spot here for you. If I had a spot I'd slam you right in, but I just don't have a single solitary spot.

[*He looks for his lighter,* WILLY *has picked it up and gives it to him. Pause.*]

WILLY [*with increasing anger*]: Howard, all I need to set my table is fifty dollars a week.

HOWARD: But where am I going to put you, kid?

WILLY: Look, it isn't a question of whether I can sell merchandise, is it?

HOWARD: No, but it's a business, kid, and everybody's gotta pull his own weight.

WILLY [*desperately*]: Just let me tell you a story, Howard –

HOWARD: 'Cause you gotta admit, business is business.

WILLY [*angrily*]: Business is definitely business, but just listen for a minute. You don't understand this. When I was a boy – eighteen, nineteen – I was already on the road. And there was a question in my mind as to whether selling had a future for me. Because in those days I had a yearning to go to Alaska. See, there were three gold strikes in one month in Alaska, and I felt like going out. Just for the ride, you might say.

HOWARD [*barely interested*]: Don't say.

WILLY: Oh, yeah, my father lived many years in Alaska. He was an adventurous man. We've got quite a little streak of self-reliance in our family. I thought I'd go out with my older brother and try to locate him, and maybe settle in the North with the old man. And I was almost decided to go, when I met a salesman in the Parker House. His name was Dave Singleman. And he was eighty-four years old, and he'd drummed merchandise in thirty-one states. And old Dave, he'd go up to his room, y'understand, put on his green velvet slippers – I'll never forget – and pick up his phone and call the buyers, and without ever leaving his room, at the age of eighty-four, he made his living. And when I saw that, I realized that selling was the greatest career a man could want. 'Cause what could be more satisfying than to be able to go, at the age of eighty-four, into twenty or thirty different cities, and pick up a phone, and be remembered and loved and helped by so many different people? Do you know? when he died – and by the way he died the death of a salesman, in his green velvet slippers in the smoker of the New York, New Haven, and Hartford, going into Boston – when he died, hundreds of salesmen and buyers were at his funeral. Things were sad on a lotta trains for months after that. [*He stands up.* HOWARD *has not looked at him.*] In those days there was personality in it, Howard. There was respect, and comradeship, and gratitude in it. Today, it's all cut and dried, and there's no chance for bringing friendship to bear – or personality. You see what I mean? They don't know me any more.

HOWARD [*moving away, toward the right*]: That's just the thing, Willy.

WILLY: If I had forty dollars a week – that's all I'd need. Forty dollars, Howard.

HOWARD: Kid, I can't take blood from a stone, I –

WILLY [*desperation is on him now*]: Howard, the year Al Smith was nominated, your father came to me and –

HOWARD [*starting to go off*]: I've got to see some people, kid.

WILLY [*stopping him*]: I'm talking about your father! There were promises made across this desk! You mustn't tell me you've got people to see – I put thirty-four years into this firm, Howard, and now I can't pay my insurance! You can't eat the orange and throw the peel away – a man is not a piece of fruit! [*After a pause*] Now pay attention. Your father – in 1928 I had a big year. I averaged a hundred and seventy dollars a week in commissions.

HOWARD [*impatiently*]: Now, Willy, you never averaged –

WILLY [*banging his hand on the desk*]: I averaged a hundred and seventy dollars a week in the year of 1928! And your father came to me – or rather, I was in the office here – it was right over this desk – and he put his hand on my shoulder –

HOWARD [*getting up*]: You'll have to excuse me, Willy, I gotta see some people. Pull yourself together. [*Going out*] I'll be back in a little while.

[*On* HOWARD'S *exit, the light on his chair grows very bright and strange.*]

WILLY: Pull myself together! What the hell did I say to him? My God, I was yelling at him! How could I! [WILLY *breaks off, staring at the light, which occupies the chair, animating it. He approaches this chair, standing across the desk from it.*] Frank, Frank, don't you remember what you told me that time? How you put your hand on my shoulder, and Frank . . . [*He leans on the desk and as he speaks the dead man's name he accidentally switches on the recorder, and instantly –*]

HOWARD'S SON: '... of New York is Albany. The capital of Ohio is Cincinnati, the capital of Rhode Island is ...' [*The recitation continues.*]

WILLY [*leaping away with fright, shouting*]: Ha! Howard! Howard! Howard!

HOWARD [*rushing in*]: What happened?

WILLY [*pointing at the machine, which continues nasally, childishly, with the capital cities*]: Shut it off! Shut it off!

HOWARD [*pulling the plug out*]: Look, Willy ...

WILLY [*pressing his hands to his eyes*]: I gotta get myself some coffee. I'll get some coffee ...

[WILLY *starts to walk out.* HOWARD *stops him.*]

HOWARD [*rolling up the cord*]: Willy, look ...

WILLY: I'll go to Boston.

HOWARD: Willy, you can't go to Boston for us.

WILLY: Why can't I go?

HOWARD: I don't want you to represent us. I've been meaning to tell you for a long time now.

WILLY: Howard, are you firing me?

HOWARD: I think you need a good long rest, Willy.

WILLY: Howard –

HOWARD: And when you feel better, come back, and we'll see if we can work something out.

WILLY: But I gotta earn money, Howard. I'm in no position to –

HOWARD: Where are your sons? Why don't your sons give you a hand?

WILLY: They're working on a very big deal.

HOWARD: This is no time for false pride, Willy. You go to your sons and you tell them that you're tired. You've got two great boys, haven't you?

WILLY: Oh, no question, no question, but in the meantime ...

HOWARD: Then that's that, heh?

WILLY: All right, I'll go to Boston tomorrow.

HOWARD: No, no.

WILLY: I can't throw myself on my sons. I'm not a cripple!

HOWARD: Look, kid, I'm busy this morning.

WILLY [*grasping* HOWARD's *arm*]: Howard, you've got to let me go to Boston!

HOWARD [*hard, keeping himself under control*]: I've got a line of people to see this morning. Sit down, take five minutes, and pull yourself together, and then go home, will ya? I need the office, Willy. [*He starts to go, turns, remembering the recorder, starts to push off the table holding the recorder.*] Oh, yeah. Whenever you can this week, stop by and drop off the samples. You'll feel better, Willy, and then come back and we'll talk. Pull yourself together, kid, there's people outside.

[HOWARD *exits, pushing the table off left.* WILLY *stares into space, exhausted. Now the music is heard –* BEN's *music – first distantly, then closer, closer. As* WILLY *speaks,* BEN *enters from the right. He carries valise and umbrella.*]

WILLY: Oh, Ben, how did you do it? What is the answer? Did you wind up the Alaska deal already?

BEN: Doesn't take much time if you know what you're doing. Just a short business trip. Boarding ship in an hour. Wanted to say good-bye.

WILLY: Ben, I've got to talk to you.

BEN [*glancing at his watch*]: Haven't the time, William.

WILLY [*crossing the apron to* BEN]: Ben, nothing's working out. I don't know what to do.

BEN: Now, look here, William. I've bought timberland in Alaska and I need a man to look after things for me.

WILLY: God, timberland! Me and my boys in those grand outdoors!

BEN: You've a new continent at your doorstep, William. Get out of these cities, they're full of talk and time payments and courts of law. Screw on your fists and you can fight for a fortune up there.

WILLY: Yes, yes! Linda, Linda!

[LINDA *enters as of old, with the wash.*]

LINDA: Oh, you're back?

BEN: I haven't much time.

WILLY: No, wait! Linda, he's got a proposition for me in Alaska.

LINDA: But you've got – [*To* BEN] He's got a beautiful job here.

WILLY: But in Alaska, kid, I could –

LINDA: You're doing well enough, Willy!

BEN [*to* LINDA]: Enough for what, my dear?

LINDA [*frightened of* BEN *and angry at him*]: Don't say those things to him! Enough to be happy right here, right now. [*To* WILLY, *while* BEN *laughs*] Why must everybody conquer the world? You're well liked, and the boys love you, and someday – [*to* BEN] – why, old man Wagner told him just the other day that if he keeps it up he'll be a member of the firm, didn't he, Willy?

WILLY: Sure, sure. I am building something with this firm, Ben, and if a man is building something he must be on the right track, mustn't he?

BEN: What are you building? Lay your hand on it. Where is it?

WILLY [*hesitantly*]: That's true, Linda, there's nothing.

LINDA: Why? [*To* BEN] There's a man eighty-four years old –

WILLY: That's right, Ben, that's right. When I look at that man I say, what is there to worry about?

BEN: Bah!

WILLY: It's true, Ben. All he has to do is go into any city, pick up the phone, and he's making his living and you know why?

BEN [*picking up his valise*]: I've got to go.

WILLY [*holding* BEN *back*]: Look at this boy!

[BIFF, *in his high-school sweater, enters carrying suitcase.* HAPPY *carries* BIFF'S *shoulder guards, gold helmet, and football pants.*]

WILLY: Without a penny to his name, three great universities are begging for him, and from there the sky's the limit, because it's not what you do, Ben. It's who you know and the smile on your face! It's contacts, Ben, contacts! The whole wealth of Alaska passes over the lunch table at the Commodore Hotel, and that's the wonder, the wonder of this country, that a man can end with diamonds here on the basis of being liked! [*He turns to* BIFF.] And that's why when you get out on that field today it's important. Because thousands of people will be rooting for you and loving you. [*To* BEN, *who has again begun to leave*] And Ben! when he walks into a business office his name will sound out like a bell and all the doors will open to him! I've seen it, Ben, I've seen it a thousand times! You can't feel it with your hand like timber, but it's there!

BEN: Good-bye, William.

WILLY: Ben, am I right? Don't you think I'm right? I value your advice.

BEN: There's a new continent at your doorstep, William. You could walk out rich. Rich! [*He is gone.*]

WILLY: We'll do it here, Ben! You hear me? We're gonna do it here!

[*Young* BERNARD *rushes in. The gay music of the boys is heard.*]

BERNARD: Oh, gee, I was afraid you left already!

WILLY: Why? What time is it?

BERNARD: It's half past one!

WILLY: Well, come on, everybody! Ebbets Field next stop! Where's the pennants? [*He rushes through the wall-line of the kitchen and out into the living-room.*]

LINDA [*to* BIFF]: Did you pack fresh underwear?

BIFF [*who has been limbering up*]: I want to go!

BERNARD: Biff, I'm carrying your helmet, ain't I?

HAPPY: No, I'm carrying the helmet.

BERNARD: Oh, Biff, you promised me.

HAPPY: I'm carrying the helmet.

BERNARD: How am I going to get in the locker room?

LINDA: Let him carry the shoulder guards. [*She puts her coat and hat on in the kitchen.*]

BERNARD: Can I, Biff? 'Cause I told everybody I'm going to be in the locker room.

HAPPY: In Ebbets Field it's the clubhouse.

BERNARD: I meant the clubhouse. Biff!

HAPPY: Biff!

BIFF [*grandly, after a slight pause*]: Let him carry the shoulder guards.

HAPPY [*as he gives* BERNARD *the shoulder guards*]: Stay close to us now.

[WILLY *rushes in with the pennants.*]

WILLY [*handing them out*]: Everybody wave when Biff comes out on the field. [HAPPY *and* BERNARD *run off.*] You set now, boys?

[*The music has died away.*]

BIFF: Ready to go, Pop. Every muscle is ready.

WILLY [*at the edge of the apron*]: You realize what this means?

BIFF: That's right, Pop.

WILLY [*feeling* BIFF'*s muscles*]: You're comin' home this afternoon captain of the All-Scholastic Championship Team of the City of New York.

BIFF: I got it, Pop. And remember, pal, when I take off my helmet, that touchdown is for you.

WILLY: Let's go! [*He is starting out, with his arm around* BIFF, *when* CHARLEY *enters, as of old, in knickers.*] I got no room for you, Charley.

CHARLEY: Room? For what?

WILLY: In the car.

CHARLEY: You goin' for a ride? I wanted to shoot some casino.

WILLY [*furiously*]: Casino! [*Incredulously*] Don't you realize what today is?

LINDA: Oh, he knows, Willy. He's just kidding you.

WILLY: That's nothing to kid about!

CHARLEY: No, Linda, what's goin' on?

LINDA: He's playing in Ebbets Field.

CHARLEY: Baseball in this weather?

WILLY: Don't talk to him. Come on, come on! [*He is pushing them out.*]

CHARLEY: Wait a minute, didn't you hear the news?

WILLY: What?

CHARLEY: Don't you listen to the radio? Ebbets Field just blew up.

WILLY: You go to hell! [CHARLEY *laughs. Pushing them out*] Come on, come on! We're late.

CHARLEY [*as they go*]: Knock a homer, Biff, knock a homer!

WILLY [*the last to leave, turning to* CHARLEY]: I don't think that was funny, Charley. This is the greatest day of his life.

CHARLEY: Willy, when are you going to grow up?

WILLY: Yeah, heh? When this game is over, Charley, you'll be laughing out of the other side of your face. They'll be calling him another Red Grange. Twenty-five thousand a year.

CHARLEY [*kidding*]: Is that so?

WILLY: Yeah, that's so.

CHARLEY: Well, then, I'm sorry, Willy. But tell me something.

WILLY: What?

CHARLEY: Who is Red Grange?

WILLY: Put up your hands. Goddam you, put up your hands!
[CHARLEY, *chuckling, shakes his head and walks away, around the left corner of the stage.* WILLY *follows him. The music rises to a mocking frenzy.*]

WILLY: Who the hell do you think you are, better than everybody else? You don't know everything, you big, ignorant, stupid . . . Put up your hands!
[*Light rises, on the right side of the forestage, on a small table in the reception room of* CHARLEY'S *office. Traffic sounds are heard.* BERNARD, *now mature, sits whistling to himself. A pair of tennis rackets and an overnight bag are on the floor beside him.*]

WILLY [*offstage*]: What are you walking away for? Don't walk away! If you're going to say something say it to my face! I know you laugh at me behind my back. You'll laugh out of the other side of your goddam face after this game. Touchdown! Touchdown! Eighty thousand people! Touchdown! Right between the goal posts.

[BERNARD *is a quiet, earnest, but self-assured young man.* WILLY'S *voice is coming from right upstage now.* BERNARD *lowers his feet off the table and listens.* JENNY, *his father's secretary, enters.*]

JENNY [*distressed*]: Say, Bernard, will you go out in the hall?

BERNARD: What is that noise? Who is it?

JENNY: Mr Loman. He just got off the elevator.

BERNARD [*getting up*]: Who's he arguing with?

JENNY: Nobody. There's nobody with him. I can't deal with him any more, and your father gets all upset everytime he comes. I've got a lot of typing to do, and your father's waiting to sign it. Will you see him?

WILLY [*entering*]: Touchdown! Touch – [*He sees* JENNY.] Jenny, Jenny, good to see you. How're ya? Workin'? Or still honest?

JENNY: Fine. How've you been feeling?

WILLY: Not much any more, Jenny. Ha, ha! [*He is surprised to see the rackets.*]

BERNARD: Hello, Uncle Willy.

WILLY [*almost shocked*]: Bernard! Well, look who's here! [*He comes quickly, guiltily, to* BERNARD *and warmly shakes his hand.*]

BERNARD: How are you? Good to see you.

WILLY: What are you doing here?

BERNARD: Oh, just stopped by to see Pop. Get off my feet till my train leaves. I'm going to Washington in a few minutes.

WILLY: Is he in?

BERNARD: Yes, he's in his office with the accountant. Sit down.

WILLY [*sitting down*]: What're you going to do in Washington?

BERNARD: Oh, just a case I've got there, Willy.

WILLY: That so? [*Indicating the rackets*] You going to play tennis there?

BERNARD: I'm staying with a friend who's got a court.

WILLY: Don't say. His own tennis court. Must be fine people, I bet.

BERNARD: They are, very nice. Dad tells me Biffs' in town.

WILLY [*with a big smile*]: Yeah, Biffs' in. Working on a very big deal, Bernard.

BERNARD: What's Biff doing?

WILLY: Well, he's been doing very big things in the West. But he decided to establish himself here. Very big. We're having dinner. Did I hear your wife had a boy?

BERNARD: That's right. Our second.

WILLY: Two boys! What do you know!

BERNARD: What kind of a deal has Biff got?

WILLY: Well, Bill Oliver – very big sporting-goods man – he wants Biff very badly. Called him in from the West. Long distance, *carte blanche*, special deliveries. Your friends have their own private tennis court?

BERNARD: You still with the old firm, Willy?

WILLY [*after a pause*]: I'm – I'm overjoyed to see how you made the grade, Bernard, overjoyed. It's an encouraging thing to see a young man really – really – Looks very good for Biff – very – [*He breaks off, then*] Bernard – [*He is so full of emotion, he breaks off again.*]

BERNARD: What is it, Willy?

WILLY [*small and alone*]: What – what's the secret?

BERNARD: What secret?

WILLY: How – how did you? Why didn't he ever catch on?

BERNARD: I wouldn't know that, Willy.

WILLY [*confidentially, desperately*]: You were his friend, his boyhood friend. There's something I don't understand about it. His life ended after that Ebbets Field game. From the age of seventeen nothing good ever happened to him.

BERNARD: He never trained himself for anything.

WILLY: But he did, he did. After high school he took so many correspondence courses. Radio mechanics; television; God knows what, and never made the slightest mark.

BERNARD [*taking off his glasses*]: Willy, do you want to talk candidly?

WILLY [*rising, faces* BERNARD]: I regard you as a very brilliant man, Bernard. I value your advice.

BERNARD: Oh, the hell with the advice, Willy. I couldn't advise you. There's just one thing I've always wanted to ask you. When he was supposed to graduate, and the math teacher flunked him –

WILLY: Oh, that son-of-a-bitch ruined his life.

BERNARD: Yeah, but, Willy, all he had to do was to go to summer school and make up that subject.

WILLY: That's right, that's right.

BERNARD: Did you tell him not to go to summer school?

WILLY: Me? I begged him to go. I ordered him to go!

BERNARD: Then why wouldn't he go?

WILLY: Why? Why? Bernard, that question has been trailing me like a ghost for the last fifteen years. He flunked the subject, and laid down and died like a hammer hit him!

BERNARD: Take it easy, kid.

WILLY: Let me talk to you – I got nobody to talk to. Bernard, Bernard, was it my fault? Y' see? It keeps going around in my mind, maybe I did something to him. I got nothing to give him.

BERNARD: Don't take it so hard.

WILLY: Why did he lay down? What is the story there? You were his friend!

BERNARD: Willy, I remember, it was June, and our grades came out. And he'd flunked math.

WILLY: That son-of-a-bitch!

BERNARD: No, it wasn't right then. Biff just got very angry, I remember, and he was ready to enrol in summer school.

WILLY [*surprised*]: He was?

BERNARD: He wasn't beaten by it at all. But then, Willy, he

disappeared from the block for almost a month. And I got the idea that he'd gone up to New England to see you. Did he have a talk with you then?

[WILLY *stares in silence.*]

BERNARD: Willy?

WILLY [*with a strong edge of resentment in his voice*]: Yeah, he came to Boston. What about it?

BERNARD: Well, just that when he came back – I'll never forget this, it always mystifies me. Because I'd thought so well of Biff, even though he'd always taken advantage of me. I loved him, Willy, y'know? And he came back after that month and took his sneakers – remember those sneakers with 'University of Virginia' printed on them? He was so proud of those, wore them every day. And he took them down in the cellar, and burned them up in the furnace. We had a fist fight. It lasted at least half an hour. Just the two of us, punching each other down the cellar, and crying right through it. I've often thought of how strange it was that I knew he'd given up his life. What happened in Boston, Willy?

[WILLY *looks at him as at an intruder.*]

BERNARD: I just bring it up because you asked me.

WILLY [*angrily*]: Nothing. What do you mean, 'What happened?' What's that got to do with anything?

BERNARD: Well, don't get sore.

WILLY: What are you trying to do, blame it on me? If a boy lays down is that my fault?

BERNARD: Now, Willy, don't get –

WILLY: Well, don't – don't talk to me that way! What does that mean, 'What happened?'

[CHARLEY *enters. He is in his vest, and he carries a bottle of bourbon.*]

CHARLEY: Hey, you're going to miss that train. [*He waves the bottle.*]

BERNARD: Yeah, I'm going. [*He takes the bottle.*] Thanks, Pop. [*He picks up his rackets and bag.*] Good-bye, Willy,

and don't worry about it. You know, 'If at first you don't
succeed . . .'

WILLY: Yes, I believe in that.

BERNARD: But sometimes, Willy, it's better for a man just
to walk away.

WILLY: Walk away?

BERNARD: That's right.

WILLY: But if you can't walk away?

BERNARD [*after a slight pause*]: I guess that's when it's tough.
[*Extending his hand*] Good-bye, Willy.

WILLY [*shaking* BERNARD'S *hand*]: Good-bye, boy.

CHARLEY [*an arm on* BERNARD'S *shoulder*]: How do you like
this kid? Gonna argue a case in front of the Supreme
Court.

BERNARD [*protesting*]: Pop!

WILLY [*genuinely shocked, pained, and happy*]: No! The
Supreme Court!

BERNARD: I gotta run. 'Bye, Dad!

CHARLEY: Knock 'em dead, Bernard!

[BERNARD *goes off.*]

WILLY [*as* CHARLEY *takes out his wallet*]: The Supreme Court!
And he didn't even mention it!

CHARLEY [*counting out money on the desk*]: He don't have to –
he's gonna do it.

WILLY: And you never told him what to do, did you? You
never took any interest in him.

CHARLEY: My salvation is that I never took any interest in
anything. There's some money – fifty dollars. I got an
accountant inside.

WILLY: Charley, look . . . [*With difficulty*] I got my insurance
to pay. If you can manage it – I need a hundred and ten
dollars.

[CHARLEY *doesn't reply for a moment, merely stops moving.*]

WILLY: I'd draw it from my bank but Linda would know, and
I . . .

CHARLEY: Sit down, Willy.

WILLY [*moving toward the chair*]: I'm keeping an account of everything, remember. I'll pay every penny back. [*He sits.*]

CHARLEY: Now listen to me, Willy.

WILLY: I want you to know I appreciate . . .

CHARLEY [*sitting down on the table*]: Willy, what're you doin'? What the hell is goin' on in your head?

WILLY: Why? I'm simply . . .

CHARLEY: I offered you a job. You can make fifty dollars a week. And I won't send you on the road.

WILLY: I've got a job.

CHARLEY: Without pay? What kind of a job is a job without pay? [*He rises.*] Now, look, kid, enough is enough. I'm no genius but I know when I'm being insulted.

WILLY: Insulted!

CHARLEY: Why don't you want to work for me?

WILLY: What's the matter with you? I've got a job.

CHARLEY: Then what're you walkin' in here every week for?

WILLY [*getting up*]: Well, if you don't want me to walk in here –

CHARLEY: I am offering you a job.

WILLY: I don't want your goddam job!

CHARLEY: When the hell are you going to grow up?

WILLY [*furiously*]: You big ignoramus, if you say that to me again I'll rap you one! I don't care how big you are! [*He's ready to fight.*]
   [*Pause.*]

CHARLEY [*kindly, going to him*]: How much do you need, Willy?

WILLY: Charley, I'm strapped, I'm strapped. I don't know what to do. I was just fired.

CHARLEY: Howard fired you?

WILLY: That snotnose. Imagine that? I named him. I named him Howard.

CHARLEY: Willy, when're you gonna realize that them things don't mean anything? You named him Howard, but you can't sell that. The only thing you got in this world is

what you can sell. And the funny thing is that you're a salesman, and you don't know that.

WILLY: I've always tried to think otherwise, I guess. I always
felt that if a man was impressive, and well liked, that
nothing –

CHARLEY: Why must everybody like you? Who liked J. P.
Morgan? Was he impressive? In a Turkish bath he'd look
like a butcher. But with his pockets on he was very well
liked. Now listen, Willy, I know you don't like me, and
nobody can say I'm in love with you, but I'll give you a
job because – just for the hell of it, put it that way. Now
what do you say?

WILLY: I – I just can't work for you, Charley.

CHARLEY: What're you, jealous of me?

WILLY: I can't work for you, that's all, don't ask me why.

CHARLEY [angered, takes out more bills]: You been jealous of
me all your life, you damned fool! Here, pay your insurance. [He puts the money in WILLY'S hand.]

WILLY: I'm keeping strict accounts.

CHARLEY: I've got some work to do. Take care of yourself.
And pay your insurance.

WILLY [moving to the right]: Funny, y'know? After all the
highways, and the trains, and the appointments, and the
years, you end up worth more dead than alive.

CHARLEY: Willy, nobody's worth nothin' dead. [After a
slight pause] Did you hear what I said?

[WILLY stands still, dreaming.]

CHARLEY: Willy!

WILLY: Apologize to Bernard for me when you see him. I
didn't mean to argue with him. He's a fine boy. They're all
fine boys, and they'll end up big – all of them. Someday
they'll all play tennis together. Wish me luck, Charley. He
saw Bill Oliver today.

CHARLEY: Good luck.

WILLY [on the verge of tears]: Charley, you're the only friend I
got. Isn't that a·remarkable thing? [He goes out.]

CHARLEY: Jesus!

[CHARLEY *stares after him a moment and follows. All light blacks out. Suddenly raucous music is heard, and a red glow rises behind the screen at right.* STANLEY, *a young waiter, appears, carrying a table, followed by* HAPPY, *who is carrying two chairs.*]

STANLEY [*putting the table down*]: That's all right, Mr Loman, I can handle it myself. [*He turns and takes the chairs from* HAPPY *and places them at the table.*]

HAPPY [*glancing around*]: Oh, this is better.

STANLEY: Sure, in the front there you're in the middle of all kinds a noise. Whenever you got a party, Mr Loman, you just tell me and I'll put you back here. Y'know, there's a lotta people they don't like it private, because when they go out they like to see a lotta action around them because they're sick and tired to stay in the house by theirself. But I know you, you ain't from Hackensack. You know what I mean?

HAPPY [*sitting down*]: So how's it coming, Stanley?

STANLEY: Ah, it's a dog's life. I only wish during the war they'd a took me in the Army. I coulda been dead by now.

HAPPY: My brother's back, Stanley.

STANLEY: Oh, he come back, heh? From the Far West.

HAPPY: Yeah, big cattle man, my brother, so treat him right. And my father's coming too.

STANLEY: Oh, your father too!

HAPPY: You got a couple of nice lobsters?

STANLEY: Hundred per cent, big.

HAPPY: I want them with the claws.

STANLEY: Don't worry, I don't give you no mice. [HAPPY *laughs.*] How about some wine? It'll put a head on the meal.

HAPPY: No. You remember, Stanley, that recipe I brought you from overseas? With the champagne in it?

STANLEY: Oh, yeah, sure. I still got it tacked up yet in the kitchen. But that'll have to cost a buck apiece anyways.

HAPPY: That's all right.

STANLEY: What'd you, hit a number or somethin'?

HAPPY: No, it's a little celebration. My brother is – I think he pulled off a big deal today. I think we're going into business together.

STANLEY: Great! That's the best for you. Because a family business, you know what I mean? – that's the best.

HAPPY: That's what I think.

STANLEY: 'Cause what's the difference? Somebody steals? It's in the family. Know what I mean? [*Sotto voce*] Like this bartender here. The boss is goin' crazy what kinda leak he's got in the cash register. You put it in but it don't come out.

HAPPY [*raising his head*]: Sh!

STANLEY: What?

HAPPY: You notice I wasn't lookin' right or left, was I?

STANLEY: No.

HAPPY: And my eyes are closed.

STANLEY: So what's the – ?

HAPPY: Strudel's comin'.

STANLEY [*catching on, looks around*]: Ah, no, there's no –
        [*He breaks off as a furred, lavishly dressed girl enters and sits at the next table. Both follow her with their eyes.*]

STANLEY: Geez, how'd ya know?

HAPPY: I got radar or something. [*Staring directly at her profile*] Oooooooo ... Stanley.

STANLEY: I think that's for you, Mr Loman.

HAPPY: Look at that mouth. Oh, God. And the binoculars.

STANLEY: Geez, you got a life, Mr Loman.

HAPPY: Wait on her.

STANLEY [*going to the girl's table*]: Would you like a menu, ma'am?

GIRL: I'm expecting someone, but I'd like a –

HAPPY: Why don't you bring her – excuse me, miss, do you mind? I sell champagne, and I'd like you to try my brand. Bring her a champagne, Stanley.

GIRL: That's awfully nice of you.

HAPPY: Don't mention it. It's all company money. [*He laughs.*]

GIRL: That's a charming product to be selling, isn't it?

HAPPY: Oh, gets to be like everything else. Selling is selling, y'know.

GIRL: I suppose.

HAPPY: You don't happen to sell, do you?

GIRL: No, I don't sell.

HAPPY: Would you object to a compliment from a stranger? You ought to be on a magazine cover.

GIRL [*looking at him a little archly*]: I have been.

[STANLEY *comes in with a glass of champagne.*]

HAPPY: What'd I say before, Stanley? You see? She's a cover girl.

STANLEY: Oh, I could see, I could see.

HAPPY [*to the* GIRL]: What magazine?

GIRL: Oh, a lot of them. [*She takes the drink.*] Thank you.

HAPPY: You know what they say in France, don't you? 'Champagne is the drink of the complexion' – Hya, Biff!

[BIFF *has entered and sits with* HAPPY.]

BIFF: Hello, kid. Sorry I'm late.

HAPPY: I just got here. Uh, Miss – ?

GIRL: Forsythe.

HAPPY: Miss Forsythe, this is my brother.

BIFF: Is Dad here?

HAPPY: His name is Biff. You might've heard of him. Great football player.

GIRL: Really? What team?

HAPPY: Are you familiar with football?

GIRL: No, I'm afraid I'm not.

HAPPY: Biff is quarterback with the New York Giants.

GIRL: Well, that is nice, isn't it? [*She drinks.*]

HAPPY: Good health.

GIRL: I'm happy to meet you.

HAPPY: That's my name. Hap. It's really Harold, but at West Point they called me Happy.

GIRL [*now really impressed*]: Oh, I see. How do you do? [*She turns her profile.*]

BIFF: Isn't Dad coming?

HAPPY: You want her?

BIFF: Oh, I could never make that.

HAPPY: I remember the time that idea would never come into your head. Where's the old confidence, Biff?

BIFF: I just saw Oliver –

HAPPY: Wait a minute. I've got to see that old confidence again. Do you want her? She's on call.

BIFF: Oh, no. [*He turns to look at the* GIRL.]

HAPPY: I'm telling you. Watch this. [*Turning to the* GIRL] Honey? [*She turns to him.*] Are you busy?

GIRL: Well, I am . . . but I could make a phone call.

HAPPY: Do that, will you, honey? And see if you can get a friend. We'll be here for a while. Biff is one of the greatest football players in the country.

GIRL [*standing up*]: Well, I'm certainly happy to meet you.

HAPPY: Come back soon.

GIRL: I'll try.

HAPPY: Don't try, honey, try hard.

[*The* GIRL *exits.* STANLEY *follows, shaking his head in bewildered admiration.*]

HAPPY: Isn't that a shame now? A beautiful girl like that? That's why I can't get married. There's not a good woman in a thousand. New York is loaded with them, kid!

BIFF: Hap, look –

HAPPY: I told you she was on call!

BIFF [*strangely unnerved*]: Cut it out, will ya? I want to say something to you.

HAPPY: Did you see Oliver?

BIFF: I saw him all right. Now look, I want to tell Dad a couple of things and I want you to help me.

HAPPY: What? Is he going to back you?

BIFF: Are you crazy? You're out of your goddam head, you know that?

HAPPY: Why? What happened?

BIFF [*breathlessly*]: I did a terrible thing today, Hap. It's been the strangest day I ever went through. I'm all numb, I swear.

HAPPY: You mean he wouldn't see you?

BIFF: Well, I waited six hours for him, see? All day. Kept sending my name in. Even tried to date his secretary so she'd get me to him, but no soap.

HAPPY: Because you're not showin' the old confidence, Biff. He remembered you, didn't he?

BIFF [*stopping* HAPPY *with a gesture*]: Finally, about five o'clock, he comes out. Didn't remember who I was or anything. I felt like such an idiot, Hap.

HAPPY: Did you tell him my Florida idea?

BIFF: He walked away. I saw him for one minute. I got so mad I could've torn the walls down! How the hell did I ever get the idea I was a salesman there? I even believed myself that I'd been a salesman for him! And then he gave me one look and – I realized what a ridiculous lie my whole life has been. We've been talking in a dream for fifteen years. I was a shipping clerk.

HAPPY: What'd you do?

BIFF [*with great tension and wonder*]: Well, he left, see. And the secretary went out. I was all alone in the waiting-room. I don't know what came over me, Hap. The next thing I know I'm in his office – panelled walls, everything. I can't explain it. I – Hap, I took his fountain pen.

HAPPY: Geez, did he catch you?

BIFF: I ran out. I ran down all eleven flights. I ran and ran and ran.

HAPPY: That was an awful dumb – what'd you do that for?

BIFF [*agonized*]: I don't know, I just – wanted to take something, I don't know. You gotta help me, Hap, I'm gonna tell Pop.

HAPPY: You crazy? What for?

BIFF: Hap, he's got to understand that I'm not the man some-body lends that kind of money to. He thinks I've been spiting him all these years and it's eating him up.

HAPPY: That's just it. You tell him something nice.

BIFF: I can't.

HAPPY: Say you got a lunch date with Oliver tomorrow.

BIFF: So what do I do tomorrow?

HAPPY: You leave the house tomorrow and come back at night and say Oliver is thinking it over. And he thinks it over for a couple of weeks, and gradually it fades away and nobody's the worse.

BIFF: But it'll go on for ever!

HAPPY: Dad is never so happy as when he's looking forward to something!

[WILLY enters.]

HAPPY: Hello, scout!

WILLY: Gee, I haven't been here in years!

[STANLEY has followed WILLY in and sets a chair for him. STANLEY starts off but HAPPY stops him.]

HAPPY: Stanley!

[STANLEY stands by, waiting for an order.]

BIFF [going to WILLY with guilt, as to an invalid]: Sit down, Pop. You want a drink?

WILLY: Sure, I don't mind.

BIFF: Let's get a load on.

WILLY: You look worried.

BIFF: N-no. [To STANLEY] Scotch all around. Make it doubles.

STANLEY: Doubles, right. [He goes.]

WILLY: You had a couple already, didn't you?

BIFF: Just a couple, yeah.

WILLY: Well, what happened, boy? [Nodding affirmatively, with a smile] Everything go all right?

BIFF [takes a breath, then reaches out and grasps WILLY's hand]: Pal ... [He is smiling bravely, and WILLY is smiling too.] I had an experience today.

HAPPY: Terrific, Pop.

WILLY: That so? What happened?

BIFF [*high, slightly alcoholic, above the earth*]: I'm going to tell you everything from first to last. It's been a strange day. [*Silence. He looks around, composes himself as best he can, but his breath keeps breaking the rhythm of his voice.*] I had to wait quite a while for him, and –

WILLY: Oliver?

BIFF: Yeah, Oliver. All day, as a matter of cold fact. And a lot of – instances – facts, Pop, facts about my life came back to me. Who was it, Pop? Who ever said I was a salesman with Oliver?

WILLY: Well, you were.

BIFF: No, Dad, I was a shipping clerk.

WILLY: But you were practically –

BIFF [*with determination*]: Dad, I don't know who said it first, but I was never a salesman for Bill Oliver.

WILLY: What're you talking about?

BIFF: Let's hold on to the facts tonight, Pop. We're not going to get anywhere bullin' around. I was a shipping clerk.

WILLY [*angrily*]: All right, now listen to me –

BIFF: Why don't you let me finish?

WILLY: I'm not interested in stories about the past or any crap of that kind because the woods are burning, boys, you understand? There's a big blaze going on all around. I was fired today.

BIFF [*shocked*]: How could you be?

WILLY: I was fired, and I'm looking for a little good news to tell your mother, because the woman has waited and the woman has suffered. The gist of it is that I haven't got a story left in my head, Biff. So don't give me a lecture about facts and aspects. I am not interested. Now what've you got to say to me?

[STANLEY *enters with three drinks. They wait until he leaves.*]

WILLY: Did you see Oliver?

BIFF: Jesus, Dad!

WILLY: You mean you didn't go up there?

HAPPY: Sure he went up there.

BIFF: I did. I – saw him. How could they fire you?

WILLY [on the edge of his chair]: What kind of a welcome did he give you?

BIFF: He won't even let you work on commission?

WILLY: I'm out! [Driving] So tell me, he gave you a warm welcome?

HAPPY: Sure, Pop, sure!

BIFF [driven]: Well, it was kind of –

WILLY: I was wondering if he'd remember you. [To HAPPY] Imagine, man doesn't see him for ten, twelve years and gives him that kind of a welcome!

HAPPY: Damn right!

BIFF [trying to return to the offensive]: Pop, look –

WILLY: You know why he remembered you, don't you? Because you impressed him in those days.

BIFF: Let's talk quietly and get this down to the facts, huh?

WILLY [as though BIFF had been interrupting]: Well, what happened? It's great news, Biff. Did he take you into his office or'd you talk in the waiting-room?

BIFF: Well, he came in, see, and –

WILLY [with a big smile]: What'd he say? Betcha he threw his arm around you.

BIFF: Well, he kinda –

WILLY: He's a fine man. [To HAPPY] Very hard man to see, y'know.

HAPPY [agreeing]: Oh, I know.

WILLY [to BIFF]: Is that where you had the drinks?

BIFF: Yeah, he gave me a couple of – no, no!

HAPPY [cutting in]: He told him my Florida idea.

WILLY: Don't interrupt. [To BIFF] How'd he react to the Florida idea?

BIFF: Dad, will you give me a minute to explain?

WILLY: I've been waiting for you to explain since I sat down here! What happened? He took you into his office and what?

BIFF: Well – I talked. And – and he listened, see.

WILLY: Famous for the way he listens, y'know. What was his answer?

BIFF: His answer was – [*He breaks off, suddenly angry.*] Dad, you're not letting me tell you what I want to tell you!

WILLY [*accusing, angered*]: You didn't see him, did you?

BIFF: I did see him!

WILLY: What'd you insult him or something? You insulted him, didn't you?

BIFF: Listen, will you let me out of it, will you just let me out of it!

HAPPY: What the hell!

WILLY: Tell me what happened!

BIFF [*to* HAPPY]: I can't talk to him!

[*A single trumpet note jars the ear. The light of green leaves stains the house, which holds the air of night and a dream.* YOUNG BERNARD *enters and knocks on the door of the house.*]

YOUNG BERNARD [*frantically*]: Mrs Loman, Mrs Loman!

HAPPY: Tell him what happened!

BIFF [*to* HAPPY]: Shut up and leave me alone!

WILLY: No, no! You had to go and flunk math!

BIFF: What math? What're you talking about?

YOUNG BERNARD: Mrs Loman, Mrs Loman!

[LINDA *appears in the house, as of old.*]

WILLY [*wildly*]: Math, math, math!

BIFF: Take it easy, Pop!

YOUNG BERNARD: Mrs Loman!

WILLY [*furiously*]: If you hadn't flunked you'd've been set by now!

BIFF: Now, look, I m gonna tell you what happened, and you're going to listen to me.

YOUNG BERNARD: Mrs Loman!

BIFF: I waited six hours –

HAPPY: What the hell are you saying?

BIFF: I kept sending in my name but he wouldn't see me. So

finally he ... [*He continues unheard as light fades low on the restaurant.*]

YOUNG BERNARD: Biff flunked math!

LINDA: No!

YOUNG BERNARD: Birnbaum flunked him! They won't graduate him!

LINDA: But they have to. He's gotta go to the university. Where is he? Biff! Biff!

YOUNG BERNARD: No, he left. He went to Grand Central.

LINDA: Grand – You mean he went to Boston!

YOUNG BERNARD: Is Uncle Willy in Boston?

LINDA: Oh, maybe Willy can talk to the teacher. Oh, the poor, poor boy!

[*Light on house area snaps out.*]

BIFF [*at the table, now audible, holding up a gold fountain pen*]: ... so I'm washed up with Oliver, you understand? Are you listening to me?

WILLY [*at a loss*]: Yeah, sure. If you hadn't flunked –

BIFF: Flunked what? What're you talking about?

WILLY: Don't blame everything on me! I didn't flunk math – you did! What pen?

HAPPY: That was awful dumb, Biff, a pen like that is worth –

WILLY [*seeing the pen for the first time*]: You took Oliver's pen?

BIFF [*weakening*]: Dad, I just explained it to you.

WILLY: You stole Bill Oliver's fountain pen!

BIFF: I didn't exactly steal it! That's just what I've been explaining to you!

HAPPY: He had it in his hand and just then Oliver walked in, so he got nervous and stuck it in his pocket!

WILLY: My God, Biff!

BIFF: I never intended to do it, Dad!

OPERATOR'S VOICE: Standish Arms, good evening!

WILLY [*shouting*]: I'm not in my room!

BIFF [*frightened*]: Dad, what's the matter? [*He and* HAPPY *stand up.*]

OPERATOR: Ringing Mr Loman for you!

WILLY: I'm not there, stop it!

BIFF [*horrified, gets down on one knee before* WILLY]: Dad, I'll make good, I'll make good. [WILLY *tries to get to his feet.* BIFF *holds him down.*] Sit down now.

WILLY: No, you're no good, you're no good for anything.

BIFF: I am, Dad, I'll find something else, you understand? Now don't worry about anything. [*He holds up* WILLY'S *face.*] Talk to me, Dad.

OPERATOR: Mr Loman does not answer. Shall I page him?

WILLY [*attempting to stand, as though to rush and silence the* OPERATOR]: No, no, no!

HAPPY: He'll strike something, Pop.

WILLY: No, no . . .

BIFF [*desperately, standing over* WILLY]: Pop, listen! Listen to me! I'm telling you something good. Oliver talked to his partner about the Florida idea. You listening? He – he talked to his partner, and he came to me . . . I'm going to be all right, you hear? Dad, listen to me, he said it was just a question of the amount!

WILLY: Then you . . . got it?

HAPPY: He's gonna be terrific, Pop!

WILLY [*trying to stand*]: Then you got it, haven't you? You got it! You got it!

BIFF [*agonized, holds* WILLY *down*]: No, no. Look, Pop. I'm supposed to have lunch with them tomorrow. I'm just telling you this so you'll know that I can still make an impression, Pop. And I'll make good somewhere, but I can't go tomorrow, see?

WILLY: Why not? You simply –

BIFF: But the pen, Pop!

WILLY: You give it to him and tell him it was an oversight!

HAPPY: Sure, have lunch tomorrow!

BIFF: I can't say that –

WILLY: You were doing a crossword puzzle and accidentally used his pen!

BIFF: Listen, kid, I took those balls years ago, now I walk in with his fountain pen? That clinches it, don't you see? I can't face him like that! I'll try elsewhere.

PAGE'S VOICE: Paging Mr Loman!

WILLY: Don't you want to be anything?

BIFF: Pop, how can I go back?

WILLY: You don't want to be anything, is that what's behind it?

BIFF [*now angry at* WILLY *for not crediting his sympathy*]: Don't take it that way! You think it was easy walking into that office after what I'd done to him? A team of horses couldn't have dragged me back to Bill Oliver!

WILLY: Then why'd you go?

BIFF: Why did I go? Why did I go? Look at you! Look at what's become of you!

[*Off left, the* WOMAN *laughs*.]

WILLY: Biff, you're going to go to that lunch tomorrow, or –

BIFF: I can't go. I've got no appointment!

HAPPY: Biff, for . . .!

WILLY: Are you spiting me?

BIFF: Don't take it that way! Goddammit!

WILLY [*strikes* BIFF *and falters away from the table*]: You rotten little louse! Are you spiting me?

THE WOMAN: Someone's at the door, Willy!

BIFF: I'm no good, can't you see what I am?

HAPPY [*separating them*]: Hey, you're in a restaurant! Now cut it out, both of you! [*The girls enter*.] Hello, girls, sit down.

[*The* WOMAN *laughs, off left*.]

MISS FORSYTHE: I guess we might as well. This is Letta.

THE WOMAN: Willy, are you going to wake up?

BIFF [*ignoring* WILLY]: How're ya, miss, sit down. What do you drink?

MISS FORSYTHE: Letta might not be able to stay long.

LETTA: I gotta get up very early tomorrow. I got jury duty. I'm so excited! Were you fellows ever on a jury?

BIFF: No, but I been in front of them! [*The girls laugh.*] This is my father.

LETTA: Isn't he cute? Sit down with us, Pop.

HAPPY: Sit him down, Biff!

BIFF [*going to him*]: Come on, slugger, drink us under the table. To hell with it! Come on, sit down, pal.

[*On* BIFF's *last insistence,* WILLY *is about to sit.*]

THE WOMAN [*now urgently*]: Willy, are you going to answer the door!

[*The* WOMAN's *call pulls* WILLY *back. He starts right, befuddled.*]

BIFF: Hey, where are you going?

WILLY: Open the door.

BIFF: The door?

WILLY: The washroom . . . the door . . . where's the door?

BIFF [*leading* WILLY *to the left*]: Just go straight down.

[WILLY *moves left.*]

THE WOMAN: Willy, Willy, are you going to get up, get up, get up, get up?

[WILLY *exits left.*]

LETTA: I think it's sweet you bring your daddy along.

MISS FORSYTHE: Oh, he isn't really your father!

BIFF [*at left, turning to her resentfully*]: Miss Forsythe, you've just seen a prince walk by. A fine, troubled prince. A hardworking, unappreciated prince. A pal, you understand? A good companion. Always for his boys.

LETTA: That's so sweet.

HAPPY: Well, girls, what's the programme? We're wasting time. Come on, Biff. Gather round. Where would you like to go?

BIFF: Why don't you do something for him?

HAPPY: Me!

BIFF: Don't you give a damn for him, Hap?

HAPPY: What're you talking about? I'm the one who –

BIFF: I sense it, you don't give a good goddam about him.

[*He takes the rolled-up hose from his pocket and puts it on the table in front of* HAPPY.] Look what I found in the cellar, for Christ's sake. How can you bear to let it go on?

HAPPY: Me? Who goes away? Who runs off and –

BIFF: Yeah, but he doesn't mean anything to you. You could help him – I can't. Don't you understand what I'm talking about? He's going to kill himself, don't you know that?

HAPPY: Don't I know it! Me!

BIFF: Hap, help him! Jesus . . . help him . . . Help me, help me, I can't bear to look at his face! [*Ready to weep, he hurries out, up right.*]

HAPPY [*starting after him*]: Where are you going?

MISS FORSYTHE: What's he so mad about?

HAPPY: Come on, girls, we'll catch up with him.

MISS FORSYTHE [*as* HAPPY *pushes her out*]: Say, I don't like that temper of his!

HAPPY: He's just a little overstrung, he'll be all right!

WILLY [*off left, as the* WOMAN *laughs*]: Don't answer! Don't answer!

LETTA: Don't you want to tell your father –

HAPPY: No, that's not my father. He's just a guy. Come on, we'll catch Biff, and, honey, we're going to paint this town! Stanley, where's the check! Hey, Stanley!

[*They exit.* STANLEY *looks toward left.*]

STANLEY [*calling to* HAPPY *indignantly*]: Mr Loman! Mr Loman!

[STANLEY *picks up a chair and follows them off. Knocking is heard off left. The* WOMAN *enters, laughing.* WILLY *follows her. She is in a black slip; he is buttoning his shirt. Raw, sensuous music accompanies their speech.*]

WILLY: Will you stop laughing? Will you stop?

THE WOMAN: Aren't you going to answer the door? He'll wake the whole hotel.

WILLY: I'm not expecting anybody.

THE WOMAN: Whyn't you have another drink, honey, and stop being so damn self-centred?

WILLY: I'm so lonely.

THE WOMAN: You know you ruined me, Willy? From now on, whenever you come to the office, I'll see that you go right through to the buyers. No waiting at my desk any more, Willy. You ruined me.

WILLY: That's nice of you to say that.

THE WOMAN: Gee, you are self-centred! Why so sad? You are the saddest, self-centredest soul I ever did see-saw. [*She laughs. He kisses her.*] Come on inside, drummer boy. It's silly to be dressing in the middle of the night. [*As knocking is heard*] Aren't you going to answer the door?

WILLY: They're knocking on the wrong door.

THE WOMAN: But I felt the knocking. And he heard us talking in here. Maybe the hotel's on fire!

WILLY [*his terror rising*]: It's a mistake.

THE WOMAN: Then tell him to go away!

WILLY: There's nobody there.

THE WOMAN: It's getting on my nerves, Willy. There's somebody standing out there and it's getting on my nerves!

WILLY [*pushing her away from him*]: All right, stay in the bathroom here, and don't come out. I think there's a law in Massachusetts about it, so don't come out. It may be that new room clerk. He looked very mean. So don't come out. It's a mistake, there's no fire.

[*The knocking is heard again. He takes a few steps away from her, and she vanishes into the wing. The light follows him, and now he is facing* YOUNG BIFF, *who carries a suitcase.* BIFF *steps toward him. The music is gone.*]

BIFF: Why didn't you answer?

WILLY: Biff! What are you doing in Boston?

BIFF: Why didn't you answer! I've been knocking for five minutes, I called you on the phone –

WILLY: I just heard you. I was in the bathroom and had the door shut. Did anything happen home?

BIFF: Dad – I let you down.

WILLY: What do you mean?

BIFF: Dad . . .

WILLY: Biffo, what's this about? [*Putting his arm around* BIFF] Come on, let's go downstairs and get you a malted.

BIFF: Dad, I flunked math.

WILLY: Not for the term?

BIFF: The term. I haven't got enough credits to graduate.

WILLY: You mean to say Bernard wouldn't give you the answers?

BIFF: He did, he tried, but I only got a sixty-one.

WILLY: And they wouldn't give you four points?

BIFF: Birnbaum refused absolutely. I begged him, Pop, but he won't give me those points. You gotta talk to him before they close the school. Because if he saw the kind of man you are, and you just talked to him in your way, I'm sure he'd come through for me. The class came right before practice, see, and I didn't go enough. Would you talk to him? He'd like you, Pop. You know the way you could talk.

WILLY: You're on. We'll drive right back.

BIFF: Oh, Dad, good work! I'm sure he'll change it for you!

WILLY: Go downstairs and tell the clerk I'm checkin' out. Go right down.

BIFF: Yes, sir! See, the reason he hates me, Pop – one day he was late for class so I got up at the blackboard and imitated him. I crossed my eyes and talked with a lithp.

WILLY [*laughing*]: You did? The kids like it?

BIFF: They nearly died laughing!

WILLY: Yeah? What'd you do?

BIFF: The thquare root of thixthy twee is . . . [WILLY *bursts out laughing;* BIFF *joins him.*] And in the middle of it he walked in!

[WILLY *laughs and the* WOMAN *joins in offstage.*]

WILLY [*without hesitation*]: Hurry downstairs and –

BIFF: Somebody in there?

WILLY: No, that was next door.

[*The* WOMAN *laughs offstage.*]

BIFF: Somebody got in your bathroom!

WILLY: No, it's the next room, there's a party –

THE WOMAN [*enters, laughing. She lisps this*]: Can I come in? There's something in the bathtub, Willy, and it's moving! [WILLY *looks at* BIFF, *who is staring open-mouthed and horrified at the* WOMAN.]

WILLY: Ah – you better go back to your room. They must be finished painting by now. They're painting her room so I let her take a shower here. Go back, go back . . . [*He pushes her.*]

THE WOMAN [*resisting*]: But I've got to get dressed, Willy, I can't –

WILLY: Get out of here! Go back, go back . . . [*Suddenly striving for the ordinary*] This is Miss Francis, Biff, she's a buyer. They're painting her room. Go back, Miss Francis, go back . . .

THE WOMAN: But my clothes, I can't go out naked in the hall!

WILLY [*pushing her offstage*]: Get outa here! Go back, go back! [BIFF *slowly sits down on his suitcase as the argument continues offstage.*]

THE WOMAN: Where's my stockings? You promised me stockings, Willy!

WILLY: I have no stockings here!

THE WOMAN: You had two boxes of size nine sheers for me, and I want them!

WILLY: Here, for God's sake, will you get outa here!

THE WOMAN [*enters holding a box of stockings*]: I just hope there's nobody in the hall. That's all I hope. [*To* BIFF] Are you football or baseball?

BIFF: Football.

THE WOMAN [*angry, humiliated*]: That's me too. G'night. [*She snatches her clothes from* WILLY, *and walks out.*]

WILLY [*after a pause*]: Well, better get going. I want to get to the school first thing in the morning. Get my suits out of the closet. I'll get my valise. [BIFF *doesn't move.*] What's the matter? [BIFF *remains motionless, tears falling.*] She's a buyer. Buys for J. H. Simmons. She lives down the hall –

they're painting. You don't imagine – [*He breaks off. After a pause*] Now listen, pal, she's just a buyer. She sees merchandise in her room and they have to keep it looking just so ... [*Pause. Assuming command*] All right, get my suits. [BIFF *doesn't move.*] Now stop crying and do as I say. I gave you an order. Biff, I gave you an order! Is that what you do when I give you an order? How dare you cry? [*Putting his arm around* BIFF] Now look, Biff, when you grow up you'll understand about these things. You mustn't – you mustn't over-emphasize a thing like this. I'll see Birnbaum first thing in the morning.

BIFF: Never mind.

WILLY [*getting down beside* BIFF]: Never mind! He's going to give you those points. I'll see to it.

BIFF: He wouldn't listen to you.

WILLY: He certainly will listen to me. You need those points for the U. of Virginia.

BIFF: I'm not going there.

WILLY: Heh? If I can't get him to change that mark you'll make it up in summer school. You've got all summer to –

BIFF [*his weeping breaking from him*]: Dad ...

WILLY [*infected by it*]: Oh, my boy ...

BIFF: Dad ...

WILLY: She's nothing to me, Biff. I was lonely, I was terribly lonely.

BIFF: You – you gave her Mama's stockings! [*His tears break through and he rises to go.*]

WILLY [*grabbing for* BIFF]: I gave you an order!

BIFF: Don't touch me, you – liar!

WILLY: Apologize for that!

BIFF: You fake! You phony little fake! You fake! [*Overcome, he turns quickly and weeping fully goes out with his suitcase.* WILLY *is left on the floor on his knees.*]

WILLY: I gave you an order! Biff, come back here or I'll beat you! Come back here! I'll whip you!

[STANLEY *comes quickly in from the right and stands in front of* WILLY.]

WILLY [*shouts at* STANLEY]: I gave you an order . . .

STANLEY: Hey, let's pick it up, pick it up, Mr Loman. [*He helps* WILLY *to his feet.*] Your boys left with the chippies. They said they'll see you home.

[*A second waiter watches some distance away.*]

WILLY: But we were supposed to have dinner together.

[*Music is heard,* WILLY'S *theme.*]

STANLEY: Can you make it?

WILLY: I'll – sure, I can make it. [*Suddenly concerned about his clothes.*] Do I – I look all right?

STANLEY: Sure, you look all right. [*He flicks a speck off* WILLY'S *lapel.*]

WILLY: Here – here's a dollar.

STANLEY: Oh, your son paid me. It's all right.

WILLY [*putting it in* STANLEY'S *hand*]: No, take it. You're a good boy.

STANLEY: Oh, no, you don't have to . . .

WILLY: Here – here's some more. I don't need it any more. [*After a slight pause*] Tell me – is there a seed store in the neighbourhood?

STANLEY: Seeds? You mean like to plant?

[*As* WILLY *turns,* STANLEY *slips the money back into his jacket pocket.*]

WILLY: Yes. Carrots, peas . . .

STANLEY: Well, there's hardware stores on Sixth Avenue, but it may be too late now.

WILLY [*anxiously*]: Oh, I'd better hurry. I've got to get some seeds. [*He starts off to the right.*] I've got to get some seeds, right away. Nothing's planted. I don't have a thing in the ground.

[WILLY *hurries out as the light goes down.* STANLEY *moves over to the right after him, watches him off. The other waiter has been staring at* WILLY.]

STANLEY [*to the waiter*]: Well, whatta you looking at?

[*The waiter picks up the chairs and moves off right.* STANLEY *takes the table and follows him. The light fades on this area. There is a long pause, the sound of the flute coming over. The light gradually rises on the kitchen, which is empty.* HAPPY *appears at the door of the house, followed by* BIFF. HAPPY *is carrying a large bunch of long-stemmed roses. He enters the kitchen, looks around for* LINDA. *Not seeing her, he turns to* BIFF, *who is just outside the house door, and makes a gesture with his hands, indicating 'Not here, I guess'. He looks into the living-room and freezes. Inside,* LINDA, *unseen, is seated,* WILLY'S *coat on her lap. She rises ominously and quietly and moves toward* HAPPY, *who backs up into the kitchen, afraid.*]

HAPPY: Hey, what're you doing up? [LINDA *says nothing but moves toward him implacably.*] Where's Pop? [*He keeps backing to the right, and now* LINDA *is in full view in the door-way to the living-room.*] Is he sleeping?

LINDA: Where were you?

HAPPY [*trying to laugh it off*]: We met two girls, Mom, very fine types. Here, we brought you some flowers. [*Offering them to her*] Put them in your room, Ma.

[*She knocks them to the floor at* BIFF'S *feet. He has now come inside and closed the door behind him. She stares at* BIFF, *silent.*]

HAPPY: Now what'd you do that for? Mom, I want you to have some flowers –

LINDA [*cutting* HAPPY *off, violently to* BIFF]: Don't you care whether he lives or dies?

HAPPY [*going to the stairs*]: Come upstairs, Biff.

BIFF [*with a flare of disgust, to* HAPPY]: Go away from me! [*To* LINDA] What do you mean, lives or dies? Nobody's dying around here, pal.

LINDA: Get out of my sight! Get out of here!

BIFF: I wanna see the boss.

LINDA: You're not going near him!

BIFF: Where is he? [*He moves into the living-room and* LINDA *follows.*]

LINDA [*shouting after* BIFF]: You invite him to dinner. He looks forward to it all day – [BIFF *appears in his parents' bedroom, looks around, and exits*] – and then you desert him there. There's no stranger you'd do that to!

HAPPY: Why? He had a swell time with us. Listen, when I – [LINDA *comes back into the kitchen*] – desert him I hope I don't outlive the day!

LINDA: Get out of here!

HAPPY: Now look, Mom . . .

LINDA: Did you have to go to women tonight? You and your lousy rotten whores!

[BIFF *re-enters the kitchen.*]

HAPPY: Mom, all we did was follow Biff around trying to cheer him up! [*To* BIFF] Boy, what a night you gave me!

LINDA: Get out of here, both of you, and don't come back! I don't want you tormenting him any more. Go on now, get your things together! [*To* BIFF] You can sleep in his apartment. [*She starts to pick up the flowers and stops herself.*] Pick up this stuff, I'm not your maid any more. Pick it up, you bum, you!

[HAPPY *turns his back to her in refusal.* BIFF *slowly moves over and gets down on his knees, picking up the flowers.*]

LINDA: You're a pair of animals! Not one, not another living soul would have had the cruelty to walk out on that man in a restaurant!

BIFF [*not looking at her*]: Is that what he said?

LINDA: He didn't have to say anything. He was so humiliated he nearly limped when he came in.

HAPPY: But, Mom, he had a great time with us –

BIFF [*cutting him off violently*]: Shut up!

[*Without another word,* HAPPY *goes upstairs.*]

LINDA: You! You didn't even go in to see if he was all right!

BIFF [*still on the floor in front of* LINDA, *the flowers in his hand; with self-loathing*]: No. Didn't. Didn't do a damned thing. How do you like that, heh? Left him babbling in a toilet.

LINDA: You louse. You . . .

BIFF: Now you hit it on the nose! [*He gets up, throws the flowers in the wastebasket.*] The scum of the earth, and you're looking at him!

LINDA: Get out of here!

BIFF: I gotta talk to the boss, Mom. Where is he?

LINDA: You're not going near him. Get out of this house!

BIFF [*with absolute assurance, determination*]: No. We're gonna have an abrupt conversation, him and me.

LINDA: You're not talking to him!

[*Hammering is heard from outside the house, off right.* BIFF *turns toward the noise.*]

LINDA [*suddenly pleading*]: Will you please leave him alone?

BIFF: What's he doing out there?

LINDA: He's planting the garden!

BIFF [*quietly*]: Now? Oh, my God!

[BIFF *moves outside,* LINDA *following. The light dies down on them and comes up on the centre of the apron as* WILLY *walks into it. He is carrying a flashlight, a hoe, and a handful of seed packets. He raps the top of the hoe sharply to fix it firmly, and then moves to the left, measuring off the distance with his foot. He holds the flashlight to look at the seed packets, reading off the instructions. He is in the blue of night.*]

WILLY: Carrots . . . quarter-inch apart. Rows . . . one-foot rows. [*He measures it off.*] One foot. [*He puts down a package and measures off.*] Beets. [*He puts down another package and measures again.*] Lettuce. [*He reads the package, puts it down.*] One foot – [*He breaks off as* BEN *appears at the right and moves slowly down to him.*] What a proposition, ts, ts. Terrific, terrific. 'Cause she's suffered, Ben, the woman has suffered. You understand me? A man can't go out the way he came in, Ben, a man has got to add up to something. You can't, you can't – [BEN *moves toward him as though to interrupt.*] You gotta consider, now. Don't answer so quick. Remember, it's a guaranteed twenty-thousand-dollar proposition. Now look, Ben, I want you to go through the ins and outs of this thing with me. I've got nobody to talk to, Ben, and the woman has suffered, you hear me?

BEN [*standing still, considering*]: What's the proposition?

WILLY: It's twenty thousand dollars on the barrelhead. Guaranteed, gilt-edged, you understand?

BEN: You don't want to make a fool of yourself. They might not honour the policy.

WILLY: How can they dare refuse? Didn't I work like a coolie to meet every premium on the nose? And now they don't pay off! Impossible!

BEN: It's called a cowardly thing, William.

WILLY: Why? Does it take more guts to stand here the rest of my life ringing up a zero?

BEN [*yielding*]: That's a point, William. [*He moves, thinking, turns.*] And twenty thousand – that *is* something one can feel with the hand, it is there.

WILLY [*now assured, with rising power*]: Oh, Ben, that's the whole beauty of it! I see it like a diamond, shining in the dark, hard and rough, that I can pick up and touch in my hand. Not like – like an appointment! This would not be another damned-fool appointment, Ben, and it changes all the aspects. Because he thinks I'm nothing, see, and so he spites me. But the funeral – [*Straightening up*] Ben, that funeral will be massive! They'll come from Maine, Massachusetts, Vermont, New Hampshire! All the old-timers with the strange licence plates – that boy will be thunderstruck, Ben, because he never realized – I am known! Rhode Island, New York, New Jersey – I am known, Ben, and he'll see it with his eyes once and for all. He'll see what I am, Ben! He's in for a shock, that boy!

BEN [*coming down to the edge of the garden*]: He'll call you a coward.

WILLY [*suddenly fearful*]: No, that would be terrible.

BEN: Yes. And a damned fool.

WILLY: No, no, he mustn't, I won't have that! [*He is broken and desperate.*]

BEN: He'll hate you, William.

[*The gay music of the boys is heard.*]

WILLY: Oh, Ben, how do we get back to all the great times? Used to be so full of light, and comradeship, the sleigh-riding in winter, and the ruddiness on his cheeks. And always some kind of good news coming up, always something nice coming up ahead. And never even let me carry the valises in the house, and simonizing, simonizing that little red car! Why, why can't I give him something and not have him hate me?

BEN: Let me think about it. [*He glances at his watch.*] I still have a little time. Remarkable proposition, but you've got to be sure you're not making a fool of yourself.

[BEN *drifts off upstage and goes out of sight.* BIFF *comes down from the left.*]

WILLY [*suddenly conscious of* BIFF, *turns and looks up at him, then begins picking up the packages of seeds in confusion*]: Where the hell is that seed? [*Indignantly*] You can't see nothing out here! They boxed in the whole goddam neighbourhood!

BIFF: There are people all around here. Don't you realize that?

WILLY: I'm busy. Don't bother me.

BIFF [*taking the hoe from* WILLY]: I'm saying good-bye to you, Pop. [WILLY *looks at him, silent, unable to move.*] I'm not coming back any more.

WILLY: You're not going to see Oliver tomorrow?

BIFF: I've got no appointment, Dad.

WILLY: He put his arm around you, and you've got no appointment?

BIFF: Pop, get this now, will you? Everytime I've left it's been a fight that sent me out of here. Today I realized something about myself and I tried to explain it to you and I – I think I'm just not smart enough to make any sense out of it for you. To hell with whose fault it is or anything like that. [*He takes* WILLY's *arm.*] Let's just wrap it up, heh? Come on in, we'll tell Mom. [*He gently tries to pull* WILLY *to left.*]

WILLY [*frozen, immobile, with guilt in his voice*]: No, I don't want to see her.

BIFF: Come on! [*He pulls again, and* WILLY *tries to pull away.*]

WILLY [*highly nervous*]: No, no, I don't want to see her.

BIFF [*tries to look into* WILLY'S *face, as if to find the answer there*]: Why don't you want to see her?

WILLY [*more harshly now*]: Don't bother me, will you?

BIFF: What do you mean, you don't want to see her? You don't want them calling you yellow, do you? This isn't your fault; it's me, I'm a bum. Now come inside! [WILLY *strains to get away.*] Did you hear what I said to you?

[WILLY *pulls away and quickly goes by himself into the house.* BIFF *follows.*]

LINDA [*to* WILLY]: Did you plant, dear?

BIFF [*at the door, to* LINDA]: All right, we had it out. I'm going and I'm not writing any more.

LINDA [*going to* WILLY *in the kitchen*]: I think that's the best way, dear. 'Cause there's no use drawing it out, you'll just never get along.

[WILLY *doesn't respond.*]

BIFF: People ask where I am and what I'm doing, you don't know, and you don't care. That way it'll be off your mind and you can start brightening up again. All right? That clears it, doesn't it? [WILLY *is silent, and* BIFF *goes to him.*] You gonna wish me luck, scout! [*He extends his hand*] What do you say?

LINDA: Shake his hand, Willy.

WILLY [*turning to her, seething with hurt*]: There's no necessity to mention the pen at all, y'know.

BIFF [*gently*]: I've got no appointment, Dad.

WILLY [*erupting fiercely*]: He put his arm around . . .?

BIFF: Dad, you're never going to see what I am, so what's the use of arguing? If I strike oil I'll send you a cheque. Meantime forget I'm alive.

WILLY [*to* LINDA]: Spite, see?

BIFF: Shake hands, Dad.

WILLY: Not my hand.

BIFF: I was hoping not to go this way.

WILLY: Well, this is the way you're going. Good-bye.

[BIFF *looks at him a moment, then turns sharply and goes to the stairs.*]

WILLY [*stops him with*]: May you rot in hell if you leave this house!

BIFF [*turning*]: Exactly what is it that you want from me?

WILLY: I want you to know, on the train, in the mountains, in the valleys, wherever you go, that you cut down your life for spite!

BIFF: No, no.

WILLY: Spite, spite, is the word of your undoing! And when you're down and out, remember what did it. When you're rotting somewhere beside the railroad tracks, remember, and don't you dare blame it on me!

BIFF: I'm not blaming it on you!

WILLY: I won't take the rap for this, you hear?

[HAPPY *comes down the stairs and stands on the bottom step, watching.*]

BIFF: That's just what I'm telling you!

WILLY [*sinking into a chair at the table, with full accusation*]: You're trying to put a knife in me – don't think I don't know what you're doing!

BIFF: All right, phony! Then let's lay it on the line. [*He whips the rubber tube out of his pocket and puts it on the table.*]

HAPPY: You crazy –

LINDA: Biff! [*She moves to grab the hose, but* BIFF *holds it down with his hand.*]

BIFF: Leave it there! Don't move it!

WILLY [*not looking at it*]: What is that?

BIFF: You know goddam well what that is.

WILLY [*caged, wanting to escape*]: I never saw that.

BIFF: You saw it. The mice didn't bring it into the cellar! What is this supposed to do, make a hero out of you? This supposed to make me sorry for you?

WILLY: Never heard of it.

BIFF: There'll be no pity for you, you hear it? No pity!

WILLY [to LINDA]: You hear the spite!

BIFF: No, you're going to hear the truth – what you are and what I am!

LINDA: Stop it!

WILLY: Spite!

HAPPY [coming down toward BIFF]: You cut it now!

BIFF [to HAPPY]: The man don't know who we are! The man is gonna know! [To WILLY] We never told the truth for ten minutes in this house!

HAPPY: We always told the truth!

BIFF [turning on him]: You big blow, are you the assistant buyer? You're one of the two assistants to the assistant, aren't you?

HAPPY: Well, I'm practically –

BIFF: You're practically full of it! We all are! And I'm through with it. [To WILLY] Now hear this, Willy, this is me.

WILLY: I know you!

BIFF: You know why I had no address for three months? I stole a suit in Kansas City and I was in jail. [To LINDA, who is sobbing] Stop crying. I'm through with it.

[LINDA turns away from them, her hands covering her face.]

WILLY: I suppose that's my fault!

BIFF: I stole myself out of every good job since high school!

WILLY: And whose fault is that?

BIFF: And I never got anywhere because you blew me so full of hot air I could never stand taking orders from anybody! That's whose fault it is!

WILLY: I hear that!

LINDA: Don't, Biff!

BIFF: It's goddam time you heard that! I had to be boss big shot in two weeks, and I'm through with it!

WILLY: Then hang yourself! For spite, hang yourself!

BIFF: No! Nobody's hanging himself, Willy! I ran down

eleven flights with a pen in my hand today. And suddenly I stopped, you hear me? And in the middle of that office building, do you hear this? I stopped in the middle of that building and I saw – the sky. I saw the things that I love in this world. The work and the food and time to sit and smoke. And I looked at the pen and said to myself, what the hell am I grabbing this for? Why am I trying to become what I don't want to be? What am I doing in an office, making a contemptuous, begging fool of myself, when all I want is out there, waiting for me the minute I say I know who I am! Why can't I say that, Willy? [*He tries to make* WILLY *face him, but* WILLY *pulls away and moves to the left.*]

WILLY [*with hatred, threateningly*]: The door of your life is wide open!

BIFF: Pop! I'm a dime a dozen, and so are you!

WILLY [*turning on him now in an uncontrolled outburst*]: I am not a dime a dozen! I am Willy Loman, and you are Biff Loman!

[BIFF *starts for* WILLY, *but is blocked by* HAPPY. *In his fury,* BIFF *seems on the verge of attacking his father.*]

BIFF: I am not a leader of men, Willy, and neither are you. You were never anything but a hard-working drummer who landed in the ash-can like all the rest of them! I'm one dollar an hour, Willy! I tried seven states and couldn't raise it. A buck an hour! Do you gather my meaning? I'm not bringing home any prizes any more, and you're going to stop waiting for me to bring them home!

WILLY [*directly to* BIFF]: You vengeful, spiteful mut!

[BIFF *breaks from* HAPPY. WILLY, *in fright, starts up the stairs.* BIFF *grabs him.*]

BIFF [*at the peak of his fury*]: Pop, I'm nothing! I'm nothing, Pop. Can't you understand that? There's no spite in it any more. I'm just what I am, that's all.

[BIFF'S *fury has spent itself, and he breaks down, sobbing, holding on to* WILLY, *who dumbly fumbles for* BIFF'S *face.*]

WILLY [*astonished*]: What're you doing? What're you doing? [*To* LINDA] Why is he crying?

BIFF [*crying, broken*]: Will you let me go, for Christ's sake? Will you take that phony dream and burn it before something happens? [*Struggling to contain himself, he pulls away and moves to the stairs.*] I'll go in the morning. Put him – put him to bed. [*Exhausted,* BIFF *moves up the stairs to his room.*]

WILLY [*after a long pause, astonished, elevated*]: Isn't that – isn't that remarkable? Biff – he likes me!

LINDA: He loves you, Willy!

HAPPY [*deeply moved*]: Always did, Pop.

WILLY: Oh, Biff! [*Staring wildly*] He cried! Cried to me. [*He is choking with his love, and now cries out his promise*] That boy – that boy is going to be magnificent!

[BEN *appears in the light just outside the kitchen.*]

BEN: Yes, outstanding, with twenty thousand behind him.

LINDA [*sensing the racing of his mind, fearfully, carefully*]: Now come to bed, Willy. It's all settled now.

WILLY [*finding it difficult not to rush out of the house*]: Yes, we'll sleep. Come on. Go to sleep, Hap.

BEN: And it does take a great kind of a man to crack the jungle.

[*In accents of dread,* BEN'S *idyllic music starts up.*]

HAPPY [*his arm around* LINDA]: I'm getting married, Pop, don't forget it. I'm changing everything. I'm gonna run that department before the year is up. You'll see, Mom. [*He kisses her.*]

BEN: The jungle is dark but full of diamonds, Willy.

[WILLY *turns, moves, listening to* BEN.]

LINDA: Be good. You're both good boys, just act that way, that's all.

HAPPY: 'Night, Pop. [*He goes upstairs.*]

LINDA [*to* WILLY]: Come, dear.

BEN [*with greater force*]: One must go in to fetch a diamond out.

WILLY [*to* LINDA, *as he moves slowly along the edge of the kitchen, toward the door*]: I just want to get settled down, Linda. Let me sit alone for a little.

LINDA [*almost uttering her fear*]: I want you upstairs.

WILLY [*taking her in his arms*]: In a few minutes, Linda. I couldn't sleep right now. Go on, you look awful tired. [*He kisses her.*]

BEN: Not like an appointment at all. A diamond is rough and hard to the touch.

WILLY: Go on now. I'll be right up.

LINDA: I think this is the only way, Willy.

WILLY: Sure, it's the best thing.

BEN: Best thing!

WILLY: The only way. Everything is gonna be – go on, kid, get to bed. You look so tired.

LINDA: Come right up.

WILLY: Two minutes.

[LINDA *goes into the living-room, then reappears in her bed-room.* WILLY *moves just outside the kitchen door.*]

WILLY: Loves me. [*Wonderingly*] Always loved me. Isn't that a remarkable thing? Ben, he'll worship me for it!

BEN [*with promise*]: It's dark there, but full of diamonds.

WILLY: Can you imagine that magnificence with twenty thousand dollars in his pocket?

LINDA [*calling from her room*]: Willy! Come up!

WILLY [*calling into the kitchen*]: Yes! Yes. Coming! It's very smart, you realize that, don't you, sweetheart? Even Ben sees it. I gotta go, baby. 'Bye! 'Bye! [*Going over to* BEN, *almost dancing*] Imagine? When the mail comes he'll be ahead of Bernard again!

BEN: A perfect proposition all around.

WILLY: Did you see how he cried to me? Oh, if I could kiss him, Ben!

BEN: Time, William, time!

WILLY: Oh, Ben, I always knew one way or another we were gonna make it, Biff and I!

BEN [*looking at his watch*]: The boat. We'll be late. [*He moves slowly off into the darkness.*]

WILLY [*elegiacally, turning to the house*]: Now when you kick off, boy, I want a seventy-yard boot, and get right down the field under the ball, and when you hit, hit low and hit hard, because it's important, boy. [*He swings around and faces the audience.*] There's all kinds of important people in the stands, and the first thing you know ... [*Suddenly realizing he is alone*] Ben! Ben, where do I ...? [*He makes a sudden movement of search.*] Ben, how do I ...?

LINDA [*calling*]: Willy, you coming up?

WILLY [*uttering a gasp of fear, whirling about as if to quiet her*]: Sh! [*He turns around as if to find his way; sounds, faces, voices, seem to be swarming in upon him and he flicks at them, crying, 'Sh! Sh!' Suddenly music, faint and high, stops him. It rises in intensity, almost to an unbearable scream. He goes up and down on his toes, and rushes off around the house.*] Shhh!

LINDA: Willy?

[*There is no answer. LINDA waits. BIFF gets up off his bed. He is still in his clothes. HAPPY sits up. BIFF stands listening.*]

LINDA [*with real fear*]: Willy, answer me! Willy!

[*There is the sound of a car starting and moving away at full speed.*]

LINDA: No!

BIFF [*rushing down the stairs*]: Pop!

[*As the car speeds off, the music crashes down in a frenzy of sound, which becomes the soft pulsation of a single 'cello string. BIFF slowly returns to his bedroom. He and HAPPY gravely don their jackets. LINDA slowly walks out of her room. The music has developed into a dead march. The leaves of day are appearing over everything. CHARLEY and BERNARD, sombrely dressed, appear and knock on the kitchen door. BIFF and HAPPY slowly descend the stairs to the kitchen as CHARLEY and BERNARD enter. All stop a moment when LINDA, in clothes of mourning, bearing a little bunch of roses,*]

*comes through the draped doorway into the kitchen. She goes
to* CHARLEY *and takes his arm. Now all move toward the
audience, through the wall-line of the kitchen. At the limit of
the apron,* LINDA *lays down the flowers, kneels, and sits back
on her heels. All stare down at the grave.*]

REQUIEM

CHARLEY: It's getting dark, Linda.

[LINDA *doesn't react. She stares at the grave.*]

BIFF: How about it, Mom? Better get some rest, heh? They'll be closing the gate soon.

[LINDA *makes no move. Pause.*]

HAPPY [*deeply angered*]: He had no right to do that. There was no necessity for it. We would've helped him.

CHARLEY [*grunting*]: Hmmm.

BIFF: Come along, Mom.

LINDA: Why didn't anybody come?

CHARLEY: It was a very nice funeral.

LINDA: But where are all the people he knew? Maybe they blame him.

CHARLEY: Naa. It's a rough world, Linda. They wouldn't blame him.

LINDA: I can't understand it. At this time especially. First time in thirty-five years we were just about free and clear. He only needed a little salary. He was even finished with the dentist.

CHARLEY: No man only needs a little salary.

LINDA: I can't understand it.

BIFF: There were a lot of nice days. When he'd come home from a trip; or on Sundays, making the stoop; finishing the cellar; putting on the new porch; when he built the extra bathroom; and put up the garage. You know something, Charley, there's more of him in that front stoop than in all the sales he ever made.

CHARLEY: Yeah. He was a happy man with a batch of cement.

LINDA: He was so wonderful with his hands.

BIFF: He had the wrong dreams. All, all, wrong.

HAPPY [*almost ready to fight* BIFF]: Don't say that!

BIFF: He never knew who he was.

CHARLEY [*stopping* HAPPY'S *movement and reply. To* BIFF]: Nobody dast blame this man. You don't understand; Willy was a salesman. And for a salesman, there is no rock bottom to the life. He don't put a bolt to a nut, he don't tell you the law or give you medicine. He's a man way out there in the blue, riding on a smile and a shoeshine. And when they start not smiling back – that's an earthquake. And then you get yourself a couple of spots on your hat, and you're finished. Nobody dast blame this man. A salesman is got to dream, boy. It comes with the territory.

BIFF: Charley, the man didn't know who he was.

HAPPY [*infuriated*]: Don't say that!

BIFF: Why don't you come with me, Happy?

HAPPY: I'm not licked that easily. I'm staying right in this city, and I'm gonna beat this racket! [*He looks at* BIFF, *his chin set.*] The Loman Brothers!

BIFF: I know who I am, kid.

HAPPY: All right, boy. I'm gonna show you and everybody else that Willy Loman did not die in vain. He had a good dream. It's the only dream you can have – to come out number-one man. He fought it out here, and this is where I'm gonna win it for him.

BIFF [*with a hopeless glance at* HAPPY, *bends toward his mother*]: Let's go, Mom.

LINDA: I'll be with you in a minute. Go on, Charley. [*He hesitates.*] I want to, just for a minute. I never had a chance to say good-bye.

[CHARLEY *moves away, followed by* HAPPY. BIFF *remains a slight distance up and left of* LINDA. *She sits there, summoning herself. The flute begins, not far away, playing behind her speech.*]

LINDA: Forgive me, dear. I can't cry. I don't know what it is, but I can't cry. I don't understand it. Why did you ever do that? Help me, Willy, I can't cry. It seems to me that you're just on another trip. I keep expecting you. Willy, dear, I can't cry. Why did you do it? I search and search and I search, and I can't understand it, Willy. I made the last payment on the house today. Today, dear. And there'll be nobody home. [*A sob rises in her throat.*] We're free and clear. [*Sobbing more fully, released*] We're free. [BIFF *comes slowly toward her.*] We're free . . . We're free . . .

[BIFF *lifts her to her feet and moves out up right with her in his arms.* LINDA *sobs quietly.* BERNARD *and* CHARLEY *come together and follow them, followed by* HAPPY. *Only the music of the flute is left on the darkening stage as over the house the hard towers of the apartment buildings rise into sharp focus.*]

CURTAIN

The Scarecrow and His Servant

Finally he stopped, and looked at Jack. It was astonishing how much expression he could manage with his gash-mouth and stone-eyes.

'Young man,' he said, 'I have a proposition to make. Here you are, an honest and willing youth, and here am I, a Scarecrow of enterprise and talent. What would you say if I offered you the position of my personal servant?'

'What would my duties be?' said Jack.

'To accompany me throughout the world, to fetch and carry, to wash, cook, and attend to my needs. In return, I have nothing to offer but excitement and glory. We might sometimes go hungry, but we shall never want for adventure. Well, my boy? What do you say?'

PHILIP PULLMAN

WINNER OF THE WHITBREAD AWARD, THE
CARNEGIE MEDAL, THE SMARTIES PRIZE AND
THE GUARDIAN CHILDREN'S FICTION PRIZE

'Philip Pullman. Is he the best storyteller ever?'
Observer

'Pullman is in a league of his own'
Jon Snow, Chairman of Whitbread judges

'Once in a lifetime a children's author emerges who is
so extraordinary that the imagination of generations is
altered. Lewis Carroll, E Nesbit, CS Lewis and Tolkien
were all of this cast. So, too, is Philip Pullman'
New Statesman

'Philip Pullman, capable of lighting up the dullest day
or greyest spirit with the incandescence of his
imagination' *Independent*

'A comic genius of children's fiction'
The Times

PHILIP PULLMAN

The Scarecrow
and his
Servant

Illustrated by Peter Bailey

CORGI YEARLING BOOKS

THE SCARECROW AND HIS SERVANT
A CORGI YEARLING BOOK 0 440 86376 7

First published in Great Britain by Doubleday,
an imprint of Random House Children's Books

Doubleday edition published 2004
Corgi Yearling edition published 2005

1 3 5 7 9 10 8 6 4 2

Copyright © Philip Pullman, 2004
Illustrations copyright © Peter Bailey, 2004

The right of Philip Pullman to be identified
as the author of this work has been asserted in accordance
with the Copyright, Designs and Patents Act 1988.

Corgi Yearling Books are published by Random House Children's Books,
61-63 Uxbridge Road, London W5 5SA,
a division of The Random House Group Ltd,
in Australia by Random House Australia (Pty) Ltd,
20 Alfred Street, Milsons Point, Sydney, NSW 2061, Australia,
in New Zealand by Random House New Zealand Ltd,
18 Poland Road, Glenfield, Auckland 10, New Zealand,
and in South Africa by Random House (Pty) Ltd,
Endulini, 5A Jubilee Road, Parktown 2193, South Africa

THE RANDOM HOUSE GROUP Limited Reg. No. 954009
www.kidsatrandomhouse.co.uk

A CIP catalogue record for this book is available from the British Library.

Printed and bound in Great Britain by
Bookmarque Ltd, Croydon, Surrey

For Freddie

Chapter One

LIGHTNING

One day old Mr Pandolfo, who hadn't been feeling at all well, decided that it was time to make a scarecrow. The birds had been very troublesome. Come to that, his rheumatism had been troublesome, and the soldiers had been troublesome, and the weather had been troublesome, and his cousins had been troublesome. It was all getting a bit too much for him. Even his old pet raven had flown away.

He couldn't do anything about his rheumatism, or the soldiers, or the weather, or his cousins, who were the biggest problem of all. There was a whole family of them, the Buffalonis, and they wanted to get hold of his land and divert all the springs and streams, and drain all the wells, and put up a factory to make weedkiller and rat poison and insecticide.

All those troubles were too big for old Mr Pandolfo to manage, but he thought he could do something about the birds, at least. So he put together a fine-looking scarecrow, with a big solid turnip for a head and a sturdy broomstick for a backbone, and dressed him in an old tweed suit, and stuffed him tightly with straw. Then he tucked a short letter inside him, wrapped in oilskin for safety.

'There you are,' he said. 'Now you remember what your job is, and remember where you belong. Be courteous, and be brave, and be honourable, and be kind. And the best of blooming luck.'

He stuck the scarecrow in the middle of the wheatfield, and went home to lie down, because he wasn't feeling well at all.

That night another farmer came along and stole the scarecrow, being too lazy to make one himself. And the next night someone else came along and stole him again.

So little by little the scarecrow moved away from the place where he was made, and he got more and more tattered and torn, and finally he didn't look nearly as smart as he'd done when Mr Pandolfo put him together. He stood in the middle of a muddy field, and he stayed there.

But one night there was a thunderstorm. It was a very violent one, and everyone in the district shivered and trembled and jumped as the thunder went off like cannon-fire and the lightning lashed down like whips. The scarecrow stood there in the wind and the rain, taking no notice.

And so he might have stayed; but then there came one of those million-to-one chances that are like winning the lottery. All his molecules and atoms and elementary particles and whatnot were lined up in exactly the right way to switch on when the lightning struck him, which it did at two in the morning, fizzing its way through his turnip and down his broomstick and into the mud.

The Scarecrow blinked with surprise and looked all around. There wasn't much to see except a field of mud, and not much light to see it by except the flashes of lightning.

Still, there wasn't a bird in sight.

'Excellent,' said the Scarecrow.

On the same night, a small boy called Jack happened to be sheltering in a barn not far away. The thunder was so loud that it woke him out of his sleep with a jump. At first he thought it was cannon-fire, and he sat up terrified with his eyes wide open. He could think of nothing worse than soldiers and guns; if it weren't for the soldiers, he'd still have a family and a home and a bed to sleep in.

But as he sat there with his heart thumping, he heard the downpour of the rain on the roof, and realized that the bang had only been thunder and not gunfire. He gave a sigh of relief and lay down again, shivering and sneezing and turning over and over in the hay trying to get warm, until finally he fell asleep.

By the morning the storm had cleared away, and the sky was a bright cold blue. Jack woke up again feeling colder than ever, and hungry too. But he knew how to look for food, and before long he'd gathered up some grains of wheat and a couple of turnip tops and a limp carrot, and he sat in the door-way of the barn in the sunlight to eat them.

'Could be worse,' he said to himself.

He ate very slowly to make it last, and then he just sat there, getting warm. Someone would come along soon to chase him away, but for the moment he was safe.

Then he heard a voice calling from across the fields. Jack was curious, so he stood up and shaded his eyes to look. The shouting came from somewhere in the field beyond the road, and since he had nothing else to do, Jack stood up and walked along towards it.

The shouts came from a scarecrow, in the middle of the muddiest field in sight, and he was waving his arms wildly and yelling at the top of his voice and leaning over at a crazy angle.

'Help!' he was shouting. 'Come and help me!'

'I think I'm going mad,' said Jack to himself. 'Still, look at that poor old thing – I'll go and help him anyway. He looks madder than I feel.'

So he stepped on to the muddy field, and struggled out to the middle, where the Scarecrow was waiting.

To tell the truth, Jack felt a little nervous, because it isn't every day you find a Scarecrow talking to you.

'Now, tell me, young man,' said the Scarecrow, as soon as Jack was close enough to hear, 'are there any birds around? Any crows, for example? I can't see behind me. Are they hiding?'

His voice was rich and sonorous. His head was made of a great knobbly turnip, with a broad crack for a mouth and a long thin sprout for a nose and two bright little stones for eyes. He had a tattered straw hat, now badly singed, and a soggy woollen scarf, and an old tweed jacket full of holes, and his rake-handle arms had gloves stuffed with straw on the ends of them, one glove leather and the other wool. He also had a pair of threadbare trousers, but since he only had one leg, the empty trouser leg trailed down beside him. Everything was the colour of mud. Jack scratched his head and looked all around.

'No,' he said, 'no crows anywhere. No birds at all.'

'That's a good job done,' said the Scarecrow. 'Now I want to move on, but I need another leg. If you go and find me a leg, I shall be very obliged. Just like this one, only the opposite,' he added, and he lifted his trouser leg daintily to show a stout stick set firmly in the earth.

'All right,' said Jack. 'I can do that.'

So he set off towards the wood at the edge of the field, and clambered through the undergrowth looking for the right sort of stick. He found one before long, and took it back to the Scarecrow.

'Let me see,' said the Scarecrow. 'Hold it up beside me. That's it. Now slide it up inside the leg of my trousers.'

The end of the stick was broken and splintered

and it wasn't easy to push it up the soggy, muddy trouser leg, but Jack finally got it all the way up, and then he jumped, because he felt it twitch in his hand.

He let go, and the new leg swung itself down beside the other. But as soon as the Scarecrow tried to move, the new foot became stuck just like the first one. The harder he struggled, the deeper he sank.

Finally he stopped, and looked at Jack. It was astonishing how much expression he could manage with his gash-mouth and stone-eyes.

'Young man,' he said, 'I have a proposition to make. Here you are, an honest and willing youth, and here am I, a Scarecrow of enterprise and talent. What would you say if I offered you the position of my personal servant?'

'What would my duties be?' said Jack.

'To accompany me throughout the world, to fetch and carry, to wash, cook, and attend to my needs. In return, I have nothing to offer but excitement and glory. We might sometimes go hungry, but we shall never want for adventure. Well, my boy? What do you say?'

'I'll do it,' said Jack. 'I've got nothing else to do except starve, and nowhere to live except ditches and empty barns. So I might as well have a job, and

thank you, Mr Scarecrow, I'll take it.'

The Scarecrow extended his hand, and Jack shook it warmly.

'Your first job is to get me out of this mud,' said the Scarecrow.

So Jack heaved the Scarecrow's two legs out of the mud and carried him to the road. He hardly weighed anything at all.

'Which way shall we go?' said Jack.

They looked both ways. In one direction there was a forest, and in the other there was a line of hills. There was no-one in sight.

'That way!' said the Scarecrow, pointing to the hills.

So they set off, with the sun on their backs, and the green hills ahead.

In a farmhouse not far behind them, a lawyer was explaining something to a farmer.

'My name is Cercorelli,' he said, 'and I specialize in finding things for my employers, the distinguished and highly respectful Buffaloni Corporation, of Bella Fontana.'

The farmer gasped. He was a stout, red-faced, idle character, and he was afraid of this lean and silky lawyer, who was dressed entirely in black.

'Oh! The Buffalonis! Yes, indeed, Mr Cercorelli,'

9

he said. 'What can I do to help? Anything! Just name it!'

'It's a small matter,' said the lawyer, 'but one of sentimental importance to my clients. It concerns a scarecrow. It was made by a distant cousin of the Chairman of the Corporation, and it seems to have vanished from its place of origin. My client Mr Giovanni Buffaloni is a very warm-hearted and family-minded man, and he would like to restore the scarecrow to its original home, in memory of his dear cousin who made it.'

The lawyer looked through some papers, and the farmer ran his finger around the inside of his shirt collar, and gulped.

'Well, I, um . . .' he said faintly.

'One might almost think that scarecrows had the power of movement!' said Mr Cercorelli, smiling in a sinister way. 'This fellow has been wandering. I've traced him through several farms already, and now I discover that he made his way to yours.'

'I – er – I think I know the scarecrow you mention,' said the farmer. 'I nick— I bought him from someone else, who didn't need him no more.'

'Oh, good. May we go and see if he is the right one?'

'Well, of course, I'd do anything for the Buffalonis, important people, wouldn't want to upset them, but . . . Well, he's gone.'

'Gone . . . *again?*' said the lawyer, narrowing his eyes.

'I went out this morning, to – er – to tidy him up a bit, and he wasn't there. Mind you, there was a big storm last night. He might have blown away.'

'Oh, dear. That is very unfortunate. Mr Buffaloni takes a dim view of people who do not look after his property. I think I can say that his degree of disappointment will be considerable.'

The farmer was quaking with alarm.

'If I ever hear anything about the scarecrow,' he said, 'anything at all, I'll report to you at once.'

'I think that would be very wise,' said Mr Cercorelli. 'Here is my card. Now show me the field from which the scarecrow vanished.'

11

Chapter Two

The Brigands

The Scarecrow and his servant set a good pace as they walked along. On the way, they passed a field of cabbages in the middle of which stood another scarecrow, but he was a mournful-looking fellow whose arms hung feebly at his side.

'Good day to you, sir!' called the Scarecrow, waving to him cheerfully.

But the scarecrow in the field took no notice.

'You see,' the Scarecrow explained to Jack, 'there's a man whose mind is on his job. He's concentrating hard. Quite right.'

'Nice-looking cabbages,' said Jack.

He left the cabbages reluctantly and ran to catch up with the Scarecrow, who was striding ahead like

12

a champion. Presently they found the road getting steeper and the fields getting rockier, and finally there were no fields at all and the road was only a track. It was very hot.

'Unless we find something to eat and drink very soon,' said Jack, 'I'm going to peg out.'

'Oh, we'll find something,' said the Scarecrow, patting him on the shoulder. 'I have every confidence in you. Besides, we understand springs and streams and wells where I come from. Fountains, too. You take it from me, we'll find a spring before long.'

They walked on, and the Scarecrow pointed out curious features of geology, such as a rock that looked like a pigeon, and botany, such as a bush with a robin's nest in it, and entomology, such as a beetle that was as black as a crow.

'You know a lot about birds, master,' said Jack.

'I've made them my lifetime study, my boy. I do believe I could scare any bird that ever lived.'

'I bet you could. Oh! Listen! What's that?'

It was the sound of someone crying, and it came from round the corner. Jack and the Scarecrow hurried on, and found an old woman sitting at a crossroads, with a basket of provisions all scattered on the ground. She was weeping and wailing at the top of her voice.

'Madam!' the Scarecrow said, raising his straw hat very politely. 'What wicked bird has done this to you?'

The old woman looked up, and gave a great gulp of astonishment. Her mouth opened and shut several times, but not a sound came out. Finally, she struggled to her feet and curtseyed nervously.

'It was the brigands,' she said, 'begging your pardon, my lord. There's a gang of terrible brigands living in these hills, robbing travellers and making life a misery for us poor people, and they just came galloping past and knocked me over and rode away laughing, the cowardly rogues.'

The Scarecrow was amazed.

'Do you mean to say that this was the work of *human beings*?' he said.

'Indeed, yes, your honour,' said the old woman.

'Jack, my boy – tell me it's not so—'

Jack was gathering up the things that had fallen out of her basket: apples, carrots, a lump of cheese, a loaf of bread. It was very difficult to do it without dribbling.

'I'm afraid it is, master,' said Jack. 'There's a lot of wicked people about. Tell you what – let's turn round and go the other way.'

'Not a bit of it!' said the Scarecrow sternly. 'We're going to teach these villains a lesson. How dare they

treat a lady in this disgraceful way? Here, madam –
take my arm . . .'

He was so courteous to the old woman, and his
manner was so graceful, that she very soon forgot
his knobbly turnip face and his rough wooden arms,
and talked to him as if he was a proper gentleman.

'Yes, sir – ever since the wars began, first the
soldiers came through and took everything, and
then the brigands came along, robbing and murder-
ing and taking what they wanted. And they say the
chief brigand is related to the Buffalonis, so they've
got political protection too. We don't know where to
turn!'

'Buffalonis, you say? I don't like the sound of
them. What are they?'

'A very powerful family, sir. We don't dare cross the Buffalonis.'

'Well, fear no more,' said the Scarecrow resolutely. 'We shall scare the brigands away, and they'll never trouble you again.'

'Nice-looking apples,' said Jack hopefully, handing the old woman her basket.

'Ooh, they are,' she said.

'Tasty-looking bread, too.'

'Yes, it is,' said the old woman, tucking it firmly under her arm.

'Lovely-looking cheese.'

'Yes, I like a piece of cheese. Goes down a treat with a drop of beer.'

'You haven't got any beer, have you?' said Jack, looking all around.

'No,' she said. 'Well, I'll be on my way. Thank you, sir,' she said, curtseying again to the Scarecrow, who raised his hat and bowed.

And off she went.

Jack sighed and followed the Scarecrow, who was already striding off towards the top of the hill.

When they reached the top, they saw a ruined castle. There was one tower that was still standing, and some walls and battlements, but everything else had tumbled down and was covered in ivy.

'What a spooky place,' said Jack. 'I wouldn't like to go near it at night.'

'Courage, Jack!' said the Scarecrow. 'Look – there's a spring. What did I tell you? Drink your fill, my boy!'

It was true. The spring bubbled out of the rocks beside the castle and flowed into a little pool, and as soon as he saw it, Jack gave a cry of delight and plunged his face deep into the icy water, swallowing and swallowing until he wasn't thirsty any more.

Finally he emerged, and heard the Scarecrow calling.

'Jack! Jack! In here! Look!'

Jack ran through the doorway at the foot of the tower, and found the Scarecrow looking around at all kinds of things: in one corner, barrels of gunpowder, muskets, swords and daggers and pikes; and in another corner, chests and boxes of gold coins and silver chains and glittering jewels of every colour; and in a third corner –

'Food!' cried Jack.

There were great smoked hams hanging from the ceiling, cheeses as big as cartwheels, onions in strings, boxes of apples, pies of every kind, bread, biscuits, and spice cakes and fruit cakes and butter cakes and honey cakes in abundance.

It was no good even trying to resist. Jack seized a

pie as big as his own head, and a moment later he was sitting in the middle of the food, chewing away merrily, while the Scarecrow watched in satisfaction.

'What a stroke of luck finding this!' he said. 'And no-one knows about it at all. If only that old lady knew about it, she could come and help herself, and she wouldn't be poor any more.'

'Well,' said Jack, swallowing a mouthful of pie and picking up a spice cake, 'it's not quite like that, master. I bet all this belongs to the brigands, and we better clear off soon, because if they catch us they'll cut our throats.'

'But I haven't got a throat.'

'Well, I have, and I don't want it cut,' said Jack. 'Look – we can't stay here – let's grab some of the food and scram.'

'Shame on you!' said the Scarecrow severely. 'Where's your courage? Where's your honour? We're going to scare these brigands away, and scare them so badly that they never come back. I wouldn't be surprised if we win a grand reward. Why, they might even make me a duke! Or give me a gold medal. No, it wouldn't surprise me a bit.'

'Well,' said Jack, 'maybe.'

Suddenly the Scarecrow pointed at a heap of straw.

'Oh – look – what's that?' he said.

There was something moving. It was a little creature the size of a mouse, which was crawling feebly around in a heap of straw on the floor. They both bent over to look at it.

'It's a baby bird,' said Jack.

'It's an owl chick, that's what it is,' said the Scarecrow severely. 'These parents have no sense of responsibility. Look at that nest up there! Downright dangerous.'

He pointed to an untidy bundle of twigs in a crack high up in the wall.

'Well, there's only one thing for it,' he said. 'You keep guard, Jack, while I return this infant to his cradle.'

'But—' Jack tried to protest.

The Scarecrow took no notice. He bent over and picked up the little bird, and tucked it tenderly into his pocket, making gentle clucking noises to soothe it. Then he began to clamber perilously up the sheer face of the wall, jamming his hands and feet into the cracks.

'Master! Take care!' called Jack, in a fever of anxiety. 'If you fall down, you'll snap like a dry stick!'

The Scarecrow didn't listen, because he was concentrating hard. Jack scampered to the door and looked around. Darkness was gathering, but there was no sign of any brigands. He scampered back in, and saw the Scarecrow high up and clinging to the wall with one hand while fumbling in his pocket with the other, and then reaching up and carefully putting the little bird back into the nest.

'Now you sit still,' he said sternly. 'No more squirming, you understand? If you can't fly, don't squirm. When I see your parents, I shall have a word with them.'

Then he began to clamber back down the wall. It looked so dangerous that Jack hardly dared watch, but finally the Scarecrow reached the floor again, and brushed his hands severely.

'I thought the birds were your enemy, master,' said Jack.

'Not the children, Jack! Good gracious me. Any man of honour would sooner bite off his own leg than hurt a child. Heaven forfend!'

'Blimey,' said Jack.

While the Scarecrow pottered about in the ruins, looking at everything with great curiosity, Jack gathered up a couple of pies, a loaf of bread, and half a dozen apples, and put them in a leather bag he found hanging on a hook next to the muskets. He hid it among the ivy growing over the tumbled wall outside.

The sun had set by this time, and it was nearly dark. Jack sat on the stones and thought about brigands. What did they do to people they caught? They weren't like scarecrows, or men of honour; they were more like soldiers, probably. They were bound to do horrible things, like tying you up and cutting bits off you, or dangling you over a fire, or putting earwigs up your nose. They might take all your ribs out. They might cram your trousers full of fireworks. They might—

Someone tapped him on the shoulder, and Jack leaped up with a yell.

'My word,' said the Scarecrow admiringly, 'that's a fine noise. I was just going to tell you that the brigands are coming.'

'What?' said Jack, in terror.

'Come, come,' said the Scarecrow. 'It's only a small flock – not more than twenty, I'd say. And I've got a plan.'

'Let's hear it, quick!'

'Very well. Here it is: we'll hide in the castle until they're all inside, and then we'll scare them, and then they'll run away. How's that?'

Jack was speechless. The Scarecrow beamed.

'Come along,' he said. 'I've found an excellent place to hide.'

Helplessly, Jack followed his master back into

the tower, and looked all around in the dimness.

'Where's this excellent place to hide?' he said.

'Why, over there!' said the Scarecrow, pointing to a corner of the room in plain sight. 'They'll never think of looking there.'

'But – but – but—'

Jack could already hear the clop of horses' hooves outside. He scrunched himself down in the corner beside the Scarecrow, and squeezed his knees together to stop them knocking, and put his hands over his eyes so that no-one could see him, and waited for the brigands to come in.

CHAPTER THREE

A STORY BY THE FIRESIDE

They were a disciplined band, those brigands. Jack watched between his fingers as they came in silently and sat around the fireplace. The chief brigand was a ferocious-looking man, with two belts full of bullets criss-cross over his shoulders, another one round his waist, a cutlass, two pistols, and three daggers: one in his belt, another strapped to his arm, and the third in the top of his boot. What's more, if he lost all his other weapons he could still stab two people with his moustache, which was waxed into long points as sharp as a pin.

His eyes glared and rolled as he looked around at his men, and Jack was almost sure they gave out sparks.

Any second now he'll see us, Jack thought. So it was despair as much as bravado that made him stand up and say:

'Good evening, gentlemen, and welcome to my master's castle!'

And he swept a low bow.

When he looked around, he saw twenty swords and twenty pistols all pointing at him, and twenty pairs of eyes, each eye just like the end of a pistol barrel.

The chief brigand roared: 'Who's this?'

'It's a mad boy, Captain,' said one of the men. 'Shall we roast him?'

'No,' said the chief, coming close and touching Jack's ribs with the point of his sword. 'There's no meat on him. He's all bone and gristle. He might flavour a stew, I suppose. Turn round, boy.'

Jack turned round and then turned back again. The chief brigand was shaking his head doubtfully.

'You say this is your master's castle?' he said.

'Indeed it is, sir, and you're most welcome,' said Jack.

'And who's your master?'

'My Lord Scarecrow,' said Jack, pointing to the Scarecrow in the corner, who was lying propped against the wall as still as a turnip, a suit of old clothes, and a few sticks could lie.

The chief brigand roared with laughter, and all his well-trained band slapped their thighs and held their sides and bellowed with mirth.

'He is mad!' cried the chief brigand. 'He's lost his wits!'

'Indeed I have, sir,' said Jack. 'I've been looking for them for months.'

'What do mad boys taste like?' said one of the brigands. 'Do they taste different from normal ones?'

'Spicier,' said another. 'More of a peppery taste.'

'No!' said the chief. 'We won't eat him. We'll keep him as a pet. We'll teach him to do tricks. Here – mad boy – turn a somersault, go on.'

Jack turned a somersault and stood up again.

'He's quick, isn't he?' said one brigand.

'Bet he can't dance, though,' said another.

'Mad boy!' roared the chief. 'Dance!'

Jack obediently capered like a monkey. Then he capered like a frog, and then he capered like a goat.

The brigands were in a good mood by now, and they roared with laughter and clapped their hands.

'Wine!' bellowed the chief. 'Mad boy, stop dancing and pour us some wine!'

Jack found a big flagon of wine and went around the circle of brigands, filling up the horn cups they were all holding out.

'A toast!' the chief brigand said. 'To plunder!'

'To plunder!' the brigands shouted, and drank the wine in one gulp, so Jack had to go all the way round and fill the cups again.

Meanwhile, some of the brigands were lighting a fire and cutting up great joints of meat. Jack looked at the meat uneasily, but it looked like proper beef, and it certainly smelled good when it started to cook.

While it was roasting, the chief brigand counted out the jewels and gold coins they'd plundered and divided them all into twenty heaps, one big one and nineteen little ones; and as he was doing that, he said, 'Here, mad boy – tell us a story.'

Well, that was a hard one for Jack. However, if he didn't do it there'd be big trouble; so he sat down and began.

'Once upon a time,' he said, 'there was a band of brigands living in a cave. They were cruel and wicked – oh, you could never imagine such terrible men. Every one of them was a qualified murderer.

'Anyway, one day they fell to quarrelling among themselves, and before they knew it, one of them lay dead on the floor of the cave.

'So the chief said, "Take him out and bury him. He makes the place look untidy."

'And they picked the dead man up and took him outside and dug a hole for him, and they put him in and shovelled the earth back on top, but he kept throwing it out.

'"You're not burying me!" he said, and he climbed out of the grave.

'"Oh yes we are!" they said, and they tried to shove him back in, but he wouldn't go. Every time they got him in the grave, he climbed out again, and he was as dead as a doornail. Finally they got him in and seven of them sat on him while the others piled rocks on top, and that did it.

'"He won't get out of that," said the chief, and they went back in the cave and lit a fire to make supper. They had a big meal and lots of wine and then they lay down to sleep.

'But in the middle of the night, one of the brigands woke up. The cave was all silent, and the moonlight was shining in through the entrance. What woke him up was a sound, like a rock moving quietly on another rock, not loud at all, just a quiet

28

sort of scraping noise. This man lay there with his eyes wide open, just listening as hard as he could. Then he heard it again.'

All the brigands were sitting stock-still, and they gazed fearfully at Jack with wide eyes.

Help, he thought. What am I going to say next?

But he didn't have to say anything, because into the silence there came a little scraping sound, like a rock moving quietly on another rock.

All the brigands jumped, and they all gave a little squeak of terror.

'And then,' said Jack, 'he saw . . . *Look! Look!*'

And he pointed dramatically to the corner where the Scarecrow was lying. Every head turned round at once.

The Scarecrow slowly lifted his head and stared at them with his knobbly turnip face.

All the brigands gasped, including the chief.

And the Scarecrow stretched out his arms and bent his legs, and stood up, and took one step towards them –

And every single brigand leaped to his feet and fled, screaming with terror. They fell over – they knocked one another out of the way – the ones that fell over got trampled on, and the ones that trampled on them got their feet caught and fell over themselves, to be trampled on in their turn – and

some of them fell in the fire and leaped up squealing with pain, and that scattered the burning logs so that the cave was dark, and that made them even more frightened, so they shrieked and yelled in mortal fear; and those who could still see a little saw the Scarecrow's great knobbly face coming towards them, and scrambled even harder to get away –

And no more than ten seconds later, the brigands were all running away down the road, screaming with terror.

Jack stood in the doorway in amazement, watching them disappear into the distance.

'Well, master,' he said, 'it happened just as you said it would.'

'Timing, you see,' said the Scarecrow. 'The secret of all good scaring. I waited till they were feeling at their ease, lulled and comfortable, you know, and then I got up and scared them good and proper. It was the last thing they expected. I expect your story helped a little,' he added. 'It probably put them in a sort of peaceful mood.'

'Hmm,' said Jack. 'But I bet they come back, because they haven't eaten their dinner. I reckon we should scarper before they do.'

'Believe me,' said the Scarecrow solemnly, 'those rascals will never come back. They're not like

31

birds, you see. With birds you need to keep scaring them afresh every day, but once is enough for brigands.'

'Well, you were right once, master. Perhaps you're right again.'

'You can depend on it, my boy! But you know, you shouldn't have told the brigands that I was the lord of this castle. That wasn't strictly true. I'm really the lord of Spring Valley.'

'Spring Valley? Where's that?'

'Oh, miles away. Ever so far. But it all belongs to me.'

'Does it?'

'Every inch. The farm, the wells, the fountains, the streams – all of it.'

'But how do you know, master? I mean, can you prove it?'

'The name of Spring Valley is written in my heart, Jack! Anyway, now I've had a rest, I'm eager to be on our way, and see the world by moonlight. Perhaps we'll meet the parents of that poor little owl chick. My word, I look forward to scaring them. Take as much food as you like – the brigands won't need it now.'

So Jack took the bag of food he'd hidden earlier, and added a pie and a cold roast chicken to it for good measure, and then followed his master out on to the high road, which was shining bright under the moon.

At that very moment, Mr Cercorelli the lawyer was sitting at a rough wooden table in a cottage kitchen, opposite an old woman who was eating bread and cheese.

'Like a scarecrow, you say?' he said, making a note.

'Yes, sir, horrible ugly brute he was. He leaped out of the bushes at me. Lord! I thought my last hour had come. He give me such a start that I dropped all me bread and cheese, and it was only when young master Buffaloni and his nice friends come along and chased him away that I felt safe again.'

'And did you see which way he went, this footpad who looked like a scarecrow?'

'Yes, sir. He went up into the hills. I shouldn't wonder if he's got a gang of marauding villains up there with him.'

'No doubt. Was he alone on this occasion?'

'No, sir. He had a young boy with him. Vicious-looking lad. Foreign, probably.'

'A young boy, eh?' said the lawyer, making another note. 'Thank you. That is very interesting. By the way,' he said, because he hadn't eaten all day, 'that cheese looks remarkably good.'

'Yes, it is,' said the old woman, putting it away. 'Very nice indeed. Nice bit of cheese.'

Mr Cercorelli sighed, and stood up.

'If you hear any more of this desperate rogue,' he said, 'be sure to let me know. Mr Buffaloni is offering a very generous reward. Good evening to you.'

CHAPTER FOUR

THE TRAVELLING PLAYERS

After a good night's sleep under a hedge, the Scarecrow and his servant woke up on a bright and sparkling morning.

'This is the life, Jack!' said the Scarecrow. 'The open road, the fresh air, and adventure just around the corner.'

'The fresh air's all right for you, master,' said Jack, removing leaves from his hair, 'but I like sleeping in a bed. I haven't seen a bed for so long, I can't remember whether the sheets go under the blankets or the blankets go under the sheets.'

'I shall just go and pay my respects to a colleague,' said the Scarecrow.

They'd woken up to find themselves close to a crossroads. A wooden sign stood where the roads

35

met; but what the four arms were pointing to was impossible to read, for years of sun and rain had completely worn away the paint.

The Scarecrow strode up to the road sign and greeted it courteously. The sign took no notice, and neither did Jack, who was busy cutting a slice of cold meat with his little pocket knife, and folding it inside a slice of bread.

Then there came a loud *crack!*

Jack looked up to see the Scarecrow, very angry, clouting the nearest arm of the signpost as hard as he could.

'Take that, you insolent rogue!' he cried, and punched it again.

Unfortunately the first punch must have loosened something in the sign, because when he punched it for the second time, all four arms swung round, and the next one clonked the Scarecrow hard on the back of the head.

The Scarecrow fell over, shouting, 'Treachery! Cowardice!' and then bounced up at once, and seized the arm that had hit him and wrenched it off the signpost altogether.

'Take that, you dastardly footpad!' he cried, belabouring the post with the broken arm. 'Fight fairly, or surrender!'

The trouble was that every time he hit the post, it

swung around again and hit him from the other side. However, he stood his ground, and fought back bravely.

'Master! Master!' called Jack, jumping up. 'That's not a footpad – that's a road sign!'

'He's in disguise,' said the Scarecrow. 'Mind out – stand back – he's a footpad all right. But don't you worry, I'll deal with him.'

'Right you are, master. Footpad he is, if you say so. But I think he's had enough now. I'm sure I heard him say, *I surrender.*'

'Did you? Are you sure?'

'Absolutely certain, master.'

'In that case—' began the Scarecrow, but stopped and looked down in horror at his own right arm, which was slipping slowly out of the sleeve of his jacket. The rake handle had come away from the broomstick that was his spine.

'I've been disarmed!' the Scarecrow said, shocked.

In fact, as Jack saw, the rake handle was so dry and brittle that it had never been much use in the first place, and the punishment it had taken in the fight with the road sign had cracked it in several places.

'I've got an idea, master,' he said. 'This fellow's arm is in better condition than your old one. Why don't we slip that up your sleeve instead?'

'What a good idea!' said the Scarecrow, cheering up at once.

So Jack did that, and just as had happened with the stick that had become his leg, the arm gave a kind of twitch when it met his shoulder, and settled into place at once.

'My word,' said the Scarecrow, admiring his new arm, trying it out by waving it around, and practising pointing at things with the finger on the end. 'What gifts you have, Jack, my boy! You could be a surgeon. Or a carpenter, even. And as for you, you scoundrel,' he added severely to the road sign, 'let that be a lesson to you.'

'I don't suppose he'll attack anyone else, master,' said Jack. 'I reckon you've sorted him out for good. Which way shall we go next?'

'That way,' said the Scarecrow, pointing confidently along one of the roads with his new arm.

So Jack shouldered his bag, and they set off.

After an hour's brisk walking, they reached the edge of a town. It must have been market day, because people were making for the town with carts full of vegetables and cheeses and other things to sell. One man was a bird-catcher. His cart was piled high with cages containing little songbirds such as linnets, larks and goldfinches. The Scarecrow was very interested.

'Prisoners of war,' he explained to Jack. 'I expect they're being sent back to their own country.'

'I don't think so, master. I think people are going to buy them and keep them in cages so they can hear them singing.'

'No!' exclaimed the Scarecrow. 'No, no, people wouldn't do that. Why, that would be dishonourable. Take it from me, they're prisoners of war.'

Presently they came to the market place, and the Scarecrow gazed around in amazement at the town hall, the church, the market stalls.

'I had no idea civilization had advanced to this point,' he said to Jack. 'Why, this almost compares to Bella Fontana. What industry! What beauty! What splendour! You wouldn't find a place like this in the kingdom of the birds, I'm sure of that.'

Jack could see children whispering and pointing at the Scarecrow.

'Listen, master,' he said, 'I don't think we—'

'What's *that*?' said the Scarecrow, full of excitement.

He was pointing at a canvas booth where a carpenter was hammering some planks together to hold up a brightly painted picture of a wild landscape.

'That's going to be a play,' said Jack. 'That's called scenery. Actors come out in front of it and act out a story.'

The Scarecrow's eyes were open as wide as they could go. He moved towards the booth as if he were being pulled on a string. There was a big colourful poster nearby, and a man was reading it aloud for those people who couldn't read themselves:

'*The Tragical History of Harlequin and Queen Dido*,' the man read out. '*To be acted by Signor Rigatelli's Celebrated Players, late from triumphs in Paris, Venice, Madrid, and Constantinople. With Effects of Battle and Shipwreck, a Dance of the Infernal Spirits, and the Eruption of Vesuvius. Daily at noon, mid-afternoon, and sunset, with special evening performance complete with Pyrotechnical Extravaganza.*'

The Scarecrow was nearly floating with excitement.

'I want to watch it *all*!' he said. 'Again and again!'

'Well, it's not free, master,' Jack explained. 'You

have to pay. And we haven't got any money.'

'In that case,' said the Scarecrow, 'I shall have to offer my services as an actor. I say!' he called. 'Signor Rigatelli!'

A fat man wearing a dressing gown and eating a piece of salami came out from behind the scenery.

'Yes?' he said.

'Signor Rigatelli,' began the Scarecrow, 'I—'

'Blimey,' said Signor Rigatelli to Jack, 'that's good. Do some more.'

'I'm not doing anything,' Jack said.

'Excuse me,' said the Scarecrow, 'but I—'

'That's it! Brilliant!' said Rigatelli.

'*What?*' said Jack. 'What are you talking about?'

'Ventriloquism,' said Rigatelli. 'Do it again, go on.'

'Signor Rigatelli,' said the Scarecrow once more, 'my patience is not inexhaustible. I have the honour to present myself to you as an actor of modest experience but boundless genius . . . What are you doing?'

Signor Rigatelli was walking around the Scarecrow, studying him from every angle. Then he lifted up the back of the Scarecrow's jacket to see how he worked, and the Scarecrow leaped away, furious.

'No – it's all right, master, don't get cross,' said

Jack hastily. 'It's just that he'd like to be an actor, you see,' he explained to Rigatelli, 'and I'm his agent,' he added.

'I've never seen anything like it,' said the great showman. 'I can't see how it works at all. Tell you what, we'll use him as a prop in the mad scene. He can stand there on the blasted heath when the queen goes barmy. Then if he looks all right he can go on again as an infernal spirit. Can you make him dance?'

'I'm not sure,' said Jack.

'Well, he can follow the others. First call in ten minutes.'

And Rigatelli crammed the rest of the salami in his mouth, and went back inside his caravan.

The Scarecrow was ecstatic.

'A prop!' he said. 'I'm going to be a *prop*! Do you realize, Jack, that this is the first step on the road to a glorious career? And already I'm playing a prop! He must have been very impressed.'

'Yes,' said Jack, 'probably.'

The Scarecrow was already disappearing behind the scenery.

'Master,' said Jack, 'wait . . .'

He found the Scarecrow watching with great interest as an actor, sitting in front of a mirror, put his greasepaint on.

'Good grief!' the actor said, suddenly catching sight of the Scarecrow, and leaped out of his chair, dropping his greasepaint.

'Good day, sir,' said the Scarecrow. 'Allow me to introduce myself. I am to play the part of a prop. May I trouble you for the use of your make-up?'

The actor swallowed hard and looked around. Then he saw Jack.

'Who's this?' he said.

'This is Lord Scarecrow,' said Jack, 'and Signor Rigatelli says he can take part in the mad scene. Listen, master,' he said to the Scarecrow, who was sitting down and looking with great interest at all the pots of greasepaint and powder. 'You know what a prop is, don't you?'

'It's a very important part,' said the Scarecrow, painting a pair of bright red lips on the front of his turnip.

'Yes, but it's what they call a silent role,' said Jack. 'You don't move and you don't speak.'

'What's going on?' said the actor.

'*I'm* going on!' said the Scarecrow proudly. 'In the mad scene.'

He outlined each of his eyes with black, and then dabbed some red powder on his cheeks. The actor was watching, goggle-eyed.

'That looks lovely, master,' Jack said, 'but you don't want to overdo it.'

'You think we should be subtle?'

'For the mad scene, definitely, master.'

'Very well. Perhaps a wig would make me look more subtle.'

'Not that one,' said Jack, taking a big blond curly wig out of the Scarecrow's hands. 'Just remember – don't move and don't speak.'

'I'll do it all with my eyes,' said the Scarecrow, taking the wig back and settling it over his turnip.

The actor gave him a horrified look and left.

'I need a costume now,' said the Scarecrow. 'This'll do.'

He picked up a scarlet cloak and twirled it around his shoulders. Jack clutched his head in despair, and followed the Scarecrow out behind the scenes, where the actors and the musicians and the stage hands were getting everything ready. There was a lot to look at, and Jack had to stop the Scarecrow explaining it all to him.

'Yes, master – hush now – the audience is out there, so we all have to be quiet . . .'

'There it is!' said an angry actress, and snatched the wig off the Scarecrow's head. 'What are you playing at?' she said to Jack. 'How dare you put my wig on that thing?'

'I beg your pardon,' said the Scarecrow, getting to his feet and bowing very low. 'I would not upset you for the world, madam, but you are already so beautiful that you need no improvement; whereas I . . .'

The actress was watching with critical interest as she settled the wig on her head.

'Not bad,' she said to Jack. 'I've seen a lot worse. I can't see how you move him at all. But don't you touch my stuff again, you hear?'

'Sorry,' said Jack.

The actress swept away.

'Such grace! Such beauty!' said the Scarecrow, gazing after her.

'Yes, master, but *shush*!' said Jack. 'Sit *down*. Be *quiet*.'

Just then they heard a crash of cymbals and a blast on a trumpet.

'Ladies and gentlemen!' came the voice of Signor Rigatelli. 'We present a performance of the doleful and piteous tragedy of Harlequin and Queen Dido, with pictorial and scenic effects never before seen, and featuring the most comical interludes ever presented on the public stage! Our performance today is sponsored by the Buffaloni Dried Meat Company, the makers of the finest salami in town, A Smile In Every Bite.'

The Buffalonis again, thought Jack. They get up to everything.

There was a roll of drums, and the curtain went up. Jack and the Scarecrow watched wide-eyed as the play began. It wasn't much of a story, but the audience enjoyed Harlequin pretending to lose a string of sausages, and then swallowing a fly by mistake and leaping around the stage as it buzzed inside him; and then Queen Dido was abandoned by her lover, Captain Fanfarone, and ran offstage mad with grief. She was the actress in the blond wig.

'Here! Boy!' came a loud whisper from Rigatelli. 'Get him on! It's the mad scene! Stick him in the middle and get off quick.'

The Scarecrow spread his arms wide as Jack carried him onstage.

'I shall be the best prop there ever was!' he declared. 'They'll be talking about my prop for years to come.'

Jack put his finger to his lips and tiptoed off-stage. As he did, he found himself face to face with the actress playing Queen Dido, who was about to come on again. She looked furious.

'What's that thing doing?' she demanded.

'He's a prop,' Jack explained.

'If you make him move or speak I'll skin you alive,' she said. 'Manually.'

Jack swallowed and nodded hard.

The curtain rose, and Jack jumped, because Queen Dido gave a wild, unearthly shriek and ran past him on to the stage.

'Oh! Ah! Woe! Misery!' she screamed, and flung herself to the ground.

The audience watched, enthralled. So did the Scarecrow. Jack could see his eyes getting wider and following her as she grovelled and shrieked and pretended to tear her hair.

'Hey nonny nonny,' she wailed, and danced up and down blowing kisses at the air. 'There's rosemary, that's for remembrance! Hey nonny nonny! O, Fanfarone, thou art a villain, forsooth! It was a lover and his lass! There's a daisy for you. La, la, la!'

Jack was very impressed. It certainly looked like great acting.

Suddenly she sat down and began to pluck the petals out of an imaginary daisy.

'He loves me – he loves me not – he loves me – he loves me not – oh, daisy, daisy, give me your answer, do! Oh, that my heart would boil over and put out the fires of my grief! La, la, la, Fanfarone, thou art a pretty villain!'

Jack was watching the Scarecrow closely. He could see the poor booby getting more and more worried, and he whispered, 'Don't, master – it's not real – keep still!'

The Scarecrow was trying, that was clear. He only moved his head very slowly to follow what Queen Dido was doing, but he did move it, and already one or two people in the audience had noticed and were nudging their neighbours to point him out.

Queen Dido struggled to her feet, clutching her heart. Suddenly the Scarecrow noticed that she had a dagger in her hand. She had her back to him, and she couldn't see him leaning sideways to peer round at her, a look of alarm on his great knobbly face.

'Oh! Ah! Woe! The pangs of my sorrow tear at my soul like red-hot hooks! Ahhhhhhhh . . .'

She gave a long despairing cry, beginning as high as she could squeal and descending to the lowest note she could reach. She was famous for that cry. Critics had said that it plumbed the depths of mortal anguish, that it would melt a heart of stone, that no-one could hear it without feeling the tears gush from their eyes.

This time, though, she had the feeling that the audience wasn't quite with her. Some of them were laughing, even, and what made it worse was that when she spun round to see if it was the Scarecrow they were laughing at, he instantly remembered to act, and fell still, staring out as if he was nothing but a turnip on a stick.

Queen Dido gave him a look of furious suspicion, and resolved to try her famous cry again.

'*Waaahhh – aahhh – aaaahhhh . . .*' she wailed, wobbling and quavering all the way from a bat-like squeak down to a groan like a cow with a belly-ache.

And behind her the Scarecrow found himself moving in time with her, and imitating the way she wobbled her head and waved her arms and sank gradually downwards. He couldn't help it – he was deeply moved. Of course, the audience thought it was hilarious, and they roared, they slapped their thighs, they clapped and whistled and cheered.

Queen Dido was furious. And so was Signor Rigatelli. He suddenly appeared beside Jack and shoved two actors out on to the stage, saying, 'Get him off! Get him off!'

Unfortunately, the two actors were dressed as brigands, and sure enough the Scarecrow thought they were real.

'You villains!' he cried, and leaped forward with his wooden arms held out like fists. 'Your Majesty, get behind me! I'll defend you!'

And he bounced around the stage, aiming blows at the actors. Queen Dido, meanwhile, had stamped in rage and hurled her wig to the ground before storming offstage to shout at Rigatelli.

The audience was loving it.

'Go it, Scarecrow!' they shouted, and 'Whack 'em, Turnip! Look behind you! Up the Scarecrow!'

The two actors didn't know what to make of it, but they kept on chasing the Scarecrow and then having to run away when he fought back.

Suddenly the Scarecrow stopped, and pointed in horror at the blond wig on the boards in front of him.

'You cut her head off when I wasn't looking!' he cried. 'How dare you! Right, that does it. I'm really angry now!'

And waving his wooden arms like a windmill, he leaped at the two actors and belaboured them mercilessly. The audience went wild. But the actors were getting cross now, and they fought back, and then Rigatelli himself came bustling up to try and restore order.

Jack rushed onstage as well, to try and pull the Scarecrow away before he got hurt. Unfortunately one of the actors had got hold of the Scarecrow's left arm, and was tugging and tugging at it, while the Scarecrow was whacking him around the head; and when Jack seized the Scarecrow around the middle and tried to tug him backwards, his master's left arm came away entirely, and the actor holding it fell back suddenly into Rigatelli, knocking him back into the other actor, who grabbed at the scenery to save himself; but the combined weight of the three of them was too much for the blasted heath, and it all came down with a screech of wood and a tearing of canvas, and in a moment there was nothing to be seen but a heap of painted scenery heaving and cursing, with arms and legs waving and disappearing and emerging again.

'This way, master!' Jack said, hauling the Scarecrow off the stage. 'Let's run for it!'

'Never!' cried the Scarecrow. 'I shall never surrender!'

'It's not surrendering, master, it's beating a retreat,' said Jack, dragging him away.

Everyone in the market place had heard what was going on, and they'd left their stalls to go and laugh at the actors and the collapsing theatre. Among them was the bird-catcher. All his cages with their linnets and goldfinches were glittering in the sun, and the little birds were singing as loud as they could, and the Scarecrow couldn't resist.

'Birds,' he said very sternly, 'I accept that a state of war exists between your kingdom and me, but there is such a thing as justice. To see you imprisoned in this cruel way makes the blood rush to my turnip with indignation. I am going to set you free, and I charge you on your honour to go straight home and not eat any farmer's grain on the way.'

Jack didn't notice what his master was doing, because he'd spotted an old man sitting at a stall selling umbrellas. He was too rheumaticky to run over to the theatre with everybody else, and he was pleased to sell one of his umbrellas to Jack, who had found a gold coin in a corner of the brigands' bag.

Then someone shouted, 'Stop thief! Get away from my birds!'

Jack turned round to see the Scarecrow opening the last of the cages. A flock of little birds was wheeling around his head, chirping merrily, and he was waving his one arm, the one that pointed nowhere.

'Fly!' he shouted. 'Fly away!'

'Come on, master!' called Jack. 'They're all after us now!' And he dragged the

Scarecrow away, and the two of them fled as fast as they could. The cries of anger, the shouts of laughter, the full-throated singing of the liberated birds all gradually faded behind them.

When they reached the open country again, they stopped. Jack was out of breath. The Scarecrow was looking at himself, trying to work out what was wrong, and then he cried, 'Oh no! My other arm's gone! I'm falling to pieces!'

'Don't worry, master, I've thought of that. I bought you a new arm – look,' said Jack, and he slipped the umbrella up the Scarecrow's sleeve, handle first.

'Good gracious,' said the Scarecrow. 'I do believe – I think I – yes, yes, I can! Look at this! Just look at this, Jack!'

And he shook his new arm, and the umbrella opened. His great turnip-face, with its bright red mouth and black-rimmed eyes, was radiant.

'Aren't I clever!' he said, marvelling. 'Look at the ingenuity of it! It goes up – it comes down – it goes up – it comes down—'

'You can keep the sun off us, master,' said Jack. 'And the rain.'

The Scarecrow looked at him proudly. 'You'll go a long way, my boy!' he said. 'I was going to think of those things in a minute, but you beat me to it. And what a triumph we had on the stage! We saw everything they said on the poster.'

'We didn't have the Shipwreck, though, or the Eruption of Vesuvius.'

'Oh, we will, Jack,' said the Scarecrow confidently. 'I'm sure we will.'

Chapter Five

Scarecrow for Hire

When the lawyer reached the town next morning, he found it full of strange rumours. After interviewing Mr Rigatelli and the actress who played Queen Dido, who were both convinced that the Scarecrow was an automaton controlled by mesmeric waves as part of a plot organized by a rival theatre company, Mr Cercorelli found his way to the elderly umbrella salesman.

'Yes, I seen it all,' said the old man. 'It was a boy with a horan-gatang. I seen one of 'em before. They live in the trees in Borneo. Almost human they are, but you wouldn't mistake him close up. What d'you want him for? Has he escaped from a zoo?'

'Not exactly,' said Mr Cercorelli. 'Which way did they go?'

'That way,' said the old man, pointing. 'You'll recognize 'em easy enough. They bought one of my umbrellas.'

The Scarecrow and his servant walked a long way that day. They spent the night under a hedge by an olive grove, and the moment they woke up, Jack knew something was wrong.

He sat up and looked all around. The sun was shining, the air smelled of thyme and sage, there was the sound of little bells around the necks of a herd of goats browsing nearby; but something was missing.

'Master! Wake up! Our bag's been stolen!' Jack cried in despair, as soon as he realized what had happened. 'All the food's gone!'

The Scarecrow sat up at once, and opened his umbrella in alarm. Jack was lifting stones, peering under the hedge, running backwards and forwards to look up and down the road.

The Scarecrow peered into the ditch, frowning at

a lizard. It took no notice. Then he bent over and looked at something among the leaves.

'A clue!' he called, and Jack came running.

'What, master?'

'There,' said the Scarecrow, using his pointing hand to indicate something small and unpleasant at his feet.

'What is it?'

'An owl pellet. You can take it from me, this was left by the culprit. No doubt about it, the thief is an owl.'

'Oh,' said Jack, scratching his head.

'Or a jackdaw,' the Scarecrow went on. 'In fact, now I think of it, it must have been a jackdaw, and he left the owl pellet to throw us off the scent. Can you believe the villainy of these birds! They have no shame.'

'No,' said Jack. 'None at all. Anyway, we haven't got any money, and we haven't got any food. I don't know what we're going to do.'

'We shall have to work for our living, dear boy,' said the Scarecrow cheerfully. 'But we are full of enterprise and both in the pink of health. Ow! Ow! What are you doing?'

His last words were spoken to a goat, which had come up behind him and started to make a meal of his trousers.

The Scarecrow turned and clouted the goat with his road sign. But the goat objected to this, and butted him hard, knocking him over before Jack could catch him. The Scarecrow was astonished.

'How dare you! What a cowardly attack!' he said, struggling up.

The goat charged him again. This time the Scarecrow was prepared. He opened his umbrella suddenly, and the goat skidded to a halt and started to eat that instead.

'Oh, really,' said the Scarecrow, 'this is too much!'

And then a tug-of-war began, with the goat at one end and the Scarecrow at the other. The rest of the

goats came over to see what was happening, and one of them started nibbling at the Scarecrow's coat tails, another at his trousers, and a third began to browse on the straw coming out of his chest.

'Go on! Scram! Clear off!' Jack shouted, clapping his hands, and reluctantly the goats slouched away.

'You expect that sort of behaviour from people with feathers,' the Scarecrow said severely, 'not people with horns. I'm very disappointed.'

'They were taking a consuming interest in you, master,' said Jack.

'Well, you can't blame them for that,' said the Scarecrow, brushing his lapels and shaking out the remains of his coat. 'But I must say, Jack, they shouldn't be allowed out without a goatherd. We shan't let that happen in Spring Valley.'

'Spring Valley? Oh, I remember. How did you manage to get a big estate, all full of – what was it? – a farm and streams and wells and so on?'

'Well, it's a puzzle, Jack,' the Scarecrow admitted, as they set off along the road. 'I've always had an inner conviction that I was a man of property. A sort of gentleman farmer, you know.'

'And is that where we're going, Spring Valley?'

'In good time, Jack. We have to make our fortunes first.'

'Oh, I see. Well, look,' said Jack, pointing ahead of them, 'there's a farm, and a farmer. Let's go and ask him for a job. That'll be a start.'

The farmer was sitting disconsolately outside his house, sharpening a scythe.

'You want a job?' he said to Jack. 'You couldn't have come at a better . . . you know. The soldiers took all my, umm, away, and the birds are eating the, er, as fast as it comes up. You set up your, that, him, in the top field, and you can take the rattle and work in the orchard.'

'The thing is,' said Jack, 'he's getting a bit tattered. If you had a spare pair of trousers he'd look a lot more realistic.'

'There's a dirty old pair of, umm, you know, in the woodshed. Help yourself. There'll be a bite to, er, at sunset, and you can sleep in the barn.'

Soon afterwards, they were at work. The Scarecrow shooed away all the birds from the cornfield, and from time to time he opened and shut his umbrella, just to teach them a lesson. Jack roamed up and down the orchard, rattling hard whenever he saw a finch or a linnet.

It was hard work. The sun was hot and there were plenty of birds to scare. Jack found himself thinking about Spring Valley, and the Scarecrow's great estate. The poor noodle must have made it up and found himself believing it, Jack thought. He was good at that. It sounded like a nice place, though.

At sunset Jack stopped rattling, and went to call the Scarecrow in. His master was very impressed by the rattle.

'Formidable!' he said when Jack showed him how it worked. 'What a weapon! I don't suppose I could use it tomorrow?'

'Well, if you do, master, I won't have anything to scare the birds with. You're an expert, and you can do it just by looking at them, but I need all the help I can get. Now you go and sit down in the barn, and I'll fetch us some supper.'

The farmer's wife gave Jack a pot of stew and a big hunk of bread, and told him not to come in the kitchen with that monster of his. New-fangled bird-scarers were all very well, but this was a respectable farm, and she couldn't be doing with mechanical monsters in the house.

'Righto, missus,' said Jack. 'Any chance of a drink?'

'There's a bucket in the well,' she said, 'and a tin cup on a string next to it.'

'Thank you,' said Jack, and took his pot of stew to the barn, pausing for a good long swig of water on the way.

But before he went into the barn, he stopped outside, because he could hear voices.

'Oh, yes,' the Scarecrow was saying, 'we fought off a dozen brigands, my servant and I.'

'Brigands?' said someone else. It was a female voice, and it was full of admiration.

Jack walked in to find the Scarecrow sitting on a bale of straw, surrounded by a dozen rakes and hoes and broomsticks and spades and pitchforks. They were all leaning on the wall, listening respectfully.

At least, that's what it looked like until they realized Jack was there. Then they went back to looking like rakes and hoes and so on.

'Ah, Jack, my boy!' said the Scarecrow.

'The farmer's wife gave me a bowl of stew for us,' said Jack doubtfully, looking around.

'You have most of it,' said the Scarecrow. 'I don't eat a great deal. A small piece of bread will be quite sufficient.'

So Jack sat down and tucked into the stew, which was full of peppers and onions and bits of gristly sausage.

'I thought I heard voices, master,' he said with his mouth full.

'And so you did. I was just telling these ladies and gentlemen about our adventures.'

Jack looked around at the rakes and hoes and brooms. None of them moved or said a word.

'Ah,' said Jack. 'Right.'

'As I was saying,' the Scarecrow went on, 'the brigands were a fearsome crew. Armed to the teeth, every single one. They trapped us in their cave and—'

'I thought you said it was a ruined castle,' said a rake.

'That's right, a ruined castle,' said the Scarecrow cheerfully.

Jack's hair was standing on end. It certainly seemed as if one of the rakes had spoken, but it was getting dark, and he was very tired. He rubbed his eyes, and felt them closing as fast as he could rub them open again.

'Well, which?' demanded the rake.

'Castle. Next to a cave. My servant and I went in to investigate, and the next thing we knew, in came two dozen brigands. Or three dozen, probably. I hid in the corner, and Jack told them a story to send them to sleep, and then I loomed up like an apparition – like this—'

The Scarecrow raised his arms and made a hideous face. Some of the smaller brooms flinched away, and a little fork squeaked in terror.

'And the brigands turned tail and fled,' the Scarecrow went on. 'I've thought about it since, and I've worked out the reason why. I think they were birds, and they were only disguised as brigands. Big birds,' he explained. 'Sort of ostrich-sized. Very dangerous,' he added.

'You must be very brave,' said a broom shyly.

'Oh, I don't know,' said the Scarecrow. 'One gets used to danger in this line of work. But soon after that, I entered a new profession. I went on the stage!'

Jack was lying down now. The last thing he noticed before he fell asleep was the Scarecrow beginning to act out the role he had taken in the play; only it seemed a much more important role than Jack remembered, and when it got to the point where Queen Dido fell in love with the Scarecrow and made him Prime Minister, Jack realized he'd been asleep for some time.

He woke up to find the sun in his eyes and the Scarecrow shaking him.

'Jack! Wake up! Time for work! The birds have been up for some time. But Jack – I need to have a word with you. In private.'

Jack rubbed his eyes and looked around.

'We *are* in private,' he said.

'No! I mean *more* private,' the Scarecrow said, in an urgent whisper. 'Away from – you know . . .'

He gestured over his shoulder and nodded backwards in a meaningful way.

'Ah, I see,' said Jack, who had no idea what he was talking about. 'Just give me a moment, and I'll meet you out by the well, master.'

The Scarecrow nodded and strode out of the barn. Jack scratched his head. The rakes and hoes and brooms were perfectly still and silent.

'Must have been dreaming,' Jack said to himself, and got up.

The farmer's wife gave him some bread and jam for breakfast, and Jack took it out to the well, where the Scarecrow was waiting impatiently.

'What is it, master?' he said.

'I've decided to get married,' the Scarecrow told him. 'As a matter of fact I've fallen in love. Oh, Jack, she's so beautiful! And such a delicate nature! You'd never believe it, but I feel almost clumsy beside her. Her grace! Her charm! Oh, my heart is lost, I love her, I worship the ground she brushes!'

'Brushes?' said Jack, his mouth full.

'She's a broom,' the Scarecrow explained. 'You

must have noticed her. The very pretty one! The lovely one! Oh, I adore her!'

'Have you told her?'

'Ah. That's what I was going to tell you. I haven't got the nerve, Jack. My courage fails me. As soon as I look at her I feel like a – like a – like an onion.'

'An onion?'

'Yes, just like an onion. But I can't think of a thing to say. So *you'll* have to tell her.'

Jack scratched his head.

'Well,' he said, 'I'm not as eloquent as you are, master. I'd probably get it all wrong. I'm sure she'd rather hear it from you.'

'Well, of course she would,' agreed the Scarecrow. 'Anyone would. But I'm struck dumb when I see her, so it'll have to be you.'

'I don't understand why you feel like an onion,' Jack said.

'No, neither do I. I had no idea that love would have that effect. Have you ever been in love, Jack?'

'I don't think so. If I fell in love, I'd probably feel like a turnip. Listen, I tell you what, master—'

'I know! You could pretend to be a bird, and attack her, and I could pretend to come and fight you off. I bet she'd be impressed by that.'

'I'm not a good actor like you, master. She'd probably guess I wasn't a real bird. Listen, let's go and do some work, and you can think about her all day long, out in the cornfield. We'll talk about it later, before we come in.'

'Yes! That's a good idea,' said the Scarecrow, and marched off proudly to start the day's work.

Chapter Six

A Serenade

Jack worked hard all morning. At midday the farmer came into the orchard to see how he was getting on, and looked around approvingly.

'That other fellow,' he said, 'your mate . . .'

'My master,' said Jack.

'As you like. Him. He's a good worker, and no mistake. But . . . well . . . you know.'

'Oh, he's good at scarecrowing,' said Jack.

'No doubt about it. But – umm – he's a bit, er, well, isn't he?'

'Only if you don't know him.'

'Oh, is that right? Then he's . . . mmm . . . is he?'

'He's a deep character,' said Jack, rattling at a blackbird.

'Ah,' said the farmer. 'Thing is, he looks almost –

71

well, if I didn't know better, I'd even say . . . you know.'

'That's part of his cleverness. See, when he's working, he never . . . kind of thing.'

'No,' said the farmer. 'Wouldn't do to . . . umm.'

'I mean, there'd be no end of a – you know.'

'Too true. You're right there. All the same, eh? I mean . . .'

'Yes,' agreed Jack. 'No. It'd be terrible if . . . er.'

'A word to the wise, eh?' said the farmer, and winked and tapped the side of his nose. Jack did the same, in case it was the private signal of a secret society. The farmer nodded and went away.

Well, it's a good thing he didn't go and say all that to the master, Jack thought. The poor booby wouldn't have understood a word.

He rattled away busily all afternoon, and as the sun was setting he went to call the Scarecrow from the top field.

'Jack,' said the Scarecrow, 'I've been thinking about her all day long, just as you suggested, and I've come to the conclusion that if she won't marry me, I'll have to do something desperate.'

'Oh dear,' said Jack. 'What would that be, master?'

'I'm saving that till tomorrow to think about.'

'Good idea. I wonder what's for supper?'

The farmer's wife gave them another bowl of stew, and she gave the Scarecrow a long hard suspicious look, too, which he didn't see, because he was gazing at the barn with a dopey expression on his turnip.

'Thank you, missus,' Jack said.

'You mind you keep him locked up at night,' said the farmer's wife. 'I don't like the look of him. If I find any hens missing . . .'

Jack and his master sat down beside the well, and once again the Scarecrow let Jack have all the stew, and only nibbled at a piece of bread.

'You ought to eat something, master,' said Jack. 'I bet she'd like you just as much if you had a full belly. You'd feel better, anyway.'

'No, I've got no appetite, Jack. I'm wasting away with love.'

'If you're sure, then,' said Jack, finishing off the stew.

'I know!' said the Scarecrow, sitting up suddenly and opening his umbrella with excitement. 'I could serenade her!'

'Well—' said Jack, but the Scarecrow was too excited to listen.

'Yes! That's it! Here's the plan. Wait till dark, and then pick her up and pretend to sweep the floor. And sweep her outside, and then sort of casually lean her against the wall, and then I'll sing to her.'

'Well—' Jack began again.

'Oh, yes. When she hears me sing, her heart will be mine!'

'You better not sing too loud. I don't think the farmer'd like it. I'm sure his old lady wouldn't.'

'Oh, I shall be very discreet,' said the Scarecrow. 'Tender, but ardent, is the note to strike.'

'That sounds about right,' said Jack.

'Start sweeping as soon as the moon shines into the farmyard. I think moonlight would show me to advantage, don't you?'

'Maybe you better let me tidy you up,' said Jack, and he dusted the Scarecrow's shoulders, and put some fresh straw in his chest, and washed his turnip. 'There – you look a treat. Remember – not too loud, now.'

The Scarecrow sat down outside the barn, and Jack went inside to lie down. Before he did, though, he found the broom and put her beside the door, so that he'd be able to find her in the dark.

'Excuse me,' he found himself saying, 'but I hope

you don't mind if I put you over here. You'll find out why when the moon comes up.'

She didn't reply, but she leaned against the wall very gracefully. Jack thought she must be shy, until he caught himself and shook his head.

He's got me believing she's alive, he thought. I better be careful, in case I go as mad as he is.

He lay down on the straw and closed his eyes. The old donkey and the cow were asleep on their feet, just breathing quietly and chewing a bit from time to time, and it was all very quiet and peaceful.

Jack woke up when the moonlight touched his eyes. He yawned and stretched and sat up.

'Well,' he said to himself, 'time to start brushing the floor. This is a daft idea. Still, he's a marvel, the master, no doubt about it.'

He took the broom and swept the floor, brushing all the straw and dust casually towards the door where the moonlight was shining through. Once he was outside, he leaned the broom against the wall and yawned again before going back to lie down.

And almost at once he went back to sleep. He must have started dreaming straight away, because it seemed as if he were watching the Scarecrow sweeping the ground outside, singing to the broom as he did so:

'Your handle so slender,
Your bristles so tender,
I have to surrender
    My heart to your charms;
Retreating, advancing,
And secretly glancing,
Oh, never stop dancing
    All night in my arms!'

Jack blinked and rubbed his eyes, but it made no difference. The Scarecrow and the broom were waltzing around the barnyard like the most graceful dancers at a ball.

'Your gentle demeanour
Sweeps everything cleaner!
I never have seen a
    More elegant Miss;
So gracious, so charming,
Completely disarming,
Oh where is the harm in
    A maidenly kiss?'

Jack thought, He's going to marry her, and then he won't want a servant any more. Mind you, he does look happy. But I don't know if I'll ever find a master I'd rather serve . . .

And while he was lying there puzzled by all those thoughts, he was woken up all of a sudden by a horrible raucous yell.

'*Hee-haw! Hee-haw!*'

He sat up, and realized first that it *had* been a dream; and second, that the old donkey in the barn was braying and stamping and creating no end of a fuss; and third, that outside in the barnyard the Scarecrow was roaring and howling and bellowing with anger, or distress, or misery.

Jack scrambled to the door of the barn to see the farmer's wife, in a long nightdress, running out of the kitchen door with a frying pan held high above her head. Behind her, the farmer, in a long nightshirt, was fumbling with a blunderbuss. The Scarecrow was clutching the broom to his heart, and real tears were streaming down his turnip.

'No, missus! No! Don't!' Jack shouted, and ran out to try and hold off the farmer's wife, who was about to wallop the Scarecrow with the frying pan. There was no danger from the farmer; as soon as he tried to aim the blunderbuss, all the lead shot fell out of the end of the barrel, and bounced on the flagstones like hail.

Jack reached the Scarecrow just as the farmer's wife did, and stood between them with his arms held wide.

'No, missus! Stop! Let me explain!' he said.

'I'll brain him!' she cried. 'I'll teach him to go caterwauling in the middle of the night and terrifying honest folk out of their beds!'

'No, don't, missus, he's a poor zany, he doesn't mean any harm – you leave him to me—'

'I told you!' said the farmer, staying safely behind his wife. 'Didn't I? Eh?'

'Yes, you did,' Jack agreed. 'You told me something, anyway.'

'None of this . . . you know,' the farmer added.

'You take that horrible thing away,' said the farmer's wife, 'and you get out of here right now, and don't you come back!'

'Certainly, missus,' said Jack, 'and what about our wages?'

'Wages?' she said. 'You're not getting any wages. Clear off, you and your monster both!'

Jack turned to the Scarecrow, who hadn't heard any of what the farmer's wife had said. In fact, he was still sobbing in despair.

'Now then, master, what's the trouble?' he said.

'She's already engaged!' the Scarecrow howled. 'She's going to marry a rake!'

'Oh, that's bad luck,' said Jack. 'Still, look on the bright side—'

'I shall do the decent thing, of course,' the

Scarecrow went on, struggling to control his emotions. 'My dear young lady,' he said to the broom, 'nothing would make me stand between you and your happiness, if your heart is already given to the gentleman in the barn. But I warn him,' he said, raising his voice and looking in at all the tools leaning on the wall, 'he had better treat this broom like the precious creature she is, and make her happiness the centre of his life, or he will face my wrath!'

With a last choking sob, he handed the broom gently to Jack. Jack took her into the barn and stood her next to the rake.

When he got back outside, the Scarecrow was speaking to the farmer and his wife.

'I am sorry for waking you up,' he said, 'but I make no excuses for the passionate expression of my feelings. After all, that is the one thing that distinguishes us from the animals.'

'Mad,' said the farmer's wife. 'Barmy. Go on, get out, clear off down the road and don't come back.'

The Scarecrow bowed as gracefully as he could.

'Well, dear,' the farmer said, 'mustn't . . . you know. Not so many, umm, about these days, eh? Sort of thing . . .'

'He's raving mad, and I want him gone!' she said. 'Also he's a horrible-looking monster, and he's

frightened the
donkey. Scram!'
she said again,
raising the frying
pan.

'Come on, master,'
said Jack. 'We'll seek
our fortune somewhere
else. We've slept under
hedges before, and it's a
nice warm night.'

So side by side the Scarecrow and his servant set
off down the moonlit road. From time to time the
Scarecrow would sigh heavily and turn to look back
with such a look of anguish on his turnip that Jack
felt sure the broom would leave her rake and fall in
love with him, if she could; but it was too late.

'Oh, yes,' said the farmer, 'he was definitely . . . you
know.'

'Mad as a hatter!' said his wife. 'A dangerous
lunatic. Foreign, too. Shouldn't have been let out.'

'I see,' said Mr Cercorelli. 'And when did he
leave?'

'When was it now?' said the farmer. 'About . . .
er . . .'

'Middle of the night,' snapped his wife. 'What

d'you want to know for, anyway? You his keeper?'

'In a manner of speaking, that is so. I am charged by my employer to bring this scarecrow back where he belongs.'

'Ah,' said the farmer. 'So it's a case of, umm, is it?'

'I beg your pardon?'

'You know, touch of the old, er, as it were. Eh?'

Mr Cercorelli gathered his papers and stood up.

'You put it very accurately, sir,' he said. 'Thank you for your help.'

'You going to lock him up when you catch him?' demanded the farmer's wife.

'Oh, I can assure you,' said Mr Cercorelli, 'that is the least of it.'

CHAPTER SEVEN

THE MISTY CART

'Jack,' said the Scarecrow next morning, 'now that my heart is broken, I think we should set out on the open road and seek our fortune.'

'What about your estate in Spring Valley, master?'

'Ah, yes, indeed. We must earn enough money to set the place in order. Then we shall go back and look after it.'

I hope there's plenty of food there, Jack thought.

The Scarecrow strode out briskly, and Jack trotted along beside him. There were plenty of things to look at, and although the Scarecrow's heart was broken, his curiosity about the world was undimmed.

'Why has that building burned down?' he'd say, or 'I wonder why that old lady is climbing a ladder,' or 'D'you know, Jack, it's an extraordinary thing, but we haven't heard a bird for hours. Why would that be, do you think?'

'I think the soldiers have been here,' Jack told him. 'They probably burned the house down, and took all the farm workers away so the old lady's got to mend the roof herself. As for the birds – why, the soldiers must have eaten up all the food and left none for the birds, not even a grain of wheat.'

'Hmm,' said the Scarecrow. 'Soldiers, eh? Do they do that sort of thing?'

'They're the worst people in the world, soldiers,' said Jack.

'Worse than birds?'

'Much worse. The only thing to do when the soldiers come is hide, and keep very very quiet.'

'What do they look like?'

'Well—'

But before Jack could answer, the Scarecrow's attention was caught by something else.

'Look!' he cried, pointing in excitement. 'What's that?'

There was a caravan coming towards them, pulled by an ancient horse that was so skinny you could count all its ribs. The caravan was covered in painted stars and moons and mystic symbols, and sitting on the box holding the reins was a man almost as skinny as the horse, wearing a long pointed hat and a robe covered in more stars and moons.

The Scarecrow gazed at it all with great admiration.

As soon as he saw them, the man waved and shook the reins to make the horse stand still. The poor old beast was only too glad to have a rest. The man jumped off the box and scampered over to the Scarecrow.

'Good day to you, sir! Good day, my lord!' he said, bowing low and plucking at the Scarecrow's sleeve.

'Good day to *you*, sir,' the Scarecrow said.

'Master,' said Jack, 'I don't think—'

But the stranger with the mystic robes had seized the Scarecrow's road-sign hand, and was scrutinizing it closely.

'Ah!' he said. 'Aha! Ha! I see great fortune in this hand!'

'Really?' said the Scarecrow, impressed. 'How do you do that?'

'By means of the mystic arts!'

'Oh!' said the Scarecrow. 'Jack, we must get a misty cart! Just like this gentleman's one. Then *we'd* know things too. We could make our fortune and find our way to Spring Valley and take it—'

'Spring Valley, did you say, sir?' said the stranger. 'Would you be a member of the celebrated Buffaloni family, my lord?'

'I don't think so,' said the Scarecrow.

'Ah! I understand! They've called you in as a consultant, to take it in hand. I hear that the Buffalonis are doing splendid things in the field of industry. Draining all those springs and wells and putting up wonderful factories! Yes? No?'

Seeing that the Scarecrow was baffled, the astrologer smoothly went on:

'But let me read your horoscope and look deep into the crystal ball. Before the power of my gaze, the veil of time is drawn aside and the mysteries of the future are revealed. Come into my caravan for a consultation!'

'Master,' Jack whispered, 'this'll cost us money, and we haven't got any. Besides, he's an old fraud—'

'Oh, no, my boy, you've got it wrong,' said the Scarecrow. 'I'm a pretty good judge, and this gentleman's mind is on higher things than fraud. His thoughts dwell in the realm of the sublime, Jack!'

'Quite right, sir! You are a profound and perceptive thinker!' said the mystic, beckoning them into the caravan, and uncovering a crystal ball on a little table.

They all sat down. Waving his fingers in a
mystical way, the astrologer peered deeply into the
crystal.

'Ah!' he said. 'As I suspected. The planetary
fluminations are dark and obscure. The only way of
disclarifying the astroplasm is to cast your
horoscope, my dear sir, which I can do for a very
modest fee.'

'Well, that's that then,' said Jack, standing up,
'because we haven't got a penny between us. Good
day—'

'No, Jack, wait!' said the Scarecrow, banging his
head.

'What are you doing, master?' said Jack. 'Stop it – you'll hurt yourself!'

'Ah – there it is!' cried the Scarecrow, and out of a crack in his turnip there fell a little gold coin.

Jack and the mystic pounced at once, but the mystic got there first.

'Excellent!' he said, nipping the coin between his long horse-like teeth. 'By a remarkable coincidence, this is exactly the right fee. I shall consult the stars at once.'

'Where did that gold coin come from, master?' said Jack, amazed.

'Oh, it's been in there for a while,' the Scarecrow told him.

'But – but – if – if –' Jack said, tearing his hair.

The Scarecrow took no notice. He was watching the astrologer, who took a dusty book from a shelf and opened it to show charts and columns of numbers, and ran a finger swiftly down them, muttering learnedly.

'You see what he's doing?' whispered the Scarecrow. 'This is clever, Jack, this is very deep.'

'Ahhhhh!' said the astrologer, in a long quavering wail. 'I see great fortune in the stars!'

'Go on, go on!' said the Scarecrow.

'Oh, yes,' said the mystic, licking a dirty finger and turning over several pages. 'And there is more!'

'You see, Jack? What a good thing we met this gentleman!' said the Scarecrow.

The astrologer suddenly drew in his breath, peering at the symbols in his book. So did the Scarecrow. They both held it for a long time, until the astrologer let it out in a long whistle. So did the Scarecrow.

Then, as if it was too heavy a burden to bear, the astrologer slowly lifted his head.

The Scarecrow's little muddy eyes were as wide as they could get – his straw was standing on end – his great gaping mouth hung open.

'I have never seen a destiny as strange and profound as this,' said the astrologer in a low, quavery voice. 'The paranomical ecliptic of the clavicle of Solomon, multiplied by the solar influence in the trine of the zaphoristical catanastomoid, divided by the meridian of the vernal azimuth and composticated by the diaphragm of Ezekiel, reveals . . .'

'Yes?'

'Means . . .'

'Yes? Yes?'

'Foretells . . .'

'Yes? Yes? Yes?'

The mystic paused for a moment, and his eyes swivelled to look at Jack, and then swivelled back to the Scarecrow.

'Danger,' he said solemnly.

'Oh no!' said the Scarecrow.

'Followed by joy –'

'Yes!'

'And then trouble –'

'No!'

'Leading to glory –'

'Yes!'

'Turning to sorrow –'

'No, no, no!'

The Scarecrow was in mortal fear.

The astrologer slowly closed the book and moved it out of Jack's reach. Then his upper lip drew back so suddenly that it made Jack jump. Beaming like a crocodile in Holy Orders, the old man said:

'But the suffering will be crowned with success –'

'Hoorah!' cried the Scarecrow.

'And the tears will end in triumph –'

'Thank goodness for that!'

'And health, wealth and happiness will be yours for as long as you live!'

'Oh, I'm so glad! Oh, what a relief!' said the

Scarecrow. 'There you are, Jack, you see, this gentleman knows what he's talking about, all right. Oh, I was worried there! But it all came right in the end. Thank you, sir! A thousand thanks! We can go on our way with confidence and fortitude. My goodness, what an experience.'

'My pleasure,' said the mystic, bowing low. 'Take care as you leave. The steps are rickety. Good day!'

He gave Jack a suspicious look, and Jack gave him one in return.

'Just think of that, Jack,' said the Scarecrow in an awed and humble voice as the caravan slowly drew away. 'We have been inside a misty cart, and we have heard the secrets of the future!'

'Never mind that, master,' said Jack. 'Have you got any more money in your head?'

'Let me see,' said the Scarecrow, and he banged his turnip vigorously. Then he shook it hard. 'Hmm,' he said, 'something's rattling. Let me see . . .'

He turned his head sideways and shook it. Something fell out and bounced on the road.

The two of them bent over to look at it.

'It's a pea,' said Jack.

'Ah, yes,' said the Scarecrow modestly. 'That's my brain, you know.'

But before either of them could pick it up and put it back, a blackbird flew down, seized the pea in his

beak, and flew up and perched on a branch.

The Scarecrow was outraged. He waved his road sign, he opened and shut his umbrella, and he stamped with fury.

'You scoundrel! You thief!' he roared. 'Give me my brain back!'

The blackbird swallowed the pea, and then, to Jack's astonishment, said, 'Get lost. I saw it first.'

'How dare you!' the Scarecrow shouted in reply. 'I've never known such unprincipled behaviour!'

'Don't shout at me,' whined the blackbird. 'You're cruel, you are. You got a horrible cruel face. I'll have the law on you if you shout at me. It's not fair.'

In fury, the Scarecrow opened and shut his umbrella several times, but in his rage he couldn't find any words, so the things he said sounded like this:

'Rrrowl – nnhnrrr – eeee – mnmnm – ngnnmmg- grrnnnggg – bbrrr – ffff – ssss – gggrrrssschhttt!'

The blackbird cringed, and uttering a feeble squeak, he flew away.

Jack scratched his head.

'I knew parrots could talk, master, but not black-birds,' he said.

'Oh, they all can, Jack. You should hear the insolent way they speak to me when they think nobody else can hear. I expect that young scoundrel thought you were a scarecrow too, and he could get away with it.'

'Well, I'm learning new things all the time,' said Jack. 'Anyway, it seems to me, master, that until we find you a new brain, you'll have to try and get on without one. We managed to find you some new arms all right, remember.'

The Scarecrow had been stamping up and down, still furious, but he stopped and looked at Jack when he heard that, and calmed down at once.

'Do you think we could find another one?' he said.

'Can't be too hard,' said Jack. 'See how you get on without it at first. You might not need one at all. Like an appendix.'

'It's very personal, though,' said the Scarecrow doubtfully.

'We'll find something, don't worry.'

'Ah, Jack, my boy, employing you was the best decision I ever made! I can do without a brain, but I don't think I could do without my servant.'

'Well, thank you, master. But I don't think I can do without food. I hope we find something to eat soon.'

Since there was nothing to eat there, they set off along the road again. But it was a bleak and deserted sort of district; the only farms they passed were burned down, and there wasn't a single person in sight.

'No birds,' said the Scarecrow, looking around. 'It's a curious thing, Jack, but I don't like it when there aren't any birds.'

'I don't like it when there isn't any food,' said Jack.

'Look!' said the Scarecrow, pointing back along the road. 'What's that?'

All they could see was a cloud of dust. But there was a sound as well, and Jack recognized it at once: a regular tramp-tramp-tramp and the beats of a snare drum accompanying it. It was a regiment of soldiers.

CHAPTER EIGHT

THE PRIDE OF THE REGIMENT

Jack tugged at the Scarecrow's sleeve.

'Come on, master!' he said urgently. 'We'll hide till they've gone past!'

The Scarecrow followed Jack into a clump of bushes.

'Are we allowed to look at them?' he said.

'Yes, but don't let them see us, master, whatever you do!' Jack begged.

The beating of the drums and the thudding of the feet came closer and closer. The Scarecrow, excited, peered out through the leaves.

'Jack! Look!' he whispered. 'It's astonishing! They're all the same!'

The soldiers, with their bright red coats and white trousers, their black boots and bearskin caps, their muskets all held at the same angle and their brass buckles gleaming, *did* all look the same. There were hundreds of them marching in step, all big and strong and well-fed.

'Magnificent!' exclaimed the Scarecrow.

'Hush!' said Jack desperately.

Ahead of the column of soldiers rode several officers on grey horses, prancing and trotting and curvetting; and behind came a dozen wagons drawn by fine black horses, all gleaming and beautifully groomed.

'What style! What panache! What vigour!' said the Scarecrow.

Jack put his hands over his ears, but the thudding of the soldiers' boots made the very earth shake. Tramp! Tramp! Tramp! Like a great mechanical monster with hundreds of legs, the regiment moved past.

When Jack dared to look, the Scarecrow was standing in the middle of the road, gazing after them with wonder and admiration.

'Jack!' he called. 'Have you ever seen anything so splendid? Tramp, tramp, tramp! And their red coats – and their shiny belts – and their helmets! Oh, that's the life for me, Jack. I'm going to be a soldier!'

'But, master—'

'Off we go! Tramp tramp tramp!'

Swinging his arms briskly, the Scarecrow set off on his wooden legs at such a pace that Jack had to run to keep up.

'Master, please listen to me! Don't be a soldier, I beg you!'

'Remember what the man in the misty cart said, Jack – great fortune! Fame, and glory!'

'Yes, and trouble and danger too – don't forget those!'

'And I'll tell you something else,' added the Scarecrow. 'The regiment is bound to have lots of food. They're such a fine-looking band of men, I'll bet they eat three times a day. If not four.'

That did it for Jack. At the thought of food, he set off after the regiment as fast as his master, soldiers or no soldiers.

It didn't take them long to catch up, because the soldiers had stopped for their midday meal, and the rich smell of beef stew made poor Jack's mouth water from several hundred yards away.

The Scarecrow strode into the camp and marched up to the cook, who was dishing out stew and potatoes to the soldiers as they stood in a smart line holding out their plates.

'I want to be a soldier,' the Scarecrow announced.

'Get away with you, turnip face!'

'I've got all the qualifications—'

'Go on, scram!'

The Scarecrow was about to lose his temper, so Jack said:

'Excuse me, sir, but who's the officer in charge?'

'Colonel Bombardo, over there,' said the cook, pointing with his ladle. 'At least, he's the commanding officer. It's the sergeant who's in charge.'

'Oh, right,' said Jack. 'I don't suppose I could have a potato?'

'Clear off! Get out of it!'

Nearly howling with hunger, Jack tugged at the Scarecrow's sleeve.

'We have to speak to the officer,' he explained. 'This way, master.'

The colonel was sitting on a canvas chair, trying to read a map upside down.

'Colonel Bombardo, sir,' said Jack, 'my master Lord Scarecrow wants to join your army. He's a good fighter, and—'

'Lord Scarecrow?' barked the colonel. 'Knew your mother. Damn fine woman. Welcome, Scarecrow. Go and speak to the sergeant over there. He'll sort you out.'

'He knew my mother!' whispered the Scarecrow, awestruck. 'Even *I* didn't know my mother. How clever he is! What a hero!'

The sergeant was a thin little man with a wrinkled face that looked as if it had seen everything there was to see, twice.

'Sergeant,' said Jack, 'this is Lord Scarecrow. Colonel Bombardo sent us over to join the regiment.'

'Lord Scarecrow, eh,' said the sergeant. 'Right, your lordship, before you join the regiment you'll have to pass an examination.'

Jack thought: Thank goodness for that! As soon as they find out what a ninny he is, they'll send us packing. But I'd love some of that stew . . .

The Scarecrow was sitting down already, with a big bass drum in front of him to write on. He looked at the exam paper, took up the pencil at once, and began to cover the page with an energetic scribble.

'What sort of questions are they?' Jack asked.

'Ballistics, navigation, fortification, tactics and strategy,' said the sergeant.

'Oh, good. I don't suppose I could have anything to eat?'

'What d'you think this is? A soup kitchen? This is an army on the march, this is. Who are you, anyway?'

'I'm Lord Scarecrow's personal servant.'

'Servant? That's a good'un. Soldiers don't have servants.'

'Colonel Bombardo's got a servant,' said Jack, looking enviously at the colonel, who was sitting with several other officers at a table outside his tent, tucking in to stew and dumplings, while a servant poured wine.

'Well, he's an officer,' said the sergeant. 'If they didn't have servants, they wouldn't be able to put their trousers on, some of 'em.'

'They get a lot to eat,' Jack said.

'Oh, for crying out loud,' said the sergeant, scribbling on a piece of paper. 'Take this chitty to the cook, go on.'

'Thank you! Thank you!' said Jack, and ran back to the cook, just in time to see the last soldier in the queue walking away with a full plate.

The cook inspected the chitty.

'Bad luck,' he said. 'There's none left.'

He showed Jack the empty stewpot. Jack felt tears springing to his eyes, but the cook winked and said:

'None of *that* rubbish, anyway. You duck under here, and I'll give you some proper Catering Corps tucker.'

Jack darted into the wagon in a moment, and was soon sitting down with the cook and his two assistants, eating braised beef *à la bourguignonne*, which was rich and hot and peppery and had little oniony things and big pools of gravy and delicate new potatoes and parsley and mint. Jack felt as if he was in heaven.

He didn't say a word till he'd finished three whole platefuls.

'Thank you!' he said finally. 'Can I take some to my master?'

'He's lunching with the colonel,' said the cook. 'While you was gobbling that up, we had a message to send over another officer's meal. So you're joining the regiment, then?'

'Well, Lord Scarecrow was taking the exam,' said Jack, 'but I don't think he can have passed it. I better go and see.'

'No hurry,' said the cook. 'They'll be there for a while yet, with their brandy and cigars.'

'Cigars?' said Jack in alarm, thinking of the Scarecrow's straw.

'Don't worry. There's a bucket-wallah to put 'em out if they catch fire to theirselves.'

'The regiment thinks of everything,' Jack said.

'Oh, it's a grand life, being a soldier.'

Jack began to think that maybe it was, after all. He thanked the cooks again, and strolled over to the sergeant, who was trimming his nails with a bayonet.

'How did Lord Scarecrow get on in the exam?' he said.

'He answered all the wrong questions. He doesn't know anything at all.'

'So he won't be able to be a soldier, then?' said Jack, relieved.

'Not a private, no, nor a sergeant, not in a hundred years. He's nowhere near clever enough. He's going to be an officer.'

'*What?*'

'Captain Scarecrow is taking his lunch with his fellow officers. You'll need to find him a horse and polish his boots and wash his uniform and keep him smart, and by the look of him you'll have your work cut out.'

'But he doesn't know how to command soldiers!'

'None of 'em do. That's why they invented sergeants. You better go and get him a uniform. The quartermaster's in that wagon over there.'

Jack explained to the quartermaster that the Scarecrow needed a captain's uniform. The quartermaster laid a set of clothes and boots on the counter.

Jack gathered them up, but the quartermaster said, 'Hold on. He'll need a sword as well if he's an officer. And a proper shako. And a pistol.'

The shako was the tall cap that the officers wore. It had a white plume in it, and a shiny black peak.

Jack's heart sank as he staggered over to the officers' table. Once he gets all this on, he'll want to be a soldier for ever, he thought.

'Ah, Jack, my boy!' said the Scarecrow happily as the officers left their table. 'Did you hear the wonderful news? I'm a captain, no less! I did so well in the examination that they made me an officer at once.'

Then he saw what Jack was carrying, and his turnip beamed with an expression of utter delight.

'Is that for me? Is that my uniform? This is the happiest day of my life! I can hardly believe it!'

Jack helped the Scarecrow put on the red coat and the white trousers, and the shiny black boots, and two white belts that went over his shoulders and crossed on his chest, and another belt to hold his trousers up just in case. The poor Scarecrow was transfigured with joy.

'Just let the birds try their tricks now!' he said,

waving his sword around. 'I bet no blackbird would dare to eat my brain if he saw me like this!'

'Mind what you're doing with the sword, master,' said Jack. 'It's just for decoration, really. Now you stay here and I'll go and find a horse for you.'

'A *horse?*' said the Scarecrow. He stopped looking joyful and looked nervous instead.

'I'll get you a slow old one,' said Jack.

'He won't want to eat me, will he? I mean, you know . . .' said the Scarecrow, delicately twiddling at the straw poking out of his collar.

'I don't think there's any hay in you, master,' said Jack, 'only straw. You'll just have to show him who's boss. Or her.'

The farrier, who was in charge of the horses, was busy putting some horseshoes on a docile old grey mare called Betsy. He said she'd be just the job for an inexperienced rider.

'Captain Scarecrow's a good fighter,' said Jack. 'He's fought brigands and actors and all sorts. But he hasn't done much riding.'

'Nothing to it. Shake the reins to make her go, pull 'em back to make her stop.'

'What about turning left and right?'

'Leave that to her. *Actors*, did you say?' said the farrier.

'Yes, he fought three of them at once. On a stage.'

'Stone the crows.'

'Yes, he can do that too,' said Jack, leading Betsy over to Captain Scarecrow.

'He's very big,' said the Scarecrow doubtfully, when he saw her.

'He's a she. She's called Betsy. She's all ready to ride. Put your foot in the stirrup – there it is – and I'll lift you up.'

They tried it three times. The first time the Scarecrow went straight over the top and down the other side, landing on his turnip and denting his shako. The second time he managed to stay there, but he was facing the wrong way round. The third time he managed to stay in the saddle, facing the right way, but he'd lost his shako and dropped his sword, and his umbrella had come open in alarm.

'Stay there, master, and I'll pick up the bits and pieces,' said Jack.

He gathered up the sword and the shako, and soon he had the Scarecrow looking very proud and martial. Around them the regiment was striking camp ready to move on, and presently the drums began to beat and the sergeant gave the order to march.

Old Betsy pricked up her ears and began to amble forward.

'Help!' cried the Scarecrow, swaying wildly.

'Look, master,' said Jack, 'I mean Captain, sir, I'm holding the bridle. She won't go any faster while I'm here.'

So they moved along behind the column of marching soldiers and the wagons and the horses, old Betsy keeping up a steady walk and the Scarecrow hanging on to the saddle with both hands.

Presently he said:

'By the way, where are we going, Jack?'

'Dunno, master. I mean Captain, sir.'

'We're off to fight the Duke of Brunswick!' said another officer, a major, riding up alongside.

'Really?' said the Scarecrow. 'And what sort of bird is he? A great big one, I expect?'

'I expect so, yes,' said the major.

'Has he got a regiment too?' said Jack.

'Oh, dozens.'

'But we're just one!'

'Ah, the King of Sardinia's army is coming to join us.'

'So there's going to be a great big battle?'

'Bound to be.'

'And when are we going to fight them?' said the Scarecrow.

'Don't know. They could attack at any moment. Ambush, you know.'

The major galloped away.

'Jack,' said the Scarecrow. 'This battle . . .'

'Yes?'

'I suppose I might get damaged?'

'Yes. We all might.'

'Could you by any chance find me some spare arms and legs? In case, you know . . .'

'I'll make sure we've got plenty of spare parts, don't you worry, master.'

'And you know, you were quite right about my brain,' the Scarecrow said reassuringly. 'I don't miss it at all.'

And on they marched, towards battle.

Some way behind, Mr Cercorelli had caught up with the astrologer.

'I warn you,' he was saying sternly, 'telling fortunes without a licence can lead to a severe penalty. What do you know of this scarecrow?'

The mystic bowed very deeply, and said in a humble voice, 'I cast his horoscope, your honour, and saw evidence of the deepest villainy. The planetary perfluminations—'

'Don't waste my time with that nonsense, or I'll have you up in front of the magistrate. What did he tell you, and where did he go?'

'He said he was going to Spring Valley, your honour.'

'Did he indeed? And did he set off in that direction?'

'No, your worship. Quite the opposite.'

'Did he say what he was going to do in Spring Valley?'

'Yes, my lord. He said he was going to make a fortune, and then go and take Spring Valley in hand. His very words! Naturally, I was going to report him as soon as I arrived at the nearest police station.'

'Naturally. Here is my card. I expect to hear at once if you see him again, you understand?'

CHAPTER NINE

THE BATTLE

M r Cercorelli wasn't the only person looking for the Scarecrow. High up above the countryside where the Scarecrow and his servant had been wandering, an elderly raven was gliding through the blue sky. She was a hundred years old, but her eyes were as sharp as they'd ever been, and when she saw a group of her cousins perching on a pine tree near a mountain top, she flew down at once.

'Granny!' they said. 'Haven't seen you for fifty years. What have you been up to?'

'Never you mind,' she said. 'What's going on over the other side of the hill? There are cousins of ours flying in from all over the place.'

'The soldiers are coming,' they explained.

111

'There's going to be a big battle. The red soldiers are going to fight the blue soldiers, and the green soldiers are coming along tomorrow to join in. But how are things over in Spring Valley?'

'Bad,' said Granny Raven. 'And getting worse. Have you seen a scarecrow? A walking one?'

'Funnily enough, we heard a young blackbird complaining about something like that just the other day. Shouldn't be allowed, he said. What d'you want to find him for?'

'None of your business. Where did you meet this blackbird?'

They told her, and she flew away.

That evening, after raiding six farms and commandeering all their food, the regiment camped by the side of a river. On the other side of the river there was a broad green meadow, and it was there that they were going to fight the Duke of Brunswick's army the next day.

While the Scarecrow joined his brother officers in a high-level discussion about tactics and strategy, Jack went to help the cooks prepare the evening meal.

'Is this how you always get food?' said Jack. 'You just take it from the farmers?'

'It's their contribution to maintaining the army,'

explained the cook. 'See, if we weren't here to defend them, the Duke of Brunswick would come and take everything from them.'

'So if you didn't take their food, he would?'

'That's it.'

'Oh, I see,' said Jack. 'What are we having for supper?'

They were going to have roast pork, and Jack sat and peeled a mound of potatoes to go with it. When he'd done that, he wandered through the camp and looked at everything.

'How are we going to get across to the battlefield?' he asked one of the gunners, who was polishing a big brass cannon.

'There's a ford,' said the gunner. 'We just hitch up the guns and drive 'em in the water and up the other side. We'll do it after breakfast.'

'Where's the Duke of Brunswick's army now?'

'Oh, they're on their way. Only we got here first, so we got what's called tactical advantage.'

'But if he gets to the meadow before we're across, then *he'll* have tactical advantage.'

'Ah, no, you don't understand,' said the gunner. 'Now clear off, I'm busy.'

So Jack went to look at the river instead. It was wide and muddy, and there might have been a ford, and there might not; because normally where there was a ford you saw a track or a road going down to the river on one side and coming out of it on the other.

He went and asked the farrier.

'No, there's no ford,' said the farrier, lighting his pipe with a glowing coal in a pair of tongs.

'Then how are we going to get across the river?'

'On a bridge. It's top secret. The Sardinians have got this new kind of bridge, movable thing, all the latest engineering. When they come, they'll put this bridge up in a moment – well, about half an hour – and we'll go straight across, form a line of battle, and engage the enemy.'

'Oh, I see. But suppose the Duke of Brunswick decides to fire all his cannons at the bridge while we're crossing it?'

'He wouldn't do that. It's against all the rules of engagement.'

'But supposing—'

'Go on, hop it. Scram. And you keep your trap shut about that bridge. It's top secret, remember.'

Jack decided not to puzzle any more, but to collect some sticks instead, so that he could repair the Scarecrow next day if he needed to.

When it was supper time, he and the other servants had to wait on the officers in their tent. Captain Scarecrow was behaving with great politeness, engaging his neighbours in lively and stimulating conversation, and sipping his wine like a connoisseur. The only thing that went wrong was when the officers took snuff after their meal. The proper way to take it was to put a little pinch on the back of your hand, sniff it briskly up your nose, and try not to sneeze; but the Scarecrow had never come across snuff before, and he sniffed up too much.

Jack could see what was going to happen, and he ran up with a tea towel – but it was too late. With a gigantic explosion, the Scarecrow sneezed so hard that all the buttons popped off his uniform, his umbrella opened in surprise, and bits of straw flew everywhere. Not only that; his turnip itself came loose, and lolled on his neck like a balloon on a stick. If Jack hadn't been there to hold it, it might have come off altogether and rolled right across the table.

As soon as the Scarecrow recovered his wits, he looked at Jack in horror.

'Dear me, what a ghastly experience!' he said. 'Was that the Duke of Brunswick attacking us? There was a terrible explosion, I'm sure of it!'

'Just a touch of gunpowder in the snuff,' said Colonel Bombardo. 'Better than snuff in the gunpowder, what? Cannons'd be sneezing, not firing. Damn poor show.'

Presently the sergeant came in and said it was time for all the officers to go to bed. Jack helped the Scarecrow to their tent.

'It'll be an exciting day tomorrow, Jack!' said the Scarecrow, as Jack tucked him up in the camp bed.

'I'm sure it will, master. I better sew all those buttons on extra tight in case you sniff some gunpowder. Goodnight!'

'Goodnight, Jack. What a good servant you are!'

So they all went to sleep.

When they woke up, there was no sign of the Sardinians, but the Duke of Brunswick's army had turned up during the night and made camp in the meadow across the river. There were lots of them.

'He's got a big army,' said Jack to the cook as they made breakfast.

'It's all show,' said the cook. 'Them big cannons they've got, they're only made of cardboard. Anyway, the Sardinians'll be here soon.'

But the Sardinians didn't show up at all. While the Duke of Brunswick's soldiers lined up their cannons pointing straight across the river, the officers of the Scarecrow's regiment rode up and down, waving their swords and shouting orders. Meanwhile, the sergeant was drilling the troops. He marched them along the riverbank and then made them about-turn and march back the other way. Not many of them fell in.

And while they were doing that, the gunners got their cannons all lined up one behind the other to go across the famous secret bridge that the Sardinians were going to bring. The Duke of Brunswick's soldiers kept looking at them and pointing and laughing.

'They won't be laughing when the Sardinians come,' said the chief gunner.

But there was no sign of the Sardinians. Finally, at about tea time, a messenger came galloping up with some shocking news. Jack was close by, and he heard the sergeant telling Colonel Bombardo all about it.

'Message here from the King of Sardinia, sir,' he said. 'He's changed his mind, and he's joining forces with the Duke of Brunswick.'

'I say! What do you think we should do, Sergeant?'

'Run away, sir.'

'Just what he'll be expecting. Very bad idea, if you ask me. We'll do just the opposite – we'll go across the ford, and before the Duke of Brunswick knows what's hit him, we'll give him a sound thrashing!'

'Very good, sir. This ford, sir—'

'Yes?'

'Where is it, sir?'

'In the river, Sergeant. Right there.'

'Right you are, sir. You're going first, are you, sir, to lead the way?'

'D'you think I should?'

'It's the usual thing, sir.'

'Then *charge!*'

And Colonel Bombardo galloped his horse right off the bank and into the water, and disappeared at once. No-one else moved.

No-one except Jack, that is. He saw the Scarecrow looking in an interested way at the river, where Colonel Bombardo's shako had just floated to the surface; and he ran through all the ranks of soldiers and past the guns and seized hold of Betsy's bridle.

It was a good thing he did, because at that very moment, there came a terrific volley of firing from the Duke of Brunswick's army across the river, and almost at once there came another volley from the other direction altogether: from behind them.

'It's the Sardinians!' someone said.

And then there were cannons going off all over the place. The regiment was trapped on the river-bank, with the Sardinians behind them and the Duke of Brunswick's army on the other side, and there was no ford at all.

The air was full of gunpowder smoke, and no-one could see anything. Soldiers were shouting and crying and running in all directions; bullets were whizzing through the air from every side; cannonballs were smashing into the tents and the wagons; and the Scarecrow was waving his sword and shouting, 'Charge!'

Luckily, no-one took any notice.

Then a stray cannonball whizzed past Betsy's flanks, giving her a nasty fright and taking some of the Scarecrow's trousers with it.

'Whoah! Help!' cried the Scarecrow.

'It's all right, master, just hold on,' said Jack.

And then a bullet clipped the Scarecrow's head, sending bits of turnip everywhere.

'Charge!' shouted the Scarecrow again, waving his sword so wildly that Jack was worried in case he cut Betsy's head off by mistake; but then another bullet came along and knocked the sword out of his hand with a loud *clang*.

'Now look what you've done!' cried the Scarecrow.

He scrambled down from Betsy's back, and he was about to run straight at the nearest soldiers and join in the fight, when Jack saw him suddenly stop and peer into a bush.

'What is it, master?' he said. 'Look, you can't hang around here – it's dangerous—'

But the Scarecrow took no notice. He was

reaching right in among the leaves, and then he very carefully lifted out a nest. Sitting in the nest was a terrified robin.

'This is quite intolerable,' the Scarecrow was saying to her. 'Madam, I offer my apologies on behalf of the regiment. It is no part of a soldier's duty to terrify a mother and her eggs. He owes a duty of care and protection to the weak and defenceless! Sit tight, madam, and I shall remove you at once to a place of safety.'

Tucking the nest into his jacket, the Scarecrow set off. There was a short pause when a stray bullet shot his leg off, and he had to lean on Jack's arm, but slowly they made their way through the battle-field. All around them soldiers in red uniforms were fighting with soldiers in blue uniforms, waving swords, firing pistols and muskets; and then along came some soldiers in green uniforms as well. The thunder of the explosions, and the groans and screams, and the crack of muskets and the whine of bullets and the crackle of flames were appalling, and the things Jack saw going on were so horrible

122

that he just closed his eyes and kept stumbling forward, leading Betsy with one hand and holding the Scarecrow up with the other, until the worst of the noise had faded behind them.

There was a bush close by, and before he did anything else the Scarecrow lifted the nest out of his jacket, with the robin still sitting on it, and placed it gently in among the leaves.

'There you are, madam,' he said politely, 'with the compliments of the regiment.'

Then he fell over.

Jack helped him up again, stuffing back the straw that was coming out all over the place.

'What a battle!' said the Scarecrow. 'Bang, crash, whiz!'

'Look at the state of you,' said Jack. 'You're full of bullet-holes, and you've only got one leg, and part of your turnip's gone. I'm going to have to tidy you up – you're badly wounded.'

'I shouldn't think anyone's more wounded than I am,' said the Scarecrow proudly.

'Not unless they're dead. Sit still.'

Jack took a good strong stick from the bundle of spare parts he'd tied on to Betsy's saddle before the battle began. He slid it inside the remains of the Scarecrow's trouser leg. The Scarecrow sprang up at once.

'Back to the battle!' he said. 'I want to win a medal, Jack, that's my dearest wish. I wouldn't mind losing all my legs and my arms and my head and everything, if only I could have a medal.'

Jack was busy tying the rest of the sticks together to make a raft.

'Well, master,' he said, 'if you turned up at that farm with no legs and no arms and no head and no sense, but with a medal shining on your chest, I don't suppose the broom would be able to resist you.'

'Don't remind me, Jack! My broken heart! In the excitement of battle I'd almost forgotten – oh! Oh! I loved her so much!'

While the Scarecrow was lamenting, Jack gave Betsy a carrot.

'Go on, old girl, you can look after yourself,' he said, and Betsy ambled away and disappeared in the bushes.

'Now, master, you come with me,' Jack went on, finishing the raft, 'because we've got a secret mission. It's very important, so just keep quiet, all right?'

'Ssh!' said the Scarecrow. 'Not a word.'

And Jack pushed the raft out on to the water, and he and the Scarecrow scrambled on board; and a few minutes later, they were floating down the river, with the sound of battle and the cries of the wounded soldiers fading quickly behind them.

CHAPTER TEN

MAROONED

While the Scarecrow and his servant were floating down the river, two important conversations were taking place.

The first one took place on the riverbank, where Mr Cercorelli was talking to the sergeant of the Scarecrow's regiment amid the wreckage of the battlefield.

'The last I seen of him, sir, he was charging into battle like a good'un,' the sergeant told him. 'He made a fine figure of an officer.'

'An officer, you say?'

'Captain Scarecrow was one of the most gallant officers I ever saw. Fearless, you might say. Or else you might say thick as a brick. But he did his duty by the regiment.'

'Did he survive the battle?'

'I couldn't tell you that, sir. I haven't seen him since.'

Mr Cercorelli looked at the devastation all around them.

'By the way,' he said, 'who won?'

'The Duke of Brunswick, sir, according to the morning paper. Very hard to tell from here. It was the King of Sardinia changing sides at the last minute that did for us.'

The lawyer made a mental note to congratulate his employers. The Buffaloni Corporation had important financial interests in Sardinia; no doubt they had reminded the King about them.

'Mind you,' the sergeant went on, 'we got a return battle next month.'

'Oh, really?'

'Yes, sir. And it'll go different next time, because the King of Naples is coming in with us.'

The lawyer made a mental note to tell his employers that as well.

'If you hear any more of Captain Scarecrow,' he said, 'here is my card. Good day.'

The other conversation took place through a window in a little farmhouse.

'Hey! You!' called Granny Raven, perching

among the geraniums in the window box.

An old man and his wife were sitting at the table, wrapping their crockery in newspaper and putting it in a cardboard box. They both looked up in astonishment.

'Here,' said the old man to his wife, 'that's old Carlo's pet, the one what escaped!'

Granny Raven clacked her beak impatiently.

'Yes, that's me,' she said, 'even if you've got it the wrong way round. He was my pet. And I didn't escape, I flew off to find a doctor, only I was too late. Now stop gaping like a pair of flytraps, and pay attention.'

'But you're *talking*!' said the old woman.

'Yes. This is an emergency.'

'Oh,' said the old man, gulping. 'Go on, then.'

'Not long before old Carlo died,' Granny Raven said, 'he asked you both to go over and do something for him. Do you remember what that was?'

'Well, yes,' said the old woman. 'He asked us to sign a piece of paper.'

'And did you?'

'Yes,' said the old man.

'Right,' said Granny Raven. Then she clacked her beak again, and looked at the table. 'What are you doing with that crockery?' she said.

'Packing,' said the old woman. 'Ever since the Buffaloni factory opened, our spring's dried up. We can't live here any more. They're taking everything over, them Buffalonis. It's not like what it used to be. Poor old Carlo's well out of it, I reckon.'

'Well, d'you want to fight the Buffalonis, or give in?'

'Give in,' said the old man, and 'Fight 'em,' said the old woman, both at once.

'Two to one,' said Granny Raven, looking at the old man very severely. 'We win. Now listen to me, and do as I say.'

When Jack woke up, the raft was floating along swiftly, together with lots of broken branches and shattered hen-coops and one or two dead dogs and other bits and pieces. The water was muddy and turbid, and the sun was beating down from a hot sky, and the Scarecrow was sitting placidly watching the distant banks go by.

'Master! Why didn't you wake me up before we drifted this far down the river?'

'Oh, we're making wonderful progress, Jack. You'd never believe how far we've come!'

'I don't think it's taking us to Spring Valley, though,' said Jack, standing up and shading his eyes to look ahead.

Very soon he couldn't even see the banks anymore, and the water, when he dipped his hand in, turned out to be too salty to drink.

'Master,' he said, 'we're drifting out to sea! I think we've left the land altogether!'

The Scarecrow was astonished.

'Just like that?' he said. 'We don't have to pay a toll, or anything? How clever! I never thought I'd go to sea. This will be very interesting.'

'Why, yes, it will, master,' said Jack. 'We don't know whether we'll drown before we starve to death, or starve to death before we drown. Or die of thirst, maybe. It'll be interesting to find out. We'd be better off getting shot to pieces by cannonballs, if you ask me.'

'Now then, you're forgetting the man in the misty

cart, Jack! Fame and glory, remember!'

'I think we've had that already, master. We're on to the danger and suffering now.'

'But it ends in triumph and happiness!'

Jack was too fed up to say anything. He sat on the edge of the raft and stared glumly all around. There was not a speck of land anywhere, and the sun glared like a furnace in the burning sky.

The Scarecrow saw his unhappiness, and said, 'Cheer up, Jack! I'm sure that success is just around the corner.'

'We're at sea, master. There aren't any corners.'

'Hmm,' said the Scarecrow. 'I think I'll scan the horizon.'

So Jack held on to his master's legs, and the Scarecrow held on to Jack's head, and peered this way and that, shading his eyes with the umbrella; but there was nothing to be seen except more and more water.

'Very dull,' said the Scarecrow, a little disappointed. 'There isn't even a seagull to scare.'

'I don't like the look of those clouds, though,' said Jack, pointing at the horizon. 'I think we're going to have a storm. Well, this is just what we need, I must say.'

The clouds got higher and bigger and darker as they watched, and presently a stiff wind began to blow, making the water lurch up and down in a very unpleasant way.

'A storm at sea, Jack!' said the Scarecrow eagerly. 'This will be a noble spectacle! All the awe-inspiring powers of nature will be unleashed over our very heads. There – you see?'

There was a flash of lightning, and only a few seconds later, the loudest crash of thunder Jack had ever heard. And then came the rain. The heavy drops hurtled down as fast as bullets, and almost as hard.

'Never mind, my boy,' shouted the Scarecrow over the noise. 'Here – shelter under my umbrella!'

'No, master! Put it down, whatever you do! We'll be struck by lightning, and that'll be the end for both of us!'

The two of them clung together on their fragile raft, with the waves getting higher and rougher, and the sky getting darker, and the thunder getting closer, and the wind getting fiercer every minute.

And then Jack felt the sticks of the raft beginning to come loose.

'Master! Hold on! Don't let go!' he cried.

'This is exciting, Jack! Boom! Crash! Whoosh! Splash!'

Then the biggest wave of all swept over them, and the raft collapsed completely.

'Oh no – it's coming apart – help! Help!'

Jack and the Scarecrow fell into the water, among the loose sticks and bits of string that were all that was left of the raft.

'Master! Help! I can't swim!'

'Don't worry, my boy. I can float. You can hold on to me! I shan't let you down!'

Jack didn't dare open his mouth again in case he swallowed more sea. In mortal terror, he clung to his master as the waves hurled them this way and that.

How long they floated he had no idea. But eventually, the storm passed over; the waves calmed down, the clouds rolled away, and the sun came out. Jack was trembling with the effort of holding tight, and weak from hunger and thirst, and still very frightened, so when the Scarecrow said something, he had to reply:

'What's that, master? I didn't hear you.'

'I said I can see a tree, Jack.'

'What? Where?'

The Scarecrow twisted around a bit in the water and stood up. Jack was too amazed to do more than lie there and look up as his master stood above him, shaking the water out of his clothes and pointing ahead.

Then Jack realized that he wasn't floating any more. In fact, he was lying in very shallow water at the edge of a beach.

'We're safe!' he cried. 'We haven't drowned! We're still alive!'

He jumped to his feet and skipped ashore, full of joy. It didn't matter that he was cold and wet and hungry – nothing like that mattered a bit. He was alive!

The Scarecrow was ahead of him, peering about with grreat interest. The tree he had seen was a palm tree, with one solitary coconut hanging high up among the leaves, and as Jack found when he joined his master, it was the only tree to be seen.

'We're on a tropical island,' he said. 'We're shipwrecked!'

'Well, Jack,' said the Scarecrow, 'I wonder what we'll find on this island. Quite often people find buried chests full of treasure, you know. I think we should start digging right away.'

'We'd be better off looking for food, master. You can't eat doubloons and pieces of eight.'

The Scarecrow looked all around. It was a very small island indeed; they could see all the way across it, and Jack reckoned that even if he walked very slowly, it would only take him ten minutes to walk all the way round the edge. 'Never despair,' said the Scarecrow. 'I shall think of something.'

Jack thought he'd better look for some water

before he died of thirst, so he wandered into the middle of the island, among the bushes, to look for something to drink.

But there was no stream, no pond, nothing. He found some little fruits, and ate one to see if it was juicy; but it was so sour and bitter that he had to spit it out at once, although he thought it was a waste of spit, because he didn't have any to spare. He looked at every different kind of leaf in case there was a cup-shaped one that had kept a drop of dew from the night before; but all the leaves were either flat and floppy or dry and hairy or thin and spiny, and none of them held a single drop of water.

'Oh, dear,' he said to himself, 'we're in big trouble now. This is the biggest trouble we've seen yet. This is a desperate situation, and no mistake.'

With a slow unhappy tread, Jack continued his short walk around the island. Less than five minutes later, he came back to the coconut palm. He tried to climb the trunk, but there were no branches to hold on to; he tried to throw stones at the coconut, but it was too high; he tried to shake the trunk, but it didn't move.

He moved into the shade and lay down, feeling so hungry and miserable and frightened that he began to cry. He found himself sobbing and weeping, and he couldn't stop, and he realized that although he was partly crying for himself, he was partly crying for the poor Scarecrow too, because his master wouldn't understand at all when he found his servant lying there dead and turning into a skeleton; he wouldn't know what to do, he'd be so distressed; and with no-one to look after him, he'd just wander about the island for ever until he fell apart.

'Oh, Jack, Jack, my dear boy!' he heard, and he felt a pair of rough wooden arms embracing him. 'Don't distress yourself! Life and hope, you know! Life and hope!'

'I'm sorry, master,' Jack said. 'I'll stop now. Did you have an interesting walk?'

'Oh, yes. I found a bush that looks just like a turkey, and another bush with little flowers the same colour as a starling's egg, and a stone exactly as big as a duck. It's full of interesting things, you know, this island. Oh! And I found a little place that looks just like Spring Valley, in miniature.'

'Spring Valley, master? I'd like to have a look at that.'

'Then follow me!'

The Scarecrow led him to a spot near the middle of the island, where the ground rose up a little way,

and some bare rocks stood above the surface. In
between them there was a little grassy hollow.

'You see,' said the Scarecrow, 'the farmhouse is
here, and *there's* the orchard, and *that's* where the
vines grow, and the olives are over *there*, and the
stream runs down *here* . . .'

'Nice-looking place, master. I wish there was a
real stream here, though.'

'Then we shall just have to dig a well, Jack.
There's bound to be some fresh water under here.
That's what we do in Spring Valley.'

'Well . . .' said Jack.

'Yes! A well. You dig there, and I'll
dig here,' said the Scarecrow, and he
began to scrape vigorously at the
ground with a dry stick.

There was nothing better to
do, so Jack found a stick too,
and scratched and poked
and scrabbled at the earth.
The sun was hot, and the
work made him even
thirstier than he was to
begin with, and besides,
the end of his stick
soon got wedged under
the corner of a big rock.

He found a stone to jam under the stick so he could lever the rock out. The Scarecrow was happily scratching away further down the miniature Spring Valley, singing to himself, and Jack heaved down on his stick with all his might.

The big rock shifted a bit. He heaved again, and it shifted some more.

It looked a bit funny for a rock. The corner was perfectly square, for one thing, and for another, it wasn't made of rock at all. It was made of wood, and bound with iron. Jack felt his eyes grow wider and wider. The iron was rusty and the wood was decaying, and there was a great big padlock holding it shut, which fell off as soon as he touched it.

Then he lifted the lid.

'Master!' he cried. 'Treasure! Look! You were right!'

The box was packed with coins, jewels, medals, necklaces, bracelets, pendants, rings for ears and rings for fingers, medallions, and every kind of gold ornament. They spilled out of the top of the box and jingled heavily as they fell on the ground. The Scarecrow's muddy little eyes couldn't open wide at the best of times, but they were fairly goggling.

'Well, that's amazing, Jack,' he said.

The Scarecrow picked up an earring and felt around the side of his turnip for an ear, but there

wasn't one. Then he picked up a necklace and tried to put it on, but it wouldn't go over his turnip at all; so he put a golden bracelet on his signpost wrist, and it fell straight off. Jack plunged his hands into the chest and filled them with coins and jewels, holding them high and letting them fall down through his fingers.

'We must be millionaires, master!' he said.

But his mouth was so dry that he couldn't speak properly.

'All the same,' he croaked, 'I'd rather have some water.'

'Would you, my boy? There should be enough in the well by now. Come and see.'

Jack thought he was hallucinating. He scrambled to his feet and ran after the Scarecrow, and sure enough, in the spot where he'd been digging, a little stream had started bubbling up.

'Oh, master! Oh, thank you! Oh! Oh! Oh!'

Jack flung himself to the ground and plunged his face into the muddy water, and drank and drank and drank until his belly could hold no more.

The Scarecrow was watching him with quiet satisfaction.

'There you are, you see,' he said. 'We understand water in Spring Valley.'

Jack lay back, bloated, and let the blessed

feeling of not being thirsty any more soak him from head to feet.

When he got up, the spring was still bubbling away, and the water was trickling down towards the beach. It didn't look as if it would get there, because most of it sank straight down into the dry earth. The Scarecrow was busy somewhere else – Jack could hear him singing to himself – so, looking carefully at the way the earth sloped and where the rocks were, Jack found another stick and began to dig.

'What are you doing, Jack?' called the Scarecrow.

'I'm making a reservoir, master. What are you doing?'

'Sorting out the treasure,' came the answer.

'Good idea.'

So Jack went on digging until there was a hole as deep as his arm and about the same size across, and he patted the earth smooth and tight all around inside it. Then he scraped a trench in the soil, and led the water from the spring down into his new hole. The Scarecrow came to watch.

'See, master, once the water's in there, all the mud will sink to the bottom, and it'll be nice and clear to drink from,' Jack explained.

'Excellent!' said the Scarecrow. 'A splendid piece of civil engineering, Jack.'

Jack scraped another trench at the other side, for the water to run away once the reservoir was full. They stood and watched the hole filling up.

'Now come and see what I've done!' said the Scarecrow proudly.

He had made a little grotto with some stones and some mud, and he'd stuck diamonds and pearls and rubies and emeralds all over it with some sticky gum from a bush. He'd made a pretty pattern in the ground with some gold coins, and another pattern with the silver ones, and then he'd made some pretend trees out of bits of stick, and draped the necklaces over them like icicles.

'That's lovely, master,' said Jack.

'And I haven't even begun to study the pictures on the coins yet. Oh, there's endless food for the mind here, Jack!'

'Food . . .'

Jack looked longingly at the coconut palm, but the coconut still hung there high up among the leaves, as if it was mocking him. He tried to put it out of his mind. At least he had something to drink.

So while the Scarecrow worked on his grotto, Jack went down to the beach and walked up and down, looking for a fish to catch. But there wasn't a fish to be seen. He could feel himself going a little crazy from hunger.

'Maybe I could eat one of my toes,' he said to himself. 'I wouldn't really miss it, not a little one. But there wouldn't be enough meat on just one. I'd need a whole foot, or two, maybe.'

He paddled up and down at the edge of the sea, sunk in misery. In the middle of the afternoon he went to the reservoir to have another drink, and the Scarecrow showed him the grotto, with great pride, pointing out all the architectural and decorative effects.

'There, Jack! What d'you think of that? Do you see how I've arranged the stones, with all the light ones here and all the dark ones there? I think I'll go and look for some shells now, to stick round the edge. But Jack – what's the matter, my boy?'

'I'm sorry, master. I've tried not to give in to

despair – but I'm starving to death – I think what you're making there must be my burial place, and a very nice one too, but I don't want to starve to death ... I don't know what to do, master, really I don't ...'

And poor Jack sank down to the ground, too weak to stand up any longer. In a moment the Scarecrow was kneeling by his side.

'Jack, Jack, what was I thinking of! If that blackbird hadn't stolen my brain, you could have made some pea soup. But as it is, the rest of my head is at your disposal, my dear servant. Cut yourself a slice of my turnip, and feast to your heart's content!'

So Jack struggled up and, not wanting to hurt the Scarecrow's feelings, took his little pocket knife and tried to find a place to cut a slice of his master's turnip. The poor thing was so battered and bruised and dried out that it was scarcely a vegetable any more,

and it was as hard as a piece of wood; but Jack managed to find a bit round the back where he could cut a little slice, and he did, and crammed it into his mouth.

'Not all at once, my boy – you'll choke!' said the Scarecrow. 'Nibble, that's the thing to do. And drink plenty of water.'

The turnip was hardly edible at all. It was dry and woody and bitter, and it took so much chewing that every mouthful took five minutes to soften and swallow.

Nevertheless, Jack ate it, and even thought he felt it doing him good.

By the time he'd finished, the Scarecrow had come back with some pretty shells from the beach. They spent an hour or so sorting them out, and then they stuck them on the ceiling of the little grotto. Then they dug a lake around it, and led some water into it from the stream, and that kept them going until sunset, and by then Jack's belly was so empty that he kept on making little moaning sounds, and the Scarecrow offered him another slice of turnip.

But there was hardly anything left to hack. A few bitter shreds were all Jack had for supper. And while he hugged his empty belly and tried to fall asleep, the Scarecrow pottered about in the moonlight, fitting every gem and every gold ornament and every piece of priceless jewellery into the grotto palace until it was perfect, and it glittered over its reflection in the tiny lake, looking fit for the queen of the fairies.

Chapter Eleven

An Invitation

Just before he woke up in the morning, Jack had a dream.

He dreamed he was just lying there on the sand, listening to a conversation in the air above. He couldn't see who was talking, but they had rusty voices, like old barbed wire being pulled through holes in a tin can.

'I'll bet you the small one goes before the day's out,' said one voice.

'I reckon the big one's gone already,' said the other.

'No. He's a monster, and they go on for ever.'

'Thin pickings these days, brother!'

'I heard there was a great battle on the mainland. Feasting for days, my cousin said.'

'All gone when I got there. Bones, nothing but bones.'

'The land's bare, brother. The soldiers move on, and who knows where they go?'

'Aye, who knows? Did you hear of the factories they're building in Spring Valley? They're making poisons, brother, poisons for the land. Is that little feller dead yet?'

Jack had been listening in his dream, and all of a sudden, with a horrible shock, he realized that it wasn't a dream at all, and that two vultures were sitting in the palm tree directly above him.

'Go away!' he managed to shout, in a voice almost as hoarse as theirs. 'Go on! Scram!'

His cry awoke the Scarecrow, who leaped up at once.

'Leave this to me, Jack!' he cried. 'This is scarecrow's work!'

And he uttered a bloodcurdling cry, and opened and shut his umbrella several times. The vultures, duly scared, spread their wings and lumbered away.

'My dear servant!' the Scarecrow said, full of compassion, as he turned to Jack. 'How long had those two villains been sitting up there?'

'I dunno, master. I heard them talking and I thought it was a dream. I wish it had been – they said I was almost a goner – Oh, master, ever since we began there's been people talking about eating me, and now the birds are at it too – and *I'm* the one that needs to eat!'

'Have another slice of my head, Jack. As long as I have a turnip on my shoulders, you shall not want for nourishment, dear boy!'

So Jack sawed away and cut himself another little scrap of his master's head, and chewed it hard with lots of water. But the poor Scarecrow was looking a great deal the worse for wear by now; Jack's knife had left deep gouges in the turnip, and the bits that were too tough to cut stuck out like splinters.

While Jack sat there gnawing the bitter root and trying to make it last a bit longer, the Scarecrow went off to inspect the grotto. He had an idea for improving the southern frontage, he said; but he'd only been gone a minute when Jack heard a furious yell.

He struggled to his feet, and hurried to see what was the matter. He found the Scarecrow stamping with fury and shouting:

'You flying fiends! How dare you! I'll bite your beaks off! I'll fill you full of stones! I'll boil you! You vagabonds, you housebreakers! Squatting – *squatting* in our *grotto*! Shoo! Begone!'

'Calm down, master! You'll do yourself a mischief,' said Jack. 'What's going on?'

He got down on his knees and peered into the grotto.

'Blimey!' he said.

For right in the centre there was a nest, and sitting on the nest was a little speckled bird. As Jack watched, another little bird flew in with a worm and gave it to the one on the nest, and as the one on the nest reached up for the worm, Jack saw that there were four eggs beneath her.

Eggs, thought Jack. *Eggs!*

'Jack?' called the Scarecrow from behind him. 'Be careful – they go for the eyes, these fiends – stand back and let me deal with them!'

The two little speckled birds were looking at Jack. He licked his lips, and swallowed. Then he sighed.

'I suppose,' he said reluctantly, 'you better stay there, since you've got some eggs to look after.'

They said nothing.

'Jack?' said the Scarecrow anxiously.

'It's all right, master,' said Jack, standing up and feeling dizzy, so that he had to hold on to the Scarecrow for a moment. 'They're sitting on some eggs.'

'Eggs, eh?' said the Scarecrow severely. 'Well, that obviously means that hostilities are suspended until they hatch. Very well,' he called, 'you, you birds in there, in view of your impending parenthood, I shall not scare you away. But you must keep

151

the place tidy, and leave as soon as your chicks have flown.'

The male bird flew out and perched on a nearby twig.

'Good morning,' he said. 'And what do you do?'

The Scarecrow blinked, and scratched his turnip.

'Well, I, um—' he began.

'Lord Scarecrow's in the agricultural business,' said Jack.

'Jolly good,' said the bird. 'And have you come a long way?'

'All the way from Spring Valley,' said the Scarecrow.

'Splendid. Well done,' said the bird, and flew away.

Now Jack was sure he was hallucinating. As a matter of fact, he didn't feel at all well.

'Jack, my boy,' said the Scarecrow, 'I wonder if I could ask you to adjust my turnip a fraction. I think it's coming loose.'

'Let's go down to the beach, master,' Jack said. 'It's too bright to see here. There's a bit of shade there, under the coconut tree.'

Leaning on his digging stick, Jack made his way through the scrubby bushes with the Scarecrow holding the umbrella over him. It really was almost too hot to bear.

When they reached the coconut tree, they had a surprise, because a flock of pigeons rose out of it noisily, making the leaves wave. And just as the pigeons flew away, the coconut fell on to the sand with a thud.

'Oh! Thank goodness!' cried Jack, and ran to pick it up.

He turned it over and over, feeling the milk sloshing this way and that. He took out his knife and dug a hole in the end, and drank every drop. There wasn't actually as much as he'd thought, and what's more, it was going rancid.

'Jack – my boy – help—'

The Scarecrow was tottering and stumbling over the sand, trying to hold his turnip on. But it had been so bashed and hacked about that it wasn't going to stay on, and besides, as Jack saw when he helped his master to sit down in the shade, the broomstick he'd had for a spine was badly cracked.

'Dear oh dear, master,

you're in a worse state than me,' Jack said. 'At least we can do something about you. Lie still, and I'll take your spine out first, and then put my digging stick there instead.'

'Is it a dangerous operation?' said the Scarecrow faintly.

'Nothing to it,' said Jack. 'Just don't wriggle.'

As soon as the new spine was in place, Jack picked up the turnip – but alas! It fell apart entirely.

And now what could he do?

There was only one thing for it.

'Here we go, master,' he said. 'Here's a new head for you.'

He jammed the coconut down on to the end of the digging stick, and at once the Scarecrow sat up.

He turned his new head from side to side, and brushed the tuft of spiky hair on the top. Oddly enough, the expressions of surprise and delight and pleasure that passed over the coconut were exactly the same as the ones Jack remembered from the turnip. The Scarecrow looked just like himself again; in fact he looked much better than before.

'You look very handsome, master,' said Jack.

'I *feel* handsome! I don't think I've ever felt so handsome. Jack, my boy, you are a wonder. Thank you a thousand times!'

But the wandering about, and the hot sun, and the rancid coconut milk on his empty stomach were all too much for Jack.

'Can I sit under your umbrella for a minute, master?' said Jack. 'I'm feeling ever so hot and dizzy.'

'Of course!'

So they sat side by side for a few minutes. But Jack couldn't keep upright; he kept slipping sideways and leaning on the Scarecrow's chest. His master let him rest there until he fell asleep.

And once again Jack had a dream, and heard voices. This time one of them belonged to the Scarecrow himself, and he was speaking quietly, but with a great deal of force:

'It's just as well for you that my servant is asleep on my breast, because otherwise I'd leap up and scare you in a moment. But I don't want to wake him. You chose your moment well, you scoundrel!'

'No, no, you've got it wrong,' said the other voice, a light and musical voice which seemed to come from a bush nearby. 'I've got a message for you, from the Grand Congress of All the Birds.'

'Grand Congress of All the Birds!' said the Scarecrow, with bottomless scorn. 'I've never heard of it.'

'Your ignorance is legendary,' said the bird.

'Well, thank you. But don't think you can get round me with your flattery. Since I can't move, I suppose I shall have to listen to your preposterous message.'

'Then I shall read it out. *The Eighty-Four Thousand Five Hundred and Seventy-Eighth Grand Congress is hereby convened on Coconut Island, that being the place chosen by Their Majesties the King and Queen of All the Birds. The President and Council send their greetings to Lord Scarecrow, and invite him to attend as principal guest of*

honour, to receive the thanks of the Congress for his gift of a Royal Palace, and to discuss the matter of Spring Valley, and—'

'Spring Valley!' cried the Scarecrow. 'What's all this?'

'I haven't finished,' said the bird. '*– To discuss the matter of Spring Valley, and to make common purpose in order to restore the good working of the land, to our mutual benefit.* There,' he concluded. 'That's it.'

'Well, I'm astonished,' said the Scarecrow. 'Spring Valley is a very important place. And if you're going to start deciding what to do about it, I insist that I have the right to speak on the subject.'

'But that's exactly what we're inviting you to do!'

'Well, why didn't you say so? Now, you understand, I shall have to bring my servant with me.'

'Out of the question.'

'What!'

'He is a human being. We birds were meeting in Congress for hundreds of thousands of years before human beings existed, and they have brought us nothing but trouble. You are welcome, as our guest of honour, because we're not scared of you, whereas we're all scared of humans. And—'

The Scarecrow leaped to his feet.

'Not scared of *me*? How dare you not be scared of me! I've got a good mind to make war on the whole kingdom of the birds!'

And he stamped away, waving his arms in a fury.

Jack couldn't keep his eyes closed any longer. He sat up and blinked in the burning sunlight, and the messenger bird flew to another bush a bit further off.

Jack said quickly, 'No, please, listen. Don't let my master's manner put you off. He's highly strung, Lord Scarecrow is, he's got nerves like piano wires. The fact is,' he added quietly, looking around to see the Scarecrow stumping up and down and gesticulating in the distance, 'I don't think he'd manage very well without me. He's a great hero, no doubt about it, but he's as simple as a baby in some ways. Ever since his heart was broken by a broom-stick he's been desperate, just desperate. His brain even fell out. I'll see if I can get him to change his mind.'

'Don't be long,' said the bird testily.

Squinting against the glare, Jack stumbled through the bushes and out on to the beach. He fell over three times before the Scarecrow saw him. His master came hurrying over the sand, his anger forgotten.

'Jack! Jack! My boy, are you ill?'

'I think I'm going to croak, master. I think I'm going to kick the bucket. But listen – I have given you good advice, haven't I? What I've said to you made sense, didn't it?'

'The best sense in the world!' said the Scarecrow warmly. 'No sense like it!'

'Then do as I suggest, and say thank you very much to this bird, and go and attend their Grand Congress. And maybe you can get to Spring Valley even if I don't.'

'Without you, my faithful servant?'

'I don't think I'll ever see it, master. I'm done for, that's what I think.'

'I shall never leave your side! And you may tell that crested charlatan so, in no uncertain terms.'

So poor Jack had to haul himself up and stagger back to the bird.

'He says he'd be delighted to accept your invitation,' he said, 'and he sends his compliments to the President and Council.'

'I should think so too,' said the bird.

'Did I . . .' Jack tried to say, but he could hardly get any words out. 'Did I hear you right, or was I dreaming? Those two little speckled birds that made their nest in the grotto – you said they were the King and Queen of all the birds?'

'That is correct.'

'Oh, good,' said Jack.

But he couldn't say anything else, because he felt himself falling sideways, and then he felt nothing at all.

CHAPTER TWELVE

THE GRAND CONGRESS

Jack woke up to find himself lying on his back and gazing up at a bright blue sky. He was lying on something soft and comfortable, so he naturally thought he was dead.

But the angels were making a lot of noise. In fact he wondered why St Peter, or the Holy Ghost, or someone, didn't come along and tell them all to stop quarrelling. They sounded like a lot of squawking birds.

Birds!

He sat up, rubbed his eyes, and looked around.

He was sitting in the middle of the island, a little way from the reservoir and the grotto palace, and under the shade of a bush whose leaves and branches had been woven together over his head.

Someone had gone to the trouble of putting a lot of soft leaves down for him to lie on, and right next to him there was a pile of fruits and nuts and berries.

'Food! Thank goodness!' he said, and ate them all up, feeling much better at once.

And everywhere there were birds: giant eagles wheeling above, herons at the edge of the reservoir, jackdaws strutting up and down, skylarks trilling in the sky, flamingos, robins, seagulls, ibises with long curved beaks, a pelican, and even an ostrich. They were flying, singing, pecking, washing themselves, fluttering their feathers, arguing, clucking, and altogether making so much noise that Jack could hardly think.

But where was the Scarecrow? Jack stood up and shaded his eyes against the brilliant sun, and gazed all around. Near the beach he saw his master's familiar shape striding along stiffly, talking and gesticulating to dozens of birds who were moving along with him.

'Well, I'm blowed,' said Jack to himself, and set off through the bushes to find out more.

'Jack, my boy!' said the Scarecrow, waving cheerfully. 'You've woken up at last! And how are you feeling, my dear servant?'

'Well, I dunno, master,' Jack said, making his way shakily over to where his master was standing.

Although the birds didn't seem afraid of the Scarecrow at all, they flew away when Jack came up, and he and the Scarecrow were able to talk without being overheard.

'I suppose I'm still alive,' Jack went on, 'and my arms and legs are all working, so I reckon I must be all right. But what's going on, master? Where did the birds come from?'

'Ah. What happens is that every ten years, the King and Queen choose somewhere to make a nest, and then they summon all the birds to the Grand Congress. Very simple, you see; primitive, really – suits their childish minds. But they were so pleased with the palace we built for them that they just wouldn't go anywhere else. Oh, and I made them let you stay, and bring you some fruit and nuts and so on. I said I wouldn't accept their gold medal otherwise.'

'They're going to give you a gold medal? That's wonderful, master!'

'Yes, they were thrilled. But look – they're calling everyone together.'

On the topmost branch of a shrub near the grotto palace, a chaffinch was calling loudly. All the other birds stopped what they were doing and flew, or strutted, or waddled, or glided into the space in front of her, and settled down to listen.

'Birds of every degree!' the chaffinch called. 'Waders, swimmers, fliers and walkers! Welcome to the Eighty-Four Thousand Five Hundred and Seventy-Eighth Congress of All the Birds! I call upon our noble President to open the proceedings and welcome our guests.'

An elderly pelican hopped on to a rock and spoke in a deep and sonorous voice.

'I declare this Congress open,' he said. 'We have much urgent and important business to discuss. But our first task is the pleasant one of announcing the winner of our gold medal. We have acclaimed many distinguished laureates in the past, but few whose accomplishments were as varied as those of our guest today. With no regard for his personal safety, he clambered high up a stone wall to restore the fallen chick of Dr and Mrs Owl to his parents' nest. Secondly, ignoring the danger of riot and pursuit, he bravely set free five linnets, six goldfinches, and seven blackbirds from their sordid and miserable captivity. Thirdly, in the midst of a deadly battle, and at great personal risk, he carried the nest of Signora Robin to a place of safety.'

Lots of little birds were gazing in admiration at the Scarecrow, who stood beside Jack with a pleased expression on his coconut.

'And finally, using the utmost resources of his architectural skill, our gold medallist built a palace of jewels for Their Majesties our King and Queen to nest in. I am happy to report the appearance of four chicks this morning. The parents and the chicks are all very well.'

The birds cheered loudly. Several took off and flew around in delight before landing again.

The chaffinch called for silence. All the birds fell still once more, and then he said:

'I now invite Lord Scarecrow to come forward and receive the gold medal, and to say a few words.'

The Scarecrow moved with great dignity between the ranks of watching birds and stood beside the President, while four hummingbirds flew up over the Scarecrow's head and dropped a scarlet ribbon very neatly around his neck. The medal hanging from it gleamed proudly on his tattered chest.

The Scarecrow cleared his throat and began, 'Your Majesties! Mr President! Birds of every kind and degree!'

Everyone fell still. Jack crossed his fingers.

'It gives me great pleasure,' the Scarecrow went on, 'to stand here today and receive this tribute. It is true, in the past we may have had our disagreements; some of your people may have stolen—'

The President coughed disapprovingly and said, 'We don't refer to it as stealing, Lord Scarecrow. Please confine yourself to general remarks of a friendly nature.'

'Oh, you're trying to censor me, are you?' said the Scarecrow, bristling. 'I must say that's typical. I come here in a spirit of friendship to do you the

honour of accepting this paltry bauble, and you treat me like—'

The birds were squawking with indignation and raising their wings and shaking their heads. The President clattered his beak loudly for silence, and said:

'Paltry bauble? How dare you! I never heard such insolence!'

The Scarecrow was about to lose his temper. There was only one thing to be done.

'Excuse me,' Jack called out, 'excuse me, Your Majesties, Mr President, Lord Scarecrow and everyone, I think there's just been a bit of trouble with the translation.'

'But we're all speaking the same language!' protested the President. 'There's no doubt whatsoever about the monstrous and unpardonable insult that this *thing* has just expressed. No doubt at all!'

'*Thing*, sir? *Thing*, did you call me?' cried the Scarecrow, and his umbrella opened and closed in a passion.

'Well, you see, that's just what I mean,' said Jack, carefully making his way through the ranks of the birds. 'Mr President, sir, it's clear to me that you're speaking in different languages. You're talking Bird, which is a rich and noble tongue worthy of the great nation of feathered heroes who speak it, and Lord Scarecrow is talking Coconut, which is a subtle and mysterious language full of wisdom and music. So if you'd let me translate for you—'

'And who are you? You're a human being. What are you doing here?' demanded the President.

'Me, sir? My name is Jack, sir, just a boy, that's right, no more than a lowly servant, sir. But I humbly offer my services, at this most dangerous time in world affairs, in the interests of peace and harmony. So if you'd just let me tell Lord Scarecrow what you're saying, and tell you what *he's* saying, I'm sure this Congress will get on very happily.'

'Hmph,' the President snorted. 'Well, you can begin by saying that unless Lord Scarecrow apologizes for that intolerable insult, we shall have no alternative but to strip him of his gold medal and declare war.'

'Certainly,' said Jack, bowing low.

He turned to the Scarecrow and said, 'Lord Scarecrow, the President offers you his profound apologies, and begs you to regard this little exchange of words as merely a storm in a teacup.'

'Oh, does he?' said the Scarecrow. 'You can tell him in return that I am a proud and free scarecrow, unused to tyranny and the despotic rule of a set of feathered popinjays, and I shall never submit to censorship.'

'Righto, master,' said Jack.

He turned to the President and said, 'Lord Scarecrow presents his most cordial and earnest compliments, and begs the Congress to regard his hasty words of a moment ago as being merely the natural and warm-hearted exuberance of one who has all his life cherished the highest and most passionate regard for all the nation of the birds. He asks me to add that he has never in his whole life received an honour that means as much to him as this gold medal, and he is already the holder of the Order of the Emerald Wurzel, the Beetroot Cup, and the Parsnip Challenge Trophy. What's more, he's a Knight of the Broomstick. But he'd gladly relinquish all those honours in favour of your gold medal, which he intends to wear with a full and grateful heart for the rest of his days.'

'He said all that, did he?' said the President suspiciously.

'It's what they call a compressed language, Coconut,' said Jack.

'Is it. Well, if that is the case, then I am happy to accept his apology,' said the President, bowing stiffly to the Scarecrow.

'He says he offers his most humble apology,' Jack told the Scarecrow.

'It didn't sound like that to me,' said his master.

'In fact—'

'No, he was speaking in Bird.'

'Ah, I see,' said the Scarecrow. 'What an extraordinary language.'

'That's why you need an interpreter, master.'

'Indeed. How lucky that you speak it so fluently! Well, in that case, I am happy to accept his apology.'

And the Scarecrow bowed very stiffly to the President.

Seeing this display of mutual respect, all the birds broke into a storm of singing and shouting and flapping and squawking and chirping and cooing. The Scarecrow responded by beaming widely and bowing in all directions. And thus everyone, for the moment, became the best of friends; but Jack thought that they would probably need a good interpreter for some time to come.

After the formalities, the Congress moved on to discuss the business of Spring Valley. But the Scarecrow didn't seem able to keep his mind on it. Several birds gave reports on the Buffaloni Corporation's poison factory, and the way they'd diverted the streams, and drained the wells, and dried up the fountains; but all the Scarecrow could do was fidget and scratch and pluck at his clothes.

When they broke for a recess, Jack said, 'Are you all right, master? You look a little out of sorts.'

'I think I'm leaking, my boy,' said the Scarecrow. 'I'm suffering a severe loss of straw.'

Jack had a look.

'It's true, master,' he said. 'Something must have loosened your stuffing. We'll have to get you some more.'

'What are you doing?' said the chaffinch, flying down to look. 'What's going on? What's the matter?'

'Lord Scarecrow's leaking,' Jack explained. 'We've got to find some more stuffing for him.'

'Nothing to it! You leave it to us!' said the chaffinch, and flew away.

'I'll take all this old straw out, master,' said Jack. 'It's been soaked and dried and battered about so much that you could do with a new filling. You'll feel much better for it, you take my word.'

He pulled out handfuls of dusty old straw, bits of twig, scraps of rag, and all the other bits and pieces the Scarecrow was so full of.

'I feel very hollow,' said the Scarecrow. 'I don't like it a bit. I can hear myself echoing.'

'Don't worry, master, we'll soon have you filled up again. Hello! What's this?'

Tucked into the middle of all the straw was a little packet of paper wrapped in oilskin.

'That's my inner conviction,' said the Scarecrow. 'Don't throw that away, whatever you do.'

Jack unwrapped the oilskin. Inside it there was a sheet of paper covered in writing.

'Oh, dear,' said Jack. 'I hoped there'd be a picture. I can't read this, master, can you?'

'Alas, no,' said the Scarecrow. 'I think my education was interrupted.'

By that time, a flock of birds had begun to fly down, each carrying a piece of straw or a twig or a bit of moss, and under the chaffinch's direction they packed them securely in the Scarecrow's inside. Each bird flew in, wove its contribution into the rest, and darted out again.

'They're doing some good stuffing, master,' said Jack. 'I'll put this back now, and then they can finish it off.'

'What's that?' said the chaffinch. 'What have you got there? What is it?'

'It's my inner conviction,' said the Scarecrow.

'What's it say? What's it all about?'

'We don't know,' said Jack. 'We can't read.'

With a loud chirrup of impatience, the chaffinch flew away. The other birds went on packing the Scarecrow, but word had got around, and the President himself came along to have a look. While the little birds flew in and out, the Scarecrow displayed his inner conviction proudly.

'You see, it's bound in oilskin,' he said proudly. 'So all through our adventures, it's been perfectly preserved. I knew it was there,' he added. 'I've been certain of it all my life.'

'Yes, but what does it say, you booby?' demanded the President. 'Are you too silly to know what your own inner conviction is?'

The Scarecrow opened his mouth to protest, but then remembered and looked at Jack for the translation.

But Jack didn't have time to say a word, because a harsh *Caw!* from behind him made him jump, and he turned round to see an elderly raven fly down and land on the grass.

She nodded to the President, who bowed very respectfully back at her.

'Good day, Granny Raven,' he said.

'Well, where is it?' she said. 'This paper from inside the Scarecrow. Come on, let's have a look.'

Jack unfolded it for her, and she put a big claw on it and read it silently.

Then she looked up.

'You, boy,' she said to Jack. 'I want a word with you. Come over here.'

Jack followed her to a quiet spot a little way away.

'I heard about your so-called translating,' she said. 'You're a bright lad, but don't push your luck. Now tell me about the Scarecrow, and don't leave anything out.'

So Jack told her everything that had happened

from the moment he heard the Scarecrow calling for help in the muddy field to the moment when he'd fainted from hunger the day before.

'Right,' she said. 'Now, there's going to be big trouble coming, and the Scarecrow's going to need that inner conviction of his more than ever. Fold it up, and put it back inside him, and don't let him lose it.'

'But why, Granny Raven? What's this trouble? And is he going to be in any danger? I mean, he's as brave as a lion, but he's not all there in the head department, if you see what I mean.'

'Not that sort of trouble. Legal trouble. Buffaloni trouble.'

'Well, we can run away!'

'No you can't, not any more. They're on your trail. We've got a couple of days' advantage, so we've got to make the most of it.'

'I don't like the sound of this at all.'

'There's a chance,' said Granny Raven, 'but only if you do exactly as I tell you. And hurry up – we haven't got a moment to lose.'

Chapter Thirteen
The Assizes

The first thing Granny Raven told them to do was get themselves back to the mainland. This turned out to be quite easy. Some seagulls who lived by the nearest fishing port found a rowing boat that wasn't being used, and they hitched it up to a team of geese, who towed it across to the island in less than a day. Once Jack and his master were on board, the birds towed it back the same way, and that very evening, the two wanderers settled down under a hedge.

'Who knows, Jack,' said the Scarecrow, 'this could be one of our last nights in the open air! We'll be sleeping in our very own farmhouse before long.'

Or jail, Jack thought.

The next thing they had to do was make their way to the town of Bella Fontana, which was the nearest town to Spring Valley. By walking hard, they did it in less than a week. Granny Raven had had to go elsewhere on urgent business, she said, but she'd see them in the town.

'You know, Jack,' the Scarecrow said as they walked towards the market place, 'I might have been mistaken about these birds. They're very good-hearted, fundamentally. No brains to speak of, but full of good intentions.'

'Now then, master,' said Jack, 'just remember: Granny Raven said she'd meet us by the fountain. And while we're in the town, I think you'd better leave the talking to me. You'll be much more impressive if you keep silent and mysterious.'

'Well, that's exactly what I am,' said the Scarecrow.

On the way, he'd managed to lose his gold medal eleven times and the oilskin package containing his inner conviction sixteen. Jack thought it would be a good idea to put them in a bank, and keep them safe till they were needed. So as soon as they got to the town centre, with its dried-up basin which had once been the municipal fountain, they looked around for the bank.

They were about to go inside when a big black

bird flew down and perched on the dusty basin and gave a loud *Caw!*

'Granny Raven!' said Jack. 'Where've you been? We were just going into the bank.'

'I've been busy,' she said. 'What d'you want a bank for?'

The Scarecrow explained: 'We're going to deposit my inner conviction. Don't worry. We know what we're doing.'

'You're luckier than you deserve,' said Granny Raven. 'D'you know what that bank's called? It's the Banco Buffaloni.'

The Scarecrow stared at it in dismay.

'These Buffalonis are everywhere!' he said. 'Well, we can't trust this bank, it's obvious. I shall have to look after my inner conviction myself. Where is it? Where's it gone? Where did I put it?'

'You've got it, master,' said Jack. 'It's safe in your straw. But what do we do now, Granny Raven? And what's going on? There's a lot of people around.'

'It's the Assizes,' she said, 'when the judge comes around judging court cases. He tries all the criminals and judges all the civil cases. There he is now.'

As Jack and the Scarecrow watched, the great doors of the town hall opened and out came an elderly man wearing a long red robe, at the head of a procession of men carrying maces and scrolls. Behind him came several men in black robes, who were the lawyers, and finally came the town clerk in a top hat. Escorted by a procession of policemen in their best uniforms, they crossed the square and went up the steps into the law court.

'Right,' said Granny Raven. 'You go in after them, and get a move on.'

'But what are we going to do in there?'

'You're going to go to court and register the Scarecrow's claim to Spring Valley.'

'An excellent idea, Jack!' said the Scarecrow. 'Let's do it at once.'

And before Jack could hold him back, the Scarecrow set off up the steps and in through the doors, with Granny Raven sitting on his shoulder.

Jack darted up behind him, and found the Scarecrow arguing with an official behind a desk.

'But I demand the right to have my case heard!' the Scarecrow was saying, banging his umbrella on the desk. 'It is an extremely important matter!'

'You're not on my list,' said the official. 'What's your name? Lord Scarecrow? Don't be ridiculous. Go away!'

Jack thought he'd better help. They were in such deep trouble already that they might as well dig a bit deeper.

'Ah, you don't understand,' he said. 'This case is a matter of extreme urgency. It all turns on the ownership of Spring Valley, and it won't take long. If it's not settled, you see, all the water'll dry up. Just like the fountain out there. Stick him on the list, and we can get through it in five minutes, and then all the water in the valley will be safe.'

'Go on!' said a man in the queue for the public seats. 'I'd like to see a scarecrow in court.'

'Yeah, let him go first,' said a woman with a shopping bag. 'He's got a nice face.'

'He's got a face like a coconut!' said the official.

'Well, it *is* a coconut,' the Scarecrow agreed.

'Go on, put him on first,' people were saying. 'It's the only laugh we'll have today.'

'Yes! Let the scarecrow have his case heard!'

'Good luck, scarecrow!'

So the man had no choice. He wrote at the top of the list:

Lord Scarecrow in the case of the ownership of Spring Valley.

No sooner had he done that than the door burst open, and in came a squad of policemen. At the head of them was a lean man in a black silk suit. It was the lawyer, Mr Cercorelli, and he said:

'One moment, if you please. Inspector, arrest this person at once.'

The Scarecrow looked around to see who was going to be arrested, only to find the chief policeman seizing his road sign and trying to put handcuffs on him.

'What are you doing? Let me go! This is an outrage!' he cried.

'Go on, boy,' said Granny Raven quietly to Jack. 'Do your stuff.'

'Oh, excuse me,' said Jack to the lawyer, 'but you can't arrest Lord Scarecrow, being as he's already in the process of going to law.'

'I beg your pardon?'

'It's true, Mr Cercorelli, sir,' said the official, showing him the list of cases to be tried.

The Scarecrow shook off the handcuffs, and dusted himself down with great dignity as a bell rang to summon everyone into the courtroom. Mr Cercorelli withdrew to talk urgently to a group of other lawyers in a huddle by the door. Jack watched them closely, and saw them all leaning over Mr Cercorelli's shoulder to read the name of the Scarecrow's case; but as soon as they read it, they all smiled and nodded with satisfaction.

Oh blimey, he thought.

Then he heard the man at the desk say something, and turned to say, 'I beg your pardon?'

'I said you're in luck,' said the official to Jack. 'This is a very distinguished judge you're up in front of. He's the most learned judge in the whole of the kingdom.'

'What's his name?' said Jack, as the doors opened and the Clerk of the Court called for silence.

'Mr Justice Buffaloni,' said the official.

'*What?*'

But it was too late to withdraw. The crowd behind

them was surging and heaving to get in, and Jack saw a lot of whispering and pointing and hurrying in and out of side doors. Soon the courtroom was full to bursting, and the Scarecrow and Jack were crammed behind a table right in the middle, with lawyers to left and right, the judge's bench high up in front of them, and a jury filing into the jury box along the side.

Everyone had to stand up as the judge came in. He bowed to the court, and everyone bowed back to him, and then he sat down.

'I'm getting a bit nervous,' Jack whispered. 'And Granny Raven's vanished. I don't know what to do.'

'No, no, Jack,' the Scarecrow whispered back. 'Have confidence in the law, my boy! Right is on our side!'

'Silence!' bellowed the Clerk. 'First case. Scarecrow versus the United Benevolent Improvement Society Chemical Works.'

The Scarecrow smiled and nodded his coconut. Jack put his hand up.

'What? What?' said the judge.

'Excuse me, your worship,' said Jack, 'but it's all going a bit fast. Who are these United Benevolent Improving people?'

'Well, if it comes to that,' said the judge, 'who are *you*?'

And he beamed at all the lawyers, and they all slapped their sides and roared with laughter at the judge's sparkling legal wit.

'I'm Lord Scarecrow's legal representative,' said Jack, 'and my client wants to know who these United Improvers are, because we never heard of them till now.'

'If I may explain, my lord,' said Mr Cercorelli, rising smoothly to his feet. 'I act for the United Benevolent Improvement Society, which is the body that holds a majority shareholding in the company known as the United Benevolent Improvement Chemical and Industrial Company, which is the operating organization that runs the United Benevolent Improvement Chemical Works, which owns and operates several factories situated in Spring Valley for the beneficial exploitation of certain mineral and water rights granted to the United Benevolent Improvement Society, which is a registered charity under the Act of 1772, and acts as a holding company in the case of the United Benevolent Improvement Chemical Works by *tenendas praedictas terras.*'

'There you are,' said the judge to Jack. 'Perfectly clear. Now be quiet while we hear this case and find for the defendant.'

'Oh, right,' said Jack. 'Well, my lord, I'd like to ask Lord Scarecrow to be a witness.'

All the other lawyers went into a huddle. Long words came buzzing out like wasps around a fruit tree. The Scarecrow smiled at everyone in the court, gazing all round with great pride and satisfaction.

Finally Mr Cercorelli said, 'We have no objection, your lordship. He will, of course, be subject to cross-examination.'

'Scarecrow to the witness box!' called the Clerk of the Court.

The Scarecrow stood up and bowed to the judge, to the jury, to the clerk, to the lawyers, and to the public.

'Stop bobbing up and down like a chicken and get into the witness box!' snapped the judge.

'A *chicken*?' said the Scarecrow.

'It's a legal term, master,' said Jack hastily.

'Oh, in that case it's perfectly all right,' said the Scarecrow, and bowed again all round.

The members of the public, watching from the gallery, were enjoying it a great deal. They settled down comfortably as Jack began.

'What is your name?' he said.

The Scarecrow looked puzzled. He scratched his coconut.

'It's Lord Scarecrow,' said Jack helpfully.

'Leading the witness!' called one of the lawyers.

'Strike it from the record,' said the judge. 'You, boy, confine yourself to questions. Don't tell the witness what to say.'

'All right,' said Jack. 'He's called Lord Scarecrow. I'm his servant, by the way.'

'And a very good one!' said the Scarecrow.

'Silence!' called the judge. 'Get on with the examination, boy, and as for you, you scoundrel, hold your tongue.'

The Scarecrow nodded approvingly, and beamed at everyone. The people in the public gallery began to giggle.

'Now then,' said Jack, 'I put it to you, Lord Scarecrow, that this United Benevolent Improvement Society is not the legal owner of Spring Valley.'

'Quite right,' said the Scarecrow.

'Then who is?'

'I am!'

'And can you prove that?'

'I hope so,' said the Scarecrow doubtfully.

The people in the gallery began to laugh.

'Silence in court!' said the judge, and glared furiously. When everyone was quiet again, he said to Jack, 'If you don't get to the point, I shall have you both arrested for wasting the court's time. Has your witness got anything useful to say, or has he not?'

'Oh, indeed he has, your lordship. Let me just ask him again.'

'You can't go on asking him the same question!'

'Just once more. Honest.'

'Once, then.'

'Thank you very much, your lordship. Right. Here goes. Lord Scarecrow, how do you know that you are the owner of Spring Valley?'

'Ah!' said the Scarecrow. 'I've got an inner conviction. I've always had it. In fact I've got it here,' he went on, fumbling in his chest. 'I know it's here somewhere. Yes! Here it is!'

'Yes, that's it,' said Jack. 'Your lordship, members of the jury, ladies and gentlemen, this piece of paper proves beyond any doubt whatsoever that Spring Valley belongs to Lord Scarecrow, and these United Benevolizers are being illegal. I rest my case.'

'But what does it say, you stupid boy?' snapped the judge. 'Get your client to read it out to the court.'

'Well, he's never learned to read, your lordship.'

'Well, *you* read it then!'

'But I never learned to read either. It's a big drawback, and if I'd known then what I know now, I'd have arranged to be born into a rich family and not into a poor one. I'm sure I'd have learned to read then.'

'If you don't know how to read,' demanded the judge, 'how do you know what's on that paper? I warn you, boy, you're in great danger!'

'My lord,' said one of the lawyers, 'all he has to do is hand it to your lordship, and your lordship can read it out for the benefit of the court.'

'Oh, no, you don't,' said Jack at once. 'We want separate verification, according to the principles of *non independentem judgi nogoodi*. So there.'

This was getting more and more difficult. But just then, Jack saw a movement out of the corner of his eye, and looked up at a high window to see Granny Raven making her way in, accompanied by a very nervous-looking blackbird. She made the blackbird sit in the

191

corner of the windowsill, and didn't let him move.

'However,' Jack went on, relieved, 'I think I can see a way out of this legal minefield. I'd like to invite my associate Granny Raven to come and take over this part of the case.'

Granny Raven glided down and perched on the table next to Jack, causing great excitement among the public, and great consternation on the part of the lawyers. They went into a huddle, and then Mr Cercorelli said:

'My lord, it is quite impossible to allow this, on the grounds of *ridiculus birdis pretendibus lawyerorum*.'

But Jack said at once, 'My client is only a poor scarecrow, without a penny to his name. Is the law of the land designed only for the rich? Surely not! And if, out of the goodness of her heart, this raven – this poor, elderly, shabby, broken-down old bird – offers to represent the Scarecrow, because she is all he can afford, then surely this great court and this noble judge will not deny my client the meagre help that she can bring? Look at the vast wealth, the profound resources, the eminent legal minds ranged against us! Your lordship, members of the jury, ladies and gentlemen of the public – is there no justice to be had in the Assizes of Bella Fontana? Is there no mercy—?'

'All right, all right,' sighed the judge, who could see that everyone in the public gallery was nodding in sympathy. 'Let the bird speak on behalf of the Scarecrow.'

'I should think so too,' said Granny Raven, and then added quietly to Jack, 'Shabby and broken-down, eh? I'll have a word with you later.'

The Scarecrow was watching everything with great interest.

'Well, go on then,' said the judge.

'Right,' said Granny Raven. 'Now pay attention. You, Scarecrow, step down from the witness box. I want to summon two more witnesses before I speak to you again. Mr and Mrs Piccolini, into the witness box.'

Nervously, arm in arm, the elderly couple who'd been packing to leave their cottage came through the courtroom and stepped up into the box.

Once they'd given their names and addresses, Granny Raven said:

'Now tell the court what happened just before your neighbour died.'

'Well, our neighbour, Mr Pandolfo,' said Mrs Piccolini, 'he hadn't been well, poor old man, and when he asked us to step over to his house we thought he was going to ask us to call the doctor. But instead he just asked us to watch him sign a

piece of paper, and then to sign it as well. So we
did.'

'Did he tell you what was on the paper?'

'No.'

'Would you recognize the paper again?'

'Yes. Mr Pandolfo was drinking some coffee, and
he spilled a drop or two on the corner of the paper.
So it would have a stain on it.'

Granny Raven turned to Jack and said, 'Go on,
open it up.'

Jack opened the oilskin package and held up the
paper. As the old woman had said, there was a
coffee-stain on the corner. Everyone gasped.

All the lawyers rose to their feet at once,
protesting, but Granny Raven clacked her beak so
loudly that they all fell still.

'Don't you want to hear what the paper says?' she
said. 'Because everybody else does.'

They went into a huddle, and after a minute one
of them said, 'We are willing to agree to the letter's
being read out by an independent witness.'

'In that case,' said Jack, 'we nominate that lady
in the jury box.'

He pointed to an old lady in a blue dress. The
Scarecrow stood up and bowed to her, and she
looked very flustered and said, 'Well, if you like, I
don't mind . . .'

She put on a pair of glasses, and Jack handed her
the letter. She quickly skimmed it through, and
said, 'Oh, dear. Poor old man!'

Then the old lady read in a clear voice:

*'This letter was written by me, Carlo Pandolfo,
being of sound mind, but not very well in the legs,
and is addressed to whom it may concern.*

*'As I am the legal owner of Spring Valley, and I
can dispose of it however I please, I choose this
manner of settling the ownership after I peg out.*

*'And I particularly want to keep the farm and all
the springs and wells and watercourses and ponds
and streams and fountains out of the hands of my
cousins those rascal Buffalonis because I don't trust*

*any of them and they are a pack of scoundrels every
one.*

'*And I have no wife or children or nieces or
nephews.*

'*And no friends either except Mr and Mrs Piccolini
down the hill.*

'*So I shall make a scarecrow and place him in the
three-acre field by the orchard and in him I shall put
this letter.*

'*And this letter shall be my last will and
testament.*

'*And I leave Spring Valley with all its buildings
and springs and wells and watercourses and ponds
and streams and fountains to the said scarecrow and
it shall belong to him in perpetuity and I wish him
good luck.*

'*That is all I have to say.*

'*Carlo Pandolfo.*'

When the lady reached the end of the letter,
there was a silence.

Then the Scarecrow said, 'Well, I did tell you I
had an inner conviction.'

And then there was an uproar. All the lawyers
began talking at once and all the people in the
public gallery turned to one another and said, 'Did
you hear that? Well I never – have you ever heard?
– and what about—?'

The Clerk of the Court called for silence, and everyone stopped to see what the judge would say. But it was Granny Raven who spoke.

'There you are,' she said. 'That's the long and the short of it. The will is legal, and properly witnessed, and Spring Valley belongs to the Scarecrow, and we can all—'

'One moment,' said Mr Cercorelli. 'Not so fast. We haven't finished yet.'

Chapter Fourteen

A Surprise Witness

A nd everyone looked at the judge. The look on his face was enough to make Jack feel that all his ribs had come loose and fallen into the pit of his stomach.

'The first witness has yet to be cross-examined,' he said. 'Mr Cercorelli, you may proceed.'

'Thank you, my lord,' said the lawyer.

Jack looked at Granny Raven. What was going to happen now? But he couldn't read any expression on the old bird's face.

The Scarecrow climbed back up into the witness box, smiling all around. Mr Cercorelli smiled back, and the two of them looked like the best of friends.

Then the lawyer began:

'You are the scarecrow mentioned in the letter we

have just heard?'

'Oh, yes,' said the Scarecrow.

'You are sure of that?'

'Absolutely sure.'

'No doubt at all?'

'No. None whatsoever. I'm certainly me, and I always have been.'

'Well, Mr Scarecrow, let us examine your claim a little more closely. Let us examine *you* a little more closely!' he said, smiling at everyone again.

The Scarecrow smiled back.

'Let's examine your left hand, for example,' said the lawyer. 'It's a remarkable hand, is it not?'

'Oh, yes. It keeps the rain off!' said the Scarecrow, opening his umbrella, and closing it again quickly when the judge frowned at him.

'And where did you get such a splendid hand?'

'From the market place in the town where I starred in *The Tragical History of Harlequin and Queen Dido*,' said the Scarecrow proudly. 'It was a great performance. First I came on as—'

'I'm sure it was enthralling. But we're talking about your hand. You lost your original hand, did you?'

'Yes. It came off, so my servant got me this one.'

'Splendid, splendid. Now can you show us your right hand?'

The Scarecrow stuck his right hand in the air.

'It looks like a road sign,' said the lawyer. 'Is that what it was?'

'Oh, yes. It points, you see. As soon as my servant got this for me, I became very good at pointing.'

'And why did your servant get you a new right hand?'

'Because the first one broke off.'

'I see. Thank you. So you have neither of the arms you were – ahem – born with?'

Jack jumped up to protest. He could see where this was leading.

'Your lordship, it doesn't make any difference which bits have been replaced – he's still the same scarecrow!'

'Oh, but it does, your lordship,' said Mr Cercorelli. 'We are seeking to establish how much of the original scarecrow created by Mr Pandolfo still remains. If there is none, then the will is null and void, and the estate of Spring Valley passes to the United Benevolent Improvement Society, according to the principle *absolutem absurditas scaribirdibus landlordum*.'

'Quite right,' said the judge. 'Carry on.'

And in spite of Jack's protests, Mr Cercorelli went through the Scarecrow's whole story, showing how every bit of him had been replaced, including the very straw inside him.

'And so, members of the jury,' he concluded, 'we can see clearly that the scarecrow made by Mr Pandolfo, the scarecrow to whom he intended to leave Spring Valley, no longer exists. Every component particle of him has been scattered to the four winds. There is nothing left. This gentleman in the witness box, so proud of his left hand that keeps the rain off and his right hand that points so well, is no more than a fraud and an impostor.'

'Hey!' said Jack. 'No, no, wait a minute!'

'Silence!' said the judge. 'Members of the jury, you have heard an account of the most shameless attempt at fraud, deception, malfeasance, embezzlement, and theft that it has ever been my misfortune to hear about. Your duty now is very simple. You have to retire to the jury room and make up your minds to do as I tell you. You must find for the defendants, and decide that the United Benevolent Improvement Society are the true owners of Spring Valley. The court will—'

'Hold on,' said a harsh old voice. 'What did that scoundrel say a minute ago? Not so fast, he said.

We haven't finished yet.'

Every head turned to look at Granny Raven.

'Everybody listening?' she said. 'I should think so too. We've got three more witnesses to call. It won't take long. The next witness is Mr Giovanni Stracciatelli.'

Jack had never heard of him, and neither had anyone else. The lawyers all huddled together and whispered, but they didn't know what to do, and when Mr Stracciatelli came to the witness box carrying a large leather-bound book, all they could do was watch suspiciously.

'You are Giovanni Stracciatelli?' said Granny Raven.

'I am.'

'And what is your occupation?'

'I am the Commissioner of Registered Charities.'

At once all the lawyers rose to their feet and protested, but Granny Raven's voice was louder than all of them.

'You stop your fuss!' she cawed. '*You* brought up the subject of charities, and *you* claimed that the United Benevolent Improvement Society was a proper charity registered under the Act, so let's have a good look at it. Mr Stracciatelli, would you please read out the names of the trustees of the United Benevolent Improvement Society?'

Mr Stracciatelli put on a pair of glasses and opened his book.

'*Trustees of the United Benevolent Improvement Society,*' he read. '*Luigi Buffaloni, Piero Buffaloni, Federico Buffaloni, Silvio Buffaloni, Giuseppe Buffaloni, and Marcello Buffaloni.*'

Gasps from the public gallery – more protests from the lawyers.

'Thank you, Mr Stracciatelli, you can step down,' said Granny Raven. 'I'd like to remind the court of Mr Pandolfo's opinion concerning the Buffalonis. This is what his letter says: *I particularly want to keep the farm and all the springs and wells and watercourses and ponds and streams and fountains out of the hands of my cousins those rascal Buffalonis because I don't trust any of them and they are a pack of scoundrels every one.*'

Still more protests. The judge was looking very sour indeed.

'Now you may say,' said Granny Raven, 'that Mr Pandolfo was wrong about the Buffalonis. You may claim that every Buffaloni born is a perfect angel. That is all beside the point. The point is that Mr Pandolfo did *not* want his land to go to the Buffalonis, and he *did* want to leave it to the scarecrow.'

'But the scarecrow no longer exists!' shouted Mr Cercorelli. 'I've just proved it!'

'You were concerned with his component particles, not with the whole entity,' said Granny Raven. 'So let us take you at your word, and assume that all that matters is the stuff he's made of. I call our next witness, Mr Bernard Blackbird.'

The blackbird flew down and perched on the witness box. He was very nervous of the Scarecrow, who was watching him closely.

'Name?' said Granny Raven.

'Bernard.'

'Tell the court about your dealings with the Scarecrow.'

'Don't want to.'

Granny Raven clacked her beak, and Bernard squeaked in terror.

'All right! I will! Just let me think. It's all gone dark in me mind.'

'You wake your ideas up, my lad,' said Granny Raven, 'or you'll be flying home with no feathers. Tell the court what you told me.'

'I'm scared of *him*,' said Bernard, looking at the Scarecrow.

'He won't hurt you. Do as you're told.'

'All right, if I have to. It was on the road somewhere. I was ever so hungry. I seen him coming out of a caravan, and then I seen him banging his head. Mind you, that was a different head. That was a turnip.'

'Never mind what sort of head it was. What was he doing?'

'Banging it. He was whacking hisself on the bonce. Then summing fell out, and him and the little geezer bent down to look at it, and—'

'My brain!' cried the Scarecrow. 'So it was *you*, you scoundrel!'

'Silence!' shouted the judge. 'Witness, carry on.'

'I forgot what I was saying,' whined the blackbird. 'When he shouts at me I get all nervous. I'm highly strung, I can't help it. You shouldn't let him shout like that. It's not fair. I'm only young.'

'Stop complaining,' said Granny Raven. 'What happened next? Something fell out of his head. What was it?'

'It was a pea. A dried pea.'

'It was my *brain*,' said the Scarecrow passionately.

'Stop him!' cried Bernard, flinching. 'He's gonna hit me! He is! He give me a really cruel look!'

'You'll get worse than that from me,' said Granny Raven. 'Tell the court what you did.'

'Well, I thought he didn't have no more use for it, so I ate it. I was hungry,' he said piteously. 'I hadn't had nothing for days, and when I seen that pea I thought he was just throwing it away. So I come down and pecked it up. I never knew it was important. It didn't taste very nice, either. It was ever so dry.'

'That'll do.'

'It give me a belly-ache.'

'I said that's enough!'

'It might have been poisoned.'

'How dare you!' said the Scarecrow.

'Stop him! Stop him!' cried Bernard, fluttering in terror. 'You seen the look he give me? You heard him? Help! He's going to murder me!'

'That's quite enough,' snapped Granny Raven.

'I need compensation, I do,' said Bernard. 'I need counselling. It's stolen all my youth and happiness away, this has. I'll never be the same. I need therapy.'

'Clear off home and stop whining,' said Granny Raven, 'or I'll give you some therapy that'll sort you out for good.'

Bernard crept along the edge of the witness box, flinching dramatically as he came near the Scarecrow, although the Scarecrow didn't move. Then he flew straight for the open window and vanished.

'Our final witness,' said Granny Raven, with a look of distaste after Bernard, 'is the Scarecrow's personal attendant.'

'What, me?' said Jack.

'Yes, boy, you. Get a move on.'

So Jack went into the witness box. The lawyers were busily objecting, but the judge wearily said, 'Let the boy give evidence. The jury will soon see what rubbish it is.'

Granny Raven said, 'Tell the jury what happened on the island where you were marooned.'

'Oh, right,' said Jack. 'We were left on this island, and there wasn't any food, and I was going to starve to death. So Lord Scarecrow very generously let me eat his head. All of it, except the brain, obviously, being as that was eaten already. So I started to eat it, and bit by bit I ate almost all of it, and it kept me alive. And then that coconut fell down and I stuck it on his neck, and very good he looks too. If it wasn't for Lord Scarecrow's generosity in letting me eat his head, I'd be nothing now but a skeleton.'

'So there, your lordship, members of the jury,' said Granny Raven, 'there is our entire case. The United Benevolent Improvement Society, which is currently running poison factories in Spring Valley, and draining all the wells, is a front organization for the Buffaloni family. Mr Pandolfo wanted to keep Spring Valley out of the hands of the Buffalonis, and leave it to the Scarecrow. The only remaining particles of the original Scarecrow are now indissolubly mingled with those of Bernard the blackbird and Jack the servant; and I shall obtain power of attorney to act for Bernard on behalf of all the birds, since he is a feckless wretch; but we maintain that the kingdom of the birds, together with Jack the servant, are now the true and undisputable owners of Spring Valley, in perpetuity.'

'The jury haven't heard my summing-up yet,' said the judge. 'They can begin by forgetting everything they have just heard. The testimony of the Scarecrow's witnesses is to be disregarded, on the grounds that it is more favourable to the Scarecrow than to the United Benevolent Improvement Society, a charity of the utmost worthiness, whose trustees are gentlemen of the highest honesty and integrity, besides employing a large number of *you*. Ladies and gentlemen of the jury, you know what's good for you – I mean, you know your duty. Go to the jury room, and decide that the Scarecrow should lose this case.'

'No need, our lordship,' said the foreman. 'We've already decided.'

'Excellent! It only remains for me to congratulate the United—'

'No,' said the foreman, 'we reckon the Scarecrow wins.'

'*What?*'

All the lawyers were on their feet at once, protesting loudly, but the foreman of the jury took no notice.

'We don't care about all that,' he said. 'It's common sense. Don't matter if he is all different bits from what he was, he's still the same Scarecrow. Any fool can see that. And we're all fed up with the fountains being dry. So what we decide is this: Spring Valley is to be owned by the birds *and* by the servant *and* by the Scarecrow equally. And that's it. That's the voice of the people.'

A great cheer broke out from the public gallery. The judge called for silence, but no-one took any notice. The lawyers were still arguing, but no-one took any notice of them either.

The Scarecrow and Jack were both lifted on the shoulders of the crowd and carried out to the square. Granny Raven went to perch on the fountain while the Scarecrow made a speech.

'Ladies and gentlemen!' he said. 'I am heartily grateful for your support, and I give you my word of honour that as soon as we have closed the poison factories, we shall let all the springs flow again, so that this fountain will run with fresh water for everyone.'

More cheers from the crowd – but then they all

fell silent and looked around. From the town hall a group of men, all wearing expensive clothes and dark glasses and looking stern, were walking towards the Scarecrow.

Jack heard whispers from the crowd.

'Luigi – Piero – Federico – Silvio – Giuseppe – Marcello! It's the whole Buffaloni family . . .'

'Well, master,' said Jack, 'it looks like a fight. Let's run away, quick.'

'Certainly not!' said the Scarecrow, and he faced the Buffalonis boldly, coconut high, umbrella poised, the very model of a people's hero.

The Buffalonis stopped right in front of him, six of them, big rich powerful men in shiny suits. Everyone held their breath.

Then the Buffaloni in the middle said, 'Our congratulations to you, my friend!' and held out his hand to shake.

The Scarecrow shook it warmly, and then all the other Buffalonis gathered round, slapping him on the back, ruffling his coconut, patting him on the shoulder, shaking his hand, embracing him warmly.

'So we lose a law case!' said the chief Buffaloni. 'It's a big world – there are plenty of other enterprises! Plenty of room in this beautiful world for Buffalonis *and* Scarecrows!'

'Good luck to you, Lord Scarecrow! Our best

wishes for all your business ventures!'

'If you ever need our help – just ask!'

'We respect a brave opponent!'

'Buffalonis and Scarecrows are good friends from now on – the best of friends!'

And then a café owner produced some wine, and the Buffalonis and the Scarecrow drank a toast to friendship, and happy laughter filled the square; and presently someone brought out an accordion, and in a moment the whole crowd was singing and dancing and laughing and drinking and throwing flowers, with the Scarecrow at the heart of the celebrations.

CHAPTER FIFTEEN

MURDER BY TERMITES

They slept that night in the farmhouse in Spring Valley. Jack woke up next morning to hear his master calling.

'Jack! Jack! Help! I don't feel at all well!'

'That's all right, master,' said Jack, hurrying along to help. 'You had too much wine last night. Come for a walk – it'll clear your head.'

'No, it's not my head,' the Scarecrow told him. 'It's my legs and my arms and my back. I've been poisoned. Help!'

And he did look in a bad way, it was perfectly true. Even his coconut had gone pale. When he stood up he fell over, when he lay down he groaned, and he was getting twitches in his arms and legs.

'Twitches, master?'

'Yes, Jack! Dreadful ghastly twitches! It's horrible! It feels as if I'm being eaten alive! Call the doctor at once!'

So Jack ran to the town and called the doctor. The Scarecrow was a celebrity now, thanks to the trial, and the doctor gathered up his bag and hurried along straight away, followed by several onlookers.

They found the Scarecrow twitching badly, and groaning at the top of his voice.

'What is it, Doctor?' said Jack. 'Listen to him! He's in a terrible state! What can it be?'

The doctor took his stethoscope and listened to the Scarecrow's chest.

'Oh, dear me,' he said. 'This is bad. Let me take your temperature.'

'No, no! Don't do that!' protested the Scarecrow. 'If you take my temperature away, I'd be cold all through. As it is, I'm hot *and* cold, both together. Oh, it's horrible! Oh, no-one knows what I'm suffering!'

'What other symptoms are you feeling?'

'Internal conniptions. And a nameless fear.'

'A nameless fear? Dear me, that's not good at all. A fear of what?'

'I don't know! Horses! Eggs! Heights! Oh! Oh! I feel terrible! Help! Help!'

And the Scarecrow leaped all over the room,
capering and skipping and prancing like a goat.

'What's he doing, Doctor?' said Jack. 'I've never
seen him like this. Is he going to die?'

'He's clearly been bitten by a spider,' explained
the doctor. 'Dancing is quite the best cure, all the
medical authorities agree.'

The Scarecrow overheard him, and sank to the
floor with terror.

'A spider! Oh, no, Doctor, anything but that! I'll
go mad with despair!'

'Better keep on dancing then, master,' said Jack.

But the poor Scarecrow couldn't dance another
step.

'No, I can't move!' he cried. 'All the strength has drained from my body – my nameless fear is going all the way down to my toes—'

'Let me feel your pulse,' said the doctor.

The Scarecrow held out his left hand. As soon as the doctor took his wrist, the umbrella opened, startling the doctor, who stepped back in alarm.

'Try the other one,' said Jack. 'Here, master, point at something.'

The doctor took his road sign in one hand, and a large silver watch in the other. Jack watched the Scarecrow, and the Scarecrow watched the doctor, and the doctor watched the watch.

After a minute the doctor solemnly declared, 'This patient has no signs of life at all.'

The Scarecrow let out a piercing yell.

'Oh no! I'm dead! Help! Help!'

'You can't be dead yet, master,' said Jack, 'not if you're making a racket like that. Can't you find anything that you can cure, Doctor?'

'Dear me, this is a very bad case, a very poor case indeed. There's only one thing for it,' said the doctor.

'What?' said the Scarecrow and Jack, together.

'I shall have to operate. Lie down on the bed, please.'

The poor Scarecrow was quivering with terror.

'Aren't you going to put him to sleep first?' said Jack.

'Of course I am,' said the doctor. 'My goodness, do you take me for a quack?'

The Scarecrow heard the word *quack* and looked around for the duck, but the doctor took a rubber hammer and knocked him on the coconut. The Scarecrow fell down, stunned.

'Now what?' said Jack.

'Undo his clothing,' said the doctor. 'Then hand me my penknife.'

Everyone gasped, and craned closer to look. Jack unfastened the Scarecrow's coat, and laid bare his shirt, with the straw sticking stiffly out of every gap, and his poor wooden neck sticking out of the top.

His master was lying so still that Jack thought he really must be dead, and before the doctor could do anything, Jack flung himself across the Scarecrow and cried and sobbed.

'Oh, master, don't be dead! Please don't be dead! I don't know what I'd do without you, master! Please don't die!'

He sobbed and howled and clung to the poor old Scarecrow, and nothing would move him. Several of the bystanders began to cry too, and before long the room was filled with weeping and wailing, and every eye was gushing with tears. Even the doctor had to find his handkerchief and blow his nose vigorously.

The birds had heard the news, and a great lament went up from all the fields round about, and the bushes and trees were full of piteous cries:

'The Scarecrow's dying!'

'He's been poisoned!'

'He's been assassinated!'

And the loudest wails of lamentation came from the room in the farmhouse in Spring Valley where the doctor and Jack and all the townsfolk were gathered around the Scarecrow. But they didn't come from the people, they came from the Scarecrow himself, because all the noise had woken him up.

He leaped off the bed and cried:

'Oh! Oh! I'm dying! I'm poisoned! Oh, what a loss to the world! Treachery! Assassination! Murder! Oh, Jack, my dear boy, has he cut me open yet?'

'He was just about to.'

'Oh! Oh! Oh! I feel terrible! I've got conniptions all up and down my spine! I feel as if a million little ghosties were nibbling me! Oh – oh – there goes my leg – I'm falling apart, Jack! Help! Help!'

The Scarecrow was running around the room in terror, and the doctor was running after him trying to hit him with the rubber hammer, to put him to sleep again. Jack was running behind them gathering up all the bits that fell on the floor – some string, a bit of wood from somewhere up his trousers, lots of straw – and everyone else was wailing and sobbing.

Then Jack heard a loud *Caw!* and looked round in relief.

'Granny Raven!' he said. 'Thank goodness you've come back! Lord Scarecrow's been taken ill, and the doctor says—'

'Never mind the doctor,' she said, perching on the windowsill. 'He doesn't need a doctor. What he needs is a carpenter. So I've gone and fetched one. Here he is.'

In came an old man wearing a carpenter's apron and carrying a bag of tools.

'Hold still, Lord Scarecrow,' he said. 'Let's have a look at you.'

'He's my patient!' said the doctor. 'Stand back!'

'I want a second opinion,' cried the Scarecrow. 'Let him look!'

Jack helped the Scarecrow back on to the bed. The carpenter put some glasses on and peered closely at the Scarecrow's legs, and then at the digging stick Jack had put in to replace his spine. He tapped them with a pencil, he felt all round them, he looked all the way up and down the faded road sign.

Then he stood up with a solemn expression. Everyone fell silent.

'In my professional opinion,' said the carpenter, 'this gentleman is suffering from an acute case of woodworm.'

The Scarecrow gave a shriek of horror. Everyone gasped.

'And if I'm not mistaken,' the carpenter went on, 'he's got termites in his stuffing, and an infestation of death-watch beetle in his backbone.'

The Scarecrow looked at Jack in despair, and reached for his hand.

'Can we save him?' Jack said.

'He needs an immediate transplant,' said the carpenter. 'He's got to have a whole new backbone, and he needs his insides cleaning out completely. This is a fresh infestation, mind. It's deeply suspicious. In my professional opinion, all them beetles and insects and woodworms got tipped down his neck yesterday.'

'The Buffalonis!' Jack cried. 'When they all came crowding round to pat him on the back! Assassins! Murderers!'

The Scarecrow was paralysed with terror. All he could do was lie there and whimper.

So Jack ran all through the farm looking for a broomstick, but the only ones he could find were already infested with woodworm, or split down the middle, or soft with dry rot.

He looked for a stick of any kind, but the only ones he could find were too short, or too bent, or too flimsy.

Then he ran back to the Scarecrow, who was lying pale and faint on the bed, twitching and whimpering.

And there were a lot more people in the room. The first visitors had now been joined by several elderly women dressed in black, weeping and wailing and tearing their hair. In those days, every town had a band of professional mourners, and

these were the mourners of Bella Fontana. They'd heard about the impending death of Lord Scarecrow, and had come to offer their services. Besides, they'd missed the death of poor old Mr Pandolfo, and they wanted to make amends.

'Ladies,' Jack said, 'I know you mean it for the best, but the thing about scarecrows is that what they really like is jolly songs. You got any jolly songs you can sing?'

'That would be disrespectful!' one of the old ladies said. 'We were always told that when someone was on the brink of death, we had to weep and wail, to remind them of where they were going next.'

'Well, that's very cheerful,' said Jack, 'and I'm sure they all appreciate it no end. But it's different with scarecrows. Songs, dances, jokes and stories, else you all go home.'

'Humph,' said the oldest old lady, but then Jack found a bottle of Mr Pandolfo's best wine, and they all agreed to try singing and dancing, just to see how it went.

'Oh, Jack,' whispered the Scarecrow, 'I'm not long for this world!'

'Well, cheer up, master, it could be worse. You're in your own bed, in your own house, on your own farm, and you might have been stuck in a muddy field or lying in splinters on a battlefield or floating about in the sea getting nibbled by fishes. Here you've got clean sheets, and these nice ladies to sing to you, and people looking high and low for a new backbone. But oh, master, don't die! Oh, oh, oh!'

And poor Jack started to wail and cry again, and flung his arms around the Scarecrow, ignoring the danger of catching woodworm.

And that started the old ladies off again. They'd been singing and dancing to 'Funiculi, Funicula', and 'Papa Piccolino', and they'd just started on 'Volare', but Jack's wails and sobs had them howling and screeching along with him, and then the Scarecrow himself joined in, and there was such a row that they didn't hear the doctor and the carpenter coming back. Only when dozens of birds flew around their heads, and Granny Raven cawed at the top of her voice, did all the crying and howling stop.

'We got a broomstick,' said the carpenter, 'and it's a good 'un. This old raven found it for us, and me and the doctor's going to transplant it right away. Everyone's got to go out of the operating theatre, for reasons of concentration and hygiene. When the operation is over, Lord Scarecrow'll need quiet and rest and recuperation, and until then, keep your fingers crossed.'

So all the townspeople left the room, and the doctor and the carpenter, with Jack's help, detached the old worm-eaten spine and emptied out all the beetle-infested straw, and gently and delicately inserted the new stick that Granny Raven had found, and packed the Scarecrow tightly with handfuls of clean fresh straw from the barn.

'Well,' said the doctor when they'd finished and washed their hands, 'we have done all that medical science can do. Now we have to rely on Mother Nature. Keep the patient warm, and make sure that his dressings are changed twice a day. If all goes well—'

'Jack, my boy,' said a well-known voice behind them, 'I feel a great deal better already! I believe I would like a bowl of soup.'

CHAPTER SIXTEEN

SPRING VALLEY

They never managed to get the Buffalonis charged with attempted murder by termites, so the case was never solved; but they didn't have any more trouble from them.

The poison factory was closed down, and re-opened as a mineral water bottling plant. Spring Valley water is famous now; every smart restaurant has it on the menu.

They cleaned up the land and cleared out all the ditches, and re-dug the wells, and opened the clogged-up drains, and now the fountains in the town are splashing good clear water all day and night, and the children play in the paddling pools and the birds wash themselves in the municipal birdbaths. Spring Valley water flows to every house, and all the houses have three kinds of tap: hot, cold, and sparkling.

As for the Scarecrow, he was the happiest of anyone. The broomstick that Granny Raven had found, the one that was transplanted to save his life, turned out to be the very one he'd fallen in love with all that time ago. Her fiancé the rake had left her for a feather duster, and, unhappy and abandoned, she had passed from hand to hand, lamenting the loss of the handsome Scarecrow who had proposed marriage to her. When the two of them found themselves united, their happiness was complete.

The Scarecrow spends all his days wandering around Spring Valley, playing with Jack's children, shooing the greedy birds away from the young corn, and enjoying the fresh air. But he only shoos the birds away to a special box of birdseed that he keeps behind the barn, and what's more, there's always a nest in his coat pocket. The little birds, the sparrows and robins, queue up for the honour; there's a waiting list. The Scarecrow and his broomstick are as proud of the eggs as if they'd laid them themselves.

'Jack's children?' I hear you say.

Yes, a few years later, when he was grown up, Jack got married. His wife is called Rosina, and their children's names are Giulietta, Roberto, and Maria. They're all as happy as fleas. Granny Raven is godmother to the children, and she stands no nonsense from any of them, and they love her dearly.

And on winter evenings, as they sit by the fire
with some good soup inside them, and the children
are playing on the hearth and the wind is roaring
round the rooftops, the Scarecrow and his servant
talk about their adventures, and bless the chance
that brought them together. There never was a
servant, Jack is sure, who had such a good master;
and in all the history of the world, the Scarecrow is
certain, there never was a scarecrow who had so
honest and faithful a servant.

ABOUT THE AUTHOR

Philip Pullman was born in 1946 in Norwich,
Norfolk. He spent a lot of his childhood on
board ships, as his father and stepfather were both
in the Royal Air Force and his mother and brother
seemed to be constantly following them around
the world by sea.

Philip read English at Oxford University and
for a long time he taught in schools before becoming
a full-time writer. He is now one of our best
storytellers. He has written many books for children
and has won numerous awards for his work.
The Firework-Maker's Daughter was a Gold Medal
Smarties prize-winner, *Clockwork* a Silver Medal
Smarties prize-winner, and *Northern Lights*, the first
volume in his trilogy, *His Dark Materials*,
won the Carnegie Medal and was joint winner of
the Guardian Children's Fiction Prize. His novel
The Amber Spyglass was the first ever children's
book to win the overall Whitbread Award.
The *His Dark Materials* trilogy has been made
into an acclaimed production at the National
Theatre and was came in third place in
the BBC's search to find the nation's favourite
book, *The Big Read*.

Philip Pullman lives in Oxford, and is married
with two sons and two grandchildren.